HALF LIFE

Half Life

A Peter Richards novel

by Dana Barney

Copyright © 2017 by Dana Barney
1st edition © 2017 by Dana Barney

Library of Congress Cataloging in Publication Data is available
ISBN 978-0-9965888-2-9

Barney, Dana
HALF LIFE

Jacket design by
April Litz

For modes,
Let's go

1.

"See you tomorrow, Ann!" Molly shouted as she stepped into the humid Austin air.

The doors to the theater shut behind her.

She shoved her phone into her jacket pocket and walked toward Guadalupe Street.

It was a few minutes after one in the morning and the final night of rehearsal for *Fame–The Musical*. The revival and Molly's involvement was long overdue. A small theater in the Hyde Park neighborhood was trying to recruit fresh talent by doing a co-production with the university's summer theater department.

Molly was playing Miss Sherman, the homeroom teacher who systematically crushes the dreams of her students. Someone had to play Miss Sherman, but everyone wanted the bigger and juicier roles. Roles that would put them on Austin's culture map. Singing, dancing, and acting, a certifiable triple threat. They would be lauded in the press only to be forgotten about weeks later and moved to the depths of the university library and remembered only on microfiche while they went to New York and Los Angeles to pursue their passion.

Molly was hoping for a bigger and more substantial role, but it's the actor that's small, not the part.

Rubbish, Molly thought. *Pure garbage you tell people who aren't accomplishing their dreams. You're doing a great job; it's the dream that's the problem.*

The technical rehearsal was scheduled to run until two a.m. for five nights. This was the last night, and they were finishing a final run-through before the dress rehearsal tomorrow night, but Molly had places to be. She was tired of being chastised for not remembering her lines—she was working on it—and didn't want to hear it from Ann, who apparently had a teleprompter pasted to her face during every rehearsal. "I'm the lead, so I learned my lines ages ago," Ann told Molly. "My mom played records of Broadway musicals for me when I was a baby, so I got this!"

Molly really had some deep-seated issues with Ann that she would have to address later, but right now, tonight, she needed to get out and relax.

Her friends were at a small, established, but not extremely well-known wine bar a few blocks down Guadalupe celebrating the end of the school year. Rehearsal wasn't over yet, but Molly wasn't going to boycott a night out on principal. Besides, the rest of the cast wasn't going to miss her. They might be mad that she bailed, and Ann would be pissed, but they'd forget about it eventually. With a long enough timeline, everything would even out. Molly would move to New York, fall in love with a soap star, and forget about her humble beginnings before the plane even left the tarmac. Ann was a few weeks away from becoming a distant memory.

The bar was a two-minute walk from the theater, so she'd be there in time to have a drink or two before someone would suggest they head down to campus and find a house party. Hopefully, Robbie would still be there because, let's be honest, that's the only reason she was going.

She and Robbie shared a Japanese studies course. A few months later she joined a study group he started. The study group met every Friday afternoon at a coffee shop on the Drag, which was the nickname for a section of Guadalupe that ran along the western edge of campus. The Drag was filled with restaurants and clothing stores that appealed to the student body. The group met for a few hours and would discuss twelfth-century politics and nineteenth-century imperialism before heading over to the Drag Bar or a small, established, but not extremely well-known wine bar to start the weekend. Robbie was smart, he played second base for the university baseball team, and had pedigree. Molly couldn't wait to see him and the smile that would erupt on his face when she walked in.

Molly stopped when she reached Guadalupe, an artery that ran from the intramural fields, through campus, and all the way to downtown Austin and the lake.

A small compact car sped towards her. It couldn't have been going less than sixty miles an hour.

It was dark blue or black and the license plates were missing.

It blew through a stop sign and someone wearing a ski mask leaned out and whistled at her.

The car glided half a block past her and came to a screeching halt as she took a left onto Guadalupe. She was standing in front of a dilapidated one-story motel, stranded between the theater and the promise and hope of the wine bar two blocks away.

The passenger side door opened.

Two people wearing ski masks got out.

"Where do you think you're going?" one of them said.

It sounded like a teenager.

Molly took a few steps back and pulled her phone out.

"I said, where do you think you're going?" the kid said again and moved closer to her.

"Leave me alone," she snapped at him.

She wasn't going to scream.

She refused to draw attention to the situation.

She could manage these boys and wouldn't allow herself to be put in a situation where she had no control. That scenario was out of the question.

"We want to talk to you," the kid retorted as he stepped onto the sidewalk. He stopped within five feet of Molly.

"You know there are cameras watching you, right?"

"Why do you think we have these masks on?" he said. "We're safe."

"Leave," she said. "I don't know who you are, but leave me alone. Do you understand that?"

"What's your name?" he asked. He reached his arm around behind his back. He was wearing a T-shirt and athletic shorts. The T-shirt had a large red W on the front. "That's all I want to know." He couldn't have been more than fourteen or fifteen years old.

"My name is get the fuck out of here," she said and walked towards the wine bar. The boy stepped up onto the sidewalk and stood between her and the wine bar.

"Now that's an awfully ugly thing for such a sweet girl like yourself to say," he said as he pulled his hand out from behind his back to reveal a pair of black panties clenched between his fingers. "I think you dropped these back there."

"Gross. Do you idiots drive around town with panties in case you happen to run into some hot girl?" she asked. The child's two friends stepped up behind him.

"Awfully high opinion of yourself you got there, huh?" one of the friends said.

"So did you lose your panties, or didn't you?"

"No, I'm fine. Thank you and now go," she said. She tried to push between them. They didn't move.

"Show us," the third guy said. The other two laughed.

"Not in your life, so please go, or do I need to call your mamas?" She waved her phone in front of them. She glanced down at the wine bar. No one was standing outside waiting to assist her.

"Show us your panties, bitch. It's not that difficult," he said and slapped the phone out of her hand. It hit the ground and the screen shattered.

"That was a mistake," Molly said as she leaned down to pick up the phone. The first boy leaned over and pushed his hand into her shoulder so she tumbled to the ground.

"You're making this much more difficult for yourself," he said.

"Am I?" she said as she looked up at him. But he wasn't looking at her. He was looking at something behind her. All three of them were. The door to one of the apartments was slightly open, and a tall figure was standing in the shadows.

"That's right! Get out of here," Molly said, but the boys didn't move. "Now!" she shouted.

"All right," one of them said. "You come with us, though," he added in a non-threatening tone.

"You don't know when to stop, do you?" she said as the three boys took a few steps back. They kept their eyes locked on the door to one of the apartments and slowly began their retreat. Molly stood up and watched them withdraw. She brushed the dirt off her knees as they got back into their car and zipped down Guadalupe. "Idiots," she said and ran her finger over the phone screen. "Bullshit and idiots."

There was a soft hissing noise behind her. She paused.

Hiss.

What the hell is that? Molly turned around.

A tall, slender figure moved toward her. It was wearing what looked like a motorcycle helmet with a black faceplate. Thin, green lights shot across the front of the faceplate. "I totally had that," Molly said, but there was no response. "Hello in there?" she said. "A girl can take care of herself these days." The figure turned its head towards her. The green lights shot back and forth across the faceplate. "Anybody home?" Molly asked, but there was no response. She looked past the slight figure and surveyed the old apartment complex.

The smell of grilled quail and radicchio from the wine bar floated under her nose as the figure took a step toward her and grabbed her by the neck.

Molly reached her hand up to grasp at the figure's wrist, but the hand squeezed down on her.

She muttered and gasped and tried to find her breath but couldn't. She wanted to scream, but the greasy hand with remnants of Sixth Street pizza clamped down on her and dragged her toward the open apartment door.

She turned her neck and looked back at the wine bar. Robbie was outside hugging and welcoming his friends. He held the door as his friends went inside. He looked up and down Guadalupe.

He was searching for something—someone. But she wasn't there.

She was a block and a half away, desperately trying to make it there, but was being held up by an unknown assailant who was choking the crap out of her.

Such a shame.

Her eyes closed.

The figure let her body drop and then took her arms and pulled her into the apartment.

The door shut once they were both inside.

2.

"I help people form themselves. I found a methodology. An approach that allows people to recognize what they're doing to themselves that creates a malady. You need to reset your physiology. Diabetes isn't collectively onset by your environment. It's inside you. I changed the eldercare industry seven years ago with this guy that's flying in tomorrow night. Trillions. There isn't a company in healthcare that wouldn't want to engage your clients," he said as his voice became softer. There were muddled sounds from across the table, followed by a few clicks of the keypad on a laptop. It sounded like they were dispensing secrets to each other. "I have thirty-five hundred written pages of this shit," he added. "It's a nightmare. I could be the next L. Ron Hubbard with the information I have."

"Certifiable," another one of them chimed in, followed by a nervous laugh.

"It's physiological. That's what I'm telling you," the first guy said as he took a swig from his vanilla latte. "How you perceive things is what matters."

I was sitting at a high top table along the back wall of a coffee shop that catered to the stay-at-home parents and aspiring entrepreneurs of Westlake, an affluent area west of downtown Austin. My phone and a cup of black coffee sat on the tabletop in front of me. Condoleezza Rice sat here years ago when she came to visit Austin. The guy who works the front counter told me it was because the location of the table provided Secret Service with a sufficient view of the coffee shop and easy access to the back in case they needed a quick escape. I didn't need a quick escape, but it was nice to sit up high and watch the morning commuters trickle in.

"Anyway, enough about me. Are you interested in coming on board?"

"Am I interested?" an older gentleman across from him said. He was wearing dark red moccasins. "Yes, of course," he said with confidence that trailed behind him like a limp dog.

I rotated my phone slightly so the microphone could pick up the audio better. I had been recording them for the past thirty minutes and tracking their every move for the last week.

"Great. We want to see this thing through. I want you to meet with David's people, and I want you to meet with Frank, too. At that point in time, when you can show me that you're committed, I'll pay you. Per hour or by retainer or whatever you prefer."

"Who is David?" said the gentleman with the red moccasins.

"He's the CFO," the quiet guy added. "He does the backend."

David was actually David Rothschild, prominent EU investment banker by day and suspicious guy by night. The guys sitting near me run a technology company in Austin called SolChem that David Rothschild owns a majority equity stake in. Rothschild and SolChem recently became sole owners of an exclusive military patent when a plane carrying ten of SolChem's scientists went missing over the Mediterranean. Two of those scientists supposedly owned a percentage of the patent when they went missing; it left the ownership of the patent in the hands of SolChem and Rothschild.

"You won't really meet with him, but with his team of advisers. They'll need to vet you."

"His financial models read like Proust."

"Not everyone knows who that is," the younger guy with the close-cropped hair said as he turned toward his coworker.

"He has the framework and has built-in knowledge of what we have to do," the coworker continued.

"This is my comfort zone. I can handle David," the older guy said.

"You'll be working with his team," the close-cropped hair guy reiterated. "You did some work for the Miles Cooperative, right? When they were first getting set up in Austin?"

"Yes, mostly operational stuff."

"How was that?"

"It was fine. Glad I am where I am now, though."

"Miles is making your city safer. Miles Ahead of the Competition. Isn't that their slogan? Or Miles Above?"

"Something like that," he said.

"We need you to handle the ownership stakes. That's it. You're not here to impress anyone, and you're not here to move up the food chain. We need your expertise and knowledge to make sure the patent law is airtight. We have an entire team of middle-management attorneys stumbling over themselves because they are so eager to move up the corporate ladder. Things are falling through the cracks, and it's unacceptable. Got it?"

"Got it," he said as he reached down and scratched the top of his foot where it met the lip of the moccasin. Since the flight and scientists disappeared last month, a theory was floating around that Rothschild and SolChem orchestrated the disappearance so they could gain full ownership and control of the patent. The theory was gaining traction online and in small circles that spent time discussing these types of things.

Conspiracies, if you will.

CNN and Erin Burnett picked up a piece of the story and their in-depth, edge-of-your-seat coverage was enough to make a few of SolChem's key investors pull out. The incident with the plane was a dent in their otherwise pristine portfolios. The investor's departure was starting to affect SolChem and Rothschild's bottom line. I was hired to prove that there was, in fact, no conspiracy at all.

My job was to bring in evidence that would reassure people and put their imaginations at bay. In fact, everything was completely normal and as it should be. It's unfortunate that a plane went missing and SolChem lost some close and valued scientists, but Rothschild and SolChem were on the up and up. They always have been.

I work freelance doing these types of things, and I never reveal the names of the companies or people who hire me.

"We speak the same language," the younger one said as he ran his hand across his hair. "You understand what I'm saying. That's why we want you. We'll do this for a month and I'll make you an offer for the full amount. We need you to make this problem go away."

"Sure."

"Put it in a place where it's manageable," he said.

"There will be a lot of eyes on this. We're probably being watched right now."

"Whatever I'm doing right now, I can still do."

"You want to be paid as a consultant. That's fine, and that's completely your choice. We can figure that out. Everyone thinks good is good enough. It's not, and I think you understand that. Everything matters. Every decision and every detail. I think you have that sensibility. Don't settle for anything."

"I know you won't understand this, a young guy like yourself, but I have to go home and talk to my wife about this."

"Sure, sure," he said. He was irritated.

"I need to run this by her," he said. "We've been married thirty-eight years, and I want to discuss this with her."

"I should get advice from you. I'm good at pushing women away. I'm not good at keeping them," he said and laughed.

I guess this is how deals are done these days. Over lattes in a strip mall coffee shop in the nice part of town.

I hit the stop button on my phone and looked down at my watch. It was half past ten, and the place was packed. From the looks of it, no one worked anymore or they all worked remote. Dialing into conference calls from laptops that didn't make it out of the zip code. Fuming away at weekly reports and status updates. Tweaking their PowerPoints to near perfection until they die of corporate ennui.

I took a bite of my kale bagel with sunflower and cucumber cream cheese.

I had black coffee. Doctor's orders.

Ten years ago I had a heart attack and flatlined in the middle of the living room of our starter home. The police rushed me to the hospital, where I was pronounced dead. The physician on call gave me a state-of-the-art mechanical heart.

I was half-human, half-machine, and I had to eat a low-fat, gluten-free, carb-free, and judgment-free diet so I didn't die. I was in my mid-thirties when my heart gave out, and my doctor wanted me to be extra careful to make sure it didn't happen again. So I gave the cheeseburger diet a fond farewell and ate chicken breast with lemon for lunch and leafy greens with crucified vegetables for dinner.

Flavor was simply a state of mind these days.

"Sorry, I'm late," he said as he sat across from me with a chai latte with a heart floating in the foam on top. "Are you Peter?"

"You're ten minutes late," I said. "I thought you weren't going to show."

"The espresso machine was having issues and—well, you see the line." He gestured his hand toward the line going out the door. It was fuming out, and the heat was creeping inside.

"It's ten minutes you lost," I added.

He was only a kid. Maybe twenty. I couldn't tell.

I still feel twenty.

"Like I said, the machine was having issues." He pulled a tablet from his bag and folded back the cover. "Anyway, let's get started. If you don't mind, I'd like your permission to record the conversation."

"Have at it."

"It makes it easier when I go back and write the article," he said and cleared his throat and took out a small digital recorder and pressed the red button. "*University Star*, Spotlight Portfolio for issue six twenty-three. I'm sitting down with Peter Richards. Caucasian male, forty-seven. Dark blue jeans, work boots, and a blue denim work shirt. Looks like it's from the Gap. Is it from the Gap?" he asked.

"Yes," I said tentatively. "Is that important?"

"For later," he said and leaned closer to the recording device. "Peter is the owner and founding partner of a website that debunks conspiracies."

"That's right. It's important to see things as they really are. It's healthy for people to immerse themselves in fiction and fantasy, but it's also important for people to understand the difference between fact and fiction. There are a handful of famous conspiracies out there: Roswell, the moon landings, the assassination of JFK, and so on. I take a hard look at the conspiracies surrounding these events and break them down and analyze them."

"Why do you do it?"

"Ninety-eight percent of conspiracies aren't credible. I want to legitimize people, places, and events. People aren't looking closely enough, and they see what they want to see. People are intrigued by conspiracies because we want chaos to be controlled by a higher power. We need to rationalize what's happening. A conspiracy lets us believe that the chaos is being controlled by someone with a higher purpose. But it's not."

"So, we're all out here on our own?"

"That's the thinking."

"Any favorite conspiracies?"

"They're all pretty interesting," I said. "Can't pick just one."

"What about Elvis?"

"What about him?"

"There's a pretty strong and widely known conspiracy that Elvis is alive and well."

"I haven't taken a look at that one yet, but I'm sure I'll get around to it."

"At that point, he might be dead."

"Case closed then, right?" I said.

"From a purely journalistic perspective, how would you go about doing it? I'm asking for my own curiosity and off the record," he said and put his hand over his recorder. "How could you debunk that theory? Go to his grave and dig the body up? What then? Go to a DNA lab and have the DNA tested? Don't forget that you illegally dug up his body."

"I assure you there are more journalistic and ethical ways of going about things."

"Very well," he said with a smear of disappointment on his face. "May we continue?"

I nodded graciously at him.

He removed his hand from the recorder. "Peter was one of the very first recipients of the Ə-zero Electro-Flux heart."

"Series 2," I added.

"Right. Series 2."

"It was the first series to be used on patients outside of a testing environment."

"The first use of these implantable medical devices was back in 2009, but this is something revolutionary."

"Ahead of its time, if you will," I said.

When he reached out to me he said he was a student at Texas State and was studying mechanical engineering. His thesis was on how machines and humans can work together to benefit society. He wanted to do a profile piece on me for the student periodical. I told him talking to me was a waste of time and that he should rent *Robocop* instead. He said he saw it a while ago, his dad made him watch it, but he got bored. It made him tired, he said. *Where was Detroit, anyway?*

"How does your heart charge? Does it come with a cord that you plug into an outlet?" He snickered, as if my heart was some sort of novelty and a thing of the past.

"I have a patch," I said and took out my wallet and pulled out a small black leather square slightly bigger than a business card. "Ə-zero sends me one of these each month and I place it on my chest to recharge the heart. It's electromagnetic, and it only takes a few minutes."

"How does it feel to be one of the first humans to go through the first phase of machine-human integration?"

"What do you mean?"

"Mechanical hearts, or hearts supported by a machine, are the very first step in a larger rollout for Ə-zero. Next month they are releasing the Electro-Flux 3 and an add-on that monitors brainwaves and cerebral blood flow. It's considered synthetic biology or cybernetic mortality. Pick your poison," he said.

I was also wearing an Ə-zero-issued wristband that connected to my heart via an RFID chip that sent radio signals between the wristband and my heart. The wristband monitors blood pressure, pulse, and stress levels. It sends the information back to Ə-zero every fifteen seconds and makes adjustments in my body as needed and within reason.

"It feels okay," I said. "I hadn't given it much thought."

"Do you think there's a conspiracy to debunk here?"

"What do you mean?"

"Ə-zero and the larger roll-out. An AI takeover perhaps?"

"If you think so," I said, and shrugged slightly for effect and looked away to show that I was somewhat disinterested.

"You can't really lead me to believe that you haven't envisioned a scenario where artificial intelligence becomes the dominant form of intelligence, and robots and computers take control of our planet? An uprising, if you will, one of the first steps being human-to-machine integration."

"That's absurd."

"Prove me wrong. The world is changing, Peter. What about the Miles Cooperative?"

"What about it?"

"Do you have an opinion on what they're doing? Fighting crime and keeping us safe with advanced technology."

"I didn't realize I needed an opinion on Miles."

"You don't. I'm just asking. You're on the forefront."

"I wouldn't put it that way. I didn't do anything."

"You died."

3.

"Not intentionally," I said and looked around the room.

The ceiling was covered with canvas coffee bags, and some sort of nouveau riche art covered the walls.

"What happens if your Electro-Flux stops working?" he asked.

"It doesn't," I said confidently.

"But it's a machine, and machines are bound to stop working at some point."

"It's a perfect system."

"It could get hacked. Your heart is part of the infrastructure now. It has a radio-frequency identifier that connects it to everything else. You're vulnerable."

"Now, *that* sounds like a conspiracy theory in the works," I said. The radio-frequency identifier, or RFID chip, is a unique identifier that connects my heart to the grid and, by design, makes my heart vulnerable to anyone who decides to hack the grid, which was pretty much impossible given how sophisticated Ɔ-zero's security was.

"Your heart stopped working. You were a young, relatively healthy man, and your heart decided to betray you," he said. "Do you ever feel like you are living on borrowed time?"

"Every day," I said and took a sip of my coffee as an icon of a small car appeared on the home screen of my watch. "I need to go." I set my coffee down and pressed my finger down on the icon. A map appeared showing me that the car was sitting at the Barton Creek Country Club, a little over two miles away. I had a few minutes before I needed to leave.

This conversation was about over anyway.

"What's it like when you die?" he asked.

"Is that something mechanical engineers are interested in? The after-life?"

"There's an afterlife?"

"I didn't say that. There isn't anything. Emptiness." I looked down at my watch.

"Are you sitting in darkness? Are you waiting for something?"

"It's nothing. Literal nothing. You're alone, but you don't have a conscience or a personality or a care in the world. You have less value than a dead bug."

"Jesus," he said, and I watched the hope sail away from him. I had no idea really, but I figured I'd give him something to mull over on his bus ride back to San Marcos, and besides, I had to leave soon. My current employer wanted me to collect as much information about Sol-Chem as I could, and the final piece was sitting at the Barton Creek Country Club. I wasn't about to put myself in a situation where my employer needed to hire a different investigator. Not that there's anyone else out there who does what I do.

"The universe, the galaxy, whatever it is, is an unending donut that keeps going around itself," I said. "This conversation, this moment, is a blip of nothingness inside a crumb of that donut."

"Is that on the record? The thing about the donut?"

"There's a record?"

"People will ask."

"Sure. Put it in there. Tell them I said it." I leaned closer to his tablet to make sure the microphone would pick it up. "Donut crumbs."

"My minor is in philosophy," he proffered.

"Of course it is."

"You're kind of a jerk. Do you know that about yourself?" he said.

"You're just a kid," I said, and rolled my eyes. A disheartened half-roll, but enough that he could see it. I heard him, and I didn't care.

"You should join one of those extremist groups. They're always looking for crazies like you. You have no discernible decision-making abilities. You're simply floating out there waiting for something to scoop you up. Debunking conspiracies? That's the most ridiculous thing I have ever heard. You think NASA will let you fly to the moon so you can prove the moon landings weren't fake?"

He went on, but my attention drifted up to a television above the bar area that was playing CNN. They had an update on a Florida family that went missing six months ago. David Creed, the dad, owned and operated a pool maintenance company in Fort Myers. He was married and had two children, a boy and a girl.

Normally, I wouldn't think anything of it, but I didn't understand why they would just disappear.

They were scheduled to visit his mother-in-law in Orlando, but when they didn't show, and didn't answer their phones, the mother-in-law called a mutual friend to go check on them. The mutual friend went to their house. The family wasn't there, and the dog was out back with a bowl full of food and a trough of water. The headline flashed across the screen:

FLORIDA FAMILY VANISHES IN BROAD DAYLIGHT

The local news runs an update on the family at least once a day, and it appears in the feed of CNN a few times a day. There wasn't anything left to report; the family was gone, but the journalists picked up every shred of evidence and every new lead they could get their hands on. Then they would turn it upside down and twist it around until they found a single shred of a story in it. Today's development was that the federal authorities discovered an abandoned Ford Explorer at the Mexican border. It matched the description of the Creed family's Ford Explorer. Same color, size, and so on. License plates were removed and the VIN numbers were obliterated, so CNN felt that was ample information for a four-minute block every twenty minutes. I'm sure they had a vault of minions calling every authority imaginable for a sound clip. If they couldn't get anyone on the record, they would decide to go with *FBI was unavailable for comment* or *President was mum on the issue* and then cut to a video feed of an empty White House press room. Maybe *Homeland Security is concerned*, because when isn't Homeland Security concerned. It's their job. LeBron is paid to make free throws and Homeland Security is paid to keep their eyebrows raised. CNN would put the quote up above the *Developing News* banner, and then they would run some commercials for paper towels and for-profit universities and watch the cash roll in.

"Do you miss it?"

"Miss what?" I asked as I kept my eye on the television. The *Developing News* banner disappeared and was replaced by a *Breaking News* banner.

17

A military base in North Carolina was attacked. Something was stolen, people were running around, but I wasn't sure because the kid kept distracting me.

"Being a journalist. Chasing the story," the kid said.

"Every day," I said, and adjusted my blue denim work shirt. My watched buzzed, and the car icon flashed.

"That's what I thought. I can see it in your eyes. You're searching for something. You married?"

"Going through some stuff, but for the sake of argument—yes. I'm married."

"Be careful," he said. "Don't want the wrong thing to find you."

"What does that have to do with me being married or not? I need to get out of here."

"It's a general harbinger," he said as he put away his stuff. "I wish I could say it was interesting meeting you. I'm not sure why you called and insisted we do a piece on you."

"You called me," I said.

"No I didn't. You made an anonymous call and said someone needed to interview Peter Richards. You said you were amazing. They knew it was you but made me come anyway."

"Hey, can I ask you something?" I placed my hand on his wrist as he began to stand up. "Do you think you could run the article with my picture? There are some good ones out there. Left profile is best. I feel like people hear the name but can't put a face to it, if you know what I mean. I think if you run it with my picture it would mean more to the readers."

"You're really something," he said and walked away.

I took my last gulp of coffee and stood up.

"See ya, Peter!" a voice shouted at me from the back. I turned around. It was the guy with the close-cropped hair. I'd have to make a note to follow up with him later.

4.

I left the coffee shop and got in my car.

I hooked a left out of the parking lot and went west on Bee Cave Parkway. I drove past The County Line as the day old brisket drifted slowly under my nose.

I turned left at the second light and headed south towards the country club. As I approached the hotel entrance a blue compact car whizzed past me with what appeared to be a short woman behind the wheel.

I slammed on my brakes and flipped my car around in the middle of the narrow road that ran between the golf course and the resort part of the country club. I accelerated until I caught up to her.

She was sitting at the stop sign at the corner of the main road.

I looked down at my notes to make sure I had the right car:

Azure Hyundai Elantra license plate 2HZ 45RE.

The car belonged to a Harold Corker, but I was more interested in who was behind the wheel: Harold's wife, Carol Corker.

A car flew by her. Once the road was clear, she slowly pulled out and took a left. I pushed my foot down on the accelerator and gunned it.

I heard her say, "Dammit!" a split second after the front of my car gently hit her rear bumper. She quickly turned her hazards on and slowly pulled over to the shoulder.

"Sorry. Sorry. Sorry," I said emphatically, as I got out of my car and went over to her driver's side window. I glanced back and looked at my front bumper. Hardly a dent.

"Are you out of your mind?" she said. I wouldn't let her small frame and short gray hair fool me; Carol Corker was a firecracker. I responded by handing her a slip of paper. She looked down at it: *US7230568.*

"We need to talk," I said.

"What is this? I don't know what this is," she exclaimed and tossed it out the window. It floated slowly towards my feet.

"It's a patent," I said. "Surely you recognize one when you see one."

She huffed and gripped her steering wheel. "That could be anything," she said. "I'm going to call the police."

"Can you confirm that a change of ownership was filed for this last week?"

"Did you not hear what I said?"

"Carol," I said. "Carol?"

"What?"

"Are you listening to me?"

"You're assaulting me."

"Can you confirm that David Rothschild and SolChem are sole owners on this patent?"

"You don't know what you're talking about, crazy man," she said, and pulled a phone out of the glove box. It was an old Motorola that had two large buttons on it: *Police* and *Fire.*

"Call the police. I'll be gone before anyone shows up."

"It'll be a hit and run. Can you live with that?" she said and she forced her finger down on the *Police* button.

"I hit you, yes, but you were slowing down when you came out of the turn. The argument goes both ways. I'm sure I'll be fine."

"That's not how the law works," she said and looked up at me.

"Come on," I said and leaned down towards her and lowered my voice. "Say yes or no. Are Rothschild and SolChem the sole owners on this bad boy?"

"You look familiar," she said and squinted her eyes.

"I get that a lot. I used to be a local television news reporter here. Investigative journalist. Peter Richards," I said and extended my hand. She didn't reciprocate the gesture.

"What did you investigate?"

"Crime and criminal activities in the city. Pure, unadulterated corruption. Yes or no, Carol?"

"I know where I know you from," she said. "You cheated on your wife."

"What?"

"That's right. You fucking cheater," the octogenarian yelled at me. "My friend Barbara knows you. She met you online, on the app. That app that everyone is using. She said you took her to the Kimber Modern and got her all liquored up."

"Sounds like a pretty good time to me. Are you going to answer my question or not?"

"You bought her vodka tonics, seventeen of them was her recollection, and then you took her back to the room, where she passed out. You wouldn't shut up about how you were an investigative journalist. You were big-time, you kept telling her. The next day she looked you up. You know what the first thing she found was?"

"A picture of me and Ben Affleck playing chicken in the swimming pool at the Venetian in Vegas?"

"What? No. You did that?"

"Was it a picture of me riding around on a wolf in the middle of prayer service at a Baptist church? I told the clergy to keep that under lock and key."

"No. It was a profile of you on CheaterStation."

"I'm sure I don't know what that is."

"It's a website that exposes filth and degenerates like yourself. People who make a vow, a promise, and then crap all over it, are put on a cross for all the world to see."

"Sounds pretty intense, Carol. Are you into stuff like that?"

"You'll pay for your crimes."

"I'm actually happily married. Going through some stuff, but happy. So whatever it is she thought she saw online, it wasn't me."

"She has good judgment."

"That's obviously not the case, now is it?"

"You better watch yourself, Mr. Richards. It's a scary world out there and I wouldn't want your lack of principals to put you in jeopardy."

"Since you haven't responded to my question, I'll take it as a yes. Rothschild and SolChem are sole owners. When did you approve the paperwork?"

"You can't hold me hostage, Mr. Richards." She reached her hand out and pushed my arm off the edge of the car door and turned off her hazard lights.

"When you approved the change of ownership, were you aware that Rothschild was behind the missing airline that the SolChem employees were on? *Possibly*. I meant to add that. Rothschild was *possibly* behind it."

5.

"Strangulation," the forensics officer said as she looked at Molly Cooper's face. "That's my guess."

"Guess?" Detective Skelly said as he hovered over the forensics officer. "Is that what they pay people to do these days? Guess?"

"I'll need to take the body down to central and have it looked at. Right now it's an unknown."

"Christ," Skelly said. There hadn't been a murder since Miles took over and now there were two.

He had been on the job for well over a decade. He knew how a crime scene worked, knew his role, and knew better than anyone to give the lead forensics officer space. He should be over by the barricades telling the new recruits to go and canvas houses and find witnesses.

He couldn't help himself today.

He shifted his focus away from the victim to the tattoo on the forearm of the forensics officer. It was a tattoo of a football helmet marked with the number nine. It was Tony Romo's number. Skelly didn't understand why fans decided to honor him by tattooing his number onto their persons. Erin was no different. She was a flawless forensics officer, graduated top of her class from the University of Dallas, and was a Cowboys fan through and through. Skelly couldn't hold it against her if she wasn't perfect.

But why did she get a tattoo of his number? Skelly thought. *Why not get a tattoo of her blood type, like all the other officers did?* It was a high-risk job, and if anything should happen and she needed a blood transfusion, the doctors wouldn't have to dig through files or call family members who didn't know, or knew incorrectly. *What a tremendous waste of space.*

23

But, then again, Skelly didn't really understand the culture of football. Especially people who liked the Dallas Cowboys.

He thought about the monstrosity of the Dallas Cowboys stadium and how much money a game ticket cost, and how maybe, for a fleeting second, he may have gotten into the wrong profession.

Being a detective was honorable and a great conversation piece, but people didn't fully understand it or, better yet, they romanticized it. To the regular people, the common folk, he was Dick Tracy and Commissioner Gordon and he could do no wrong. Everyone wanted to talk to him about the Manson Family and Jeffrey Dahmer, which he thought was weird. Most of the job was complicated and full of unnecessary paperwork brought on by an inhuman bureaucracy. When people asked, which they frequently did, he told them he became a detective because he wanted to connect with victims and help tell their story. The victims' stories and their justice were all that mattered.

But that's just what he told people.

The fact was, he was driven more by a morbid curiosity than anything else. The victims were important, but the victims were already dead, so there was little he could do. Retribution and a clean and friendly narrative for family and friends was always nice. He knew how to wrap it up in a nice little package so it was digestible and logical. The reality was, Skelly was driven by a morbid curiosity and fascination. Victims were important, but he wanted to know what made people tick.

His mind rushed back to the most recent … incident.

H-E-B was a Texas grocery store chain that promoted the sourcing of local ingredients, competitive pay, and an occasional corpse in aisle seven.

Early last Thursday morning, the meat manager found a body lying in the middle of aisle seven, next to a stack of fresh locally sourced cage-free, hormone-free chickens. No obvious signs of struggle. The meat manager put his hand on the victim's wrist. She had smooth skin and was wearing a charm bracelet. He guessed that she was probably in her early twenties or late teens. She had a pulse, so he called 911.

"Police, Fire, or EMS?"

"This is Raul at the Mueller H-E-B," he said into the phone. "I'm the manager of the meat department and I'd like to report a body. I found a body here. Right between the roasters and turkey legs," he said.

He was put on hold almost immediately, so he had time to run over to the bakery department and grab something to eat. They were out of the donut-bagel Godsends, so he settled for a chocolate croissant. He had a suspicion that Vicki took a dozen or so home each night for her two unappreciative, bulging children, but he had no way of knowing for sure.

"Yes," he said when someone came back on the line. "She had a pulse, but I'm not sure about that anymore." The operator asked him to check again, but between the croissant in one hand and the phone in the other, he simply couldn't bother. "She was here when I came in this morning. I'm usually the first one in." It was getting light outside and other people were slowly coming in. He tossed an apron over the body. "No, I don't think she works here, but there's a lot of turnover so, who knows."

Initially, Skelly thought the body at the H-E-B was an isolated incident.

His intuition told him to classify it as suspicious, but the paper pushers downtown told him to file it under FB and deal with it later. FB stood for "found body," and it was the most boring and indistinct classification you could use. FB meant it could be any variety of things except murder. It was never murder.

People weren't murdered anymore in Austin, not for at least two years.

"People aren't murdered anymore, so please realign your point of view, Skelly," is what he was told.

The department issued a small press release to a few news outlets but didn't let any media on the scene. In fact, it wasn't even a considered a crime scene. H-E-B was closed for twenty-four hours while the police conducted a routine investigation, is what people were told.

This was going to be no different.

It was three in the morning, but there were students and onlookers and people recording all sorts of video and taking pictures.

Miles would tell the department to deny it and insist that people were sensationalizing things.

Eventually, people would forget and find something else.

The distractions were out there.

It was almost too easy.

"This is bad, Skelly," the forensics officer said as she turned away from Molly Cooper's body and gave Skelly a concerned looked.

"Tell me what you have," Skelly said as he looked at the onlookers staring at them. "Start at the beginning."

"Time of death was less than two hours ago. There's clear bruising around the neck and traces of skin under her fingernails. There was a struggle, and it's clear that she was overpowered. There is also bruising on her calves."

"What is that from?"

"I think she was grabbed outside and started fighting. There are clear indentation marks on the calves that could be from her hitting the steps," she said and pointed to the step leading into one of the rooms.

"You want to call it?" he asked.

"I think we should take her to the lab. Get a second opinion. You know, given the current state of things. We don't want to alarm anyone."

"Of course not," Skelly said and smiled at her.

They had a thing once, a few years ago, when she was transferred in from Dallas. Even though she had some family in Austin, and grew up in Lakeway, she didn't know anyone. Not really, at least. She didn't have anyone to hang out with and talk shop with, so Skelly took a liking to her. Most days, after her shift was over, Skelly would take her to the JW Marriott on Congress and they would sip scotch and he would listen with his seasoned cop face as she talked about the various corpses and crime scenes she had seen in her day. She would talk about how murders in Dallas were more pitiless than in Austin, the rich and upper class were truly filthy animals. Six years on the job and she had seen it all.

"And to think I was about to say things were boring around here," she said. "I was beginning to think you hired a forensics officer for appearances."

"That's right. Appearance. That's what's important. How we see things, not as they happened," Skelly said as an officer came up to him.

The officer held a piece of paper between department-issued tweezers.

"I think this is for you," the officer said. Skelly took the paper and held it up. Looked like Cream Vellum Bristol 67 lb, but Skelly couldn't tell for sure.

He flipped it over so he could see what was written on the back: *Skelly, you're next.* "Where did you find this?"

"It was in the room," the officer said and pointed his finger across Skelly's chest towards Room 11.

Blue Bonnet Court Hotel is an historic motor court-style motel on the northwestern corner of the Hyde Park neighborhood in the north-central part of the city. In the 1930s it featured Austin's first neon sign, which still hangs from the front in all its dilapidated glory. It only has eleven rooms, and Molly Cooper's body was found behind the motel.

Skelly looked out at the crowd of onlookers. "Anyone out there have any info?"

"No. They're pretty upset," the officer said as Skelly thought about the note. It wasn't the first threat he received and it didn't bother him the way it used to. People get upset, enraged even, and the police are accessible targets. Skelly understood that, so he decided to let the threats roll off his back.

People didn't care for the police these days.

Popular opinion and media coverage over the last decade didn't work in their favor and officers were told through the chain of command to treat daily occurrences and suspects with kid gloves. Police officers, and employees of the department, weren't to offend anyone and put the station at risk of a lawsuit, even a frivolous one. After all, the police weren't protecting people. The city was being protected by the constant watch and surveillance of the Miles Cooperative. This resulted in a community who didn't think it needed the police. Miles was protecting them and helping create a dry spell of violent and petty crime. Or so the community thought.

Fact was, people became inert from consistent and interminable technological dependency, which caused them to lash out and rebel against their passivity in the most unpredictable, and often, violent ways.

Homicides were down, but suicides were as prevalent as they were ten and twenty years ago. But people only saw what was on the screens in front of them. They saw what the media and the Miles Cooperative wanted them to see: "Bad weather is on the horizon," "Watch out for flash floods this weekend," and the favorite, "Local politician is involved in a scandal with a transsexual lounge singer." The public was immersed in an ever-growing augmented reality and consistently desensitized to the physical world around them.

People blame the police when things go wrong and praise the Miles Cooperative for keeping their city safe.

Miles has a full-scale communications network throughout most of the city, with surveillance cameras and various types of telecommunication systems that connect to a wide array of public and private systems.

Their network also allow for easy and accessible communication for responding officers. Officers can get to a crime scene faster and with more information. They also have drone-mounted cameras and other vehicle devices that allow surveillance from a wide variety of places not previously available.

Nevertheless, Skelly was in the business of solving crimes and catching criminals no matter what. He had a peripheral understanding of computer technology and smart devices, but he wasn't a user. He felt the knowledge was only needed to help him be better at his job. He didn't have family or friends or a cacophony of people who he needed to be in touch with. He'd started taking drum lessons, but that was to help him transition into his inevitable retirement.

"Do you want to talk about this?" Erin shouted after him.

His life in the balance now.

A vague threat against him, and his colleague wanted to discuss it with him. Sort through his feelings only to land on one that might be accurate but was still only a guess as far as he was concerned. Skelly didn't know how he felt; he rarely did. He enjoyed his time with Erin, liked the camaraderie and liked having someone to share a drink with. But a full-on sidebar of his feelings, a deep dive into his emotional cortex, was simply out of the question. He didn't know how he felt but, he could probably make a guess and a guess was as good as anything. He was annoyed. He was annoyed the note showed up, annoyed he got the call when he wasn't even on duty, and annoyed there was another corpse on his watch. All this after a body showed up in a grocery store last week. Austin was supposed to be safe. A haven for people escaping the violence and gore of Big City America. At least that's what they told the tourists.

By design, Skelly was going to spend the rest of his career sitting behind a desk filling out paperwork. He loved his job and finding the criminals and putting them in jail.

He was put on this earth to solve crimes. He wasn't here to sit behind a desk and collect dust. Sure, a few onlookers would ask questions.

"Did someone get murdered here?"

"What happened to Austin being a safe place to live?"

The city hired PR to deal with that sort of stuff and propel a large volume of confusing and misleading information. People would become confused and they would eventually focus on something else and forget about it. Meanwhile, Skelly would have to go downtown and classify this as a FB.

"Hey—" Skelly said to one of the officers standing lazily along the police tape. "There's some evidence that needs to be bagged back there. Get some evidence bags from the truck and help Erin out."

"What is it?" the officer asked.

"Evidence. That's what it is," Skelly snapped. "Don't worry about it. In fact, don't even look at it. It's not your job to ask questions." Skelly pushed his hands out to signal that the officer should start moving along.

"I was told I should watch the police tape. Hold my ground, they told me."

"And you're doing a great job. Once you help her with the evidence you can come right back. She found a note on the victim. Make sure you have the lab run a handwriting sample on it. You know how to get the lab to do that?"

"Sure."

"Check the box on the form that says *handwriting sample*. You're already doing an amazing job, kid. In fact, make it a rush job. Check that box, too. Critically urgent work we're doing here."

"What does the note say?"

"It says you're doing a great job not asking questions," Skelly said as he felt a soft buzz in his pocket. He turned his back to the recruit and pulled his phone out and answered it. "What do you want, Cleft?"

"You busy, Skelly?" the voice said on the other end of the phone.

It was Cleft Duvall.

Suddenly, Skelly had another item to add to the list of annoyances. It wasn't that he disliked Cleft, he simply didn't have the energy to manage him. Skelly and Cleft had known each other for a few years. They were acquainted when Cleft aided and abetted a known fugitive who was on the run. Cleft and the suspect, Peter Richards, worked at a local television station until it was decommissioned largely because of the trivial behavior of its reporter, Peter Richards, and news director, Cleft Duvall. Peter was charged with murdering his next-door neighbor. It was a crime Skelly knew intimately. He was the detective assigned to the case by a complicated lottery system that assigned cases based on the geographic proximity of an investigating officer to the crime scene and possible interest and enthusiasm level of said investigating officer.

When 911 called dispatch, Skelly was down the street from the crime scene apathetically eating sushi whilst fighting the distinct desire to get into bed, so it only made sense that he would be chosen. Peter, allegedly, saw his neighbor being murdered and then called the police. When the police arrived, they discovered his neighbor's body buried in Peter's backyard. Skelly read him his rights and then Peter faked having a heart attack. It was a clever way to skirt the law but Skelly knew all the tricks. The paramedics came and took Peter to the hospital, where he was pronounced dead.

The doctor was on retainer with a company that manufactured electronic hearts, a fairly new endeavor after some success in the home automation business. They gave Peter a new heart, and when no one was looking, Peter escaped from the hospital and went looking for the person he thought he saw kill his neighbor. He engaged the help of his friend, Cleft, and managed to avoid the law for a few days, but Skelly was closing in. In the day or so it took Skelly to catch up to Peter, Peter exposed the Korean mob, and he'll tell you this himself, also uncovered the true killer of his neighbor. Skelly thought he deserved the credit for some of it, but Peter and Cleft were lauded as national heroes.

That went on for about a week until everyone forgot about them.

The morning shows started talking about awards season and theorizing who was going to win the Super Bowl. So Peter and Cleft faded; a light gust of wind blew them into obscurity. Skelly, on the other hand, was reprimanded for not doing a good enough job: "Don't let criminals solve crimes," they told him. He was an embarrassment for the institution and was put on administrative leave. He spent his time tending to his garden and sampling cocktails at eating establishments on the east side.

"What is it, Cleft?" Skelly said into the phone.

"How are the drum lessons going?"

"Fine," Skelly said. "I'm in the middle of something."

"I have a name for you."

"Okay," Skelly said as he looked back at Erin hovering over Molly Cooper's body. She flashed him a smile. "What's the name?" he said softly into the phone.

"Jacob Cutler."

"What about him?"

"You know that string of robberies up north?"

"What about them?"

"He's the guy. Well, not him, but the old him. Jacob used to go by the name of Thomas Golbez. That was until yesterday, when I issued him a new identity. Re-identified, if you will."

"How much?"

"Five grand."

"Cleft—"

"The payday is bigger for you on this, so I charge more."

"Greed."

"Hey, you came to me," Cleft said and hung up the phone.

6.

After KVAN fired and denied the existence of Cleft Duval and Peter Richards, Cleft started a company that helped people establish new identities. He likes to refer to it as a "re-identity" service that helps people recreate themselves. For a price.

"This Golbez guy came into my office yesterday afternoon," Cleft said into the phone. "He said he heard about me through a friend of his. I said cool, and he said he wanted the full treatment. Package deluxe. I said no problem, and he handed me a handful a cash and told me to do it quick. I gave him the full ride: new social security card, driver's license, credit and debit cards under the new name connected to a highly trusted and valued financial institution. I know what you're thinking, but I can't tell you the name, it's strictly confidential. That is, unless you're a client. I asked him, nonchalant, as if it were none of my business and I didn't care which way he went, I asked him what he was so desperate to get away from. What was he escaping? I asked. You know, because everyone is escaping something. It's a matter of how bad you want to get away.

"He said—and his voice got real quiet. *Paranoid fucker*, I thought— He said he robbed a few establishments up north and accidentally shot someone. A boy, a kid, he thought. He was scared. He was trying to get some loot, cash for his grandma or something, but now he's got this dead kid on his conscience. Some people are pretty terrible at understanding cause and effect, I swear, man: 'I'll bring a gun, but no way will it ever create a situation for me.'

"Anyway, this Golbez guy, he was sure, 100 percent confident, that the police and Miles were hot on his tail. He was freaking out. Too paranoid to get out of town. Didn't want to take a bus anywhere, didn't even want to hitch a ride.

"They were waiting for him after all. The exits were being watched. Miles probably had footage of it. A buddy of his said he should come see me and I would take care of everything. So that's what I did. He's all set up now. Jacob Cutler, everyman. He has a studio apartment half a mile off the interstate. It's part of the package. One month paid rent at a place of my choosing. If he likes it, then he can extend the lease. I don't give a flying crap what he does as soon as he walks out of my office. I'll text you the address."

"Thanks," Skelly said on the other end of the phone. "It's pretty low what you're doing, Cleft."

"Hey, you came to me. You made the deal. You wanted to leverage your career or whatever. Solve more crimes and get a better retirement package?"

"These people are getting a second chance and you're selling them out."

"They're the lowest of the low. They should expect that I'll sell them out. If they don't, if they aren't surprised that I did something like this, then they aren't worth the ground they walk on and should be put away. Besides, I help get these people jobs as part of their re-identity."

"Really?" Skelly asked. "What types are jobs are you getting these people?"

"Classified information, my friend," Cleft said.

There was a knock on his office door.

He had a small office on the second floor of a shopping center in the Hyde Park neighborhood, a well-established and highly regarded area of Austin.

It's right where Cleft wanted to be.

His clientele were people who were holding on for dear life and Cleft was their only hope. He wanted to be in an area that offered clients promise and a sense of what their lives could be. Plus, residents wouldn't know a criminal from a hole in the wall so people mostly went unnoticed.

"Who is it?" Cleft shouted as he cupped the mouthpiece of the phone. He was standing behind a small legal desk that had a phone, laptop computer, and an unopened case of baseball cards sitting on the edge. The case of baseball cards had *PETER* written across the shrink-wrap on the side.

"It's me," a voice said from the other side of the door, followed by another knock.

"I heard you," Cleft said. "Who goes there?"

"Seriously?" said the voice.

"Who goes there?!" Cleft said again, as he removed his hand from the mouthpiece. "I gotta go, Skelly. Good luck with your impending retirement or whatever it is you do these days," he said. He hung up and looked back at the door. "Who goes there?" he said.

"Jesus," the voice muttered. "I come from a world with a bluer sun."

"What?!"

"I come from a world with a bluer sun, Cleft! Let me in!"

"Thee shall enter," Cleft said as he pressed a large red button on his desk. A loud buzzing sound echoed through the room followed by the clicking of multiple locks. Cleft waved his hands in the air as the door opened.

Peter stood at the precipice.

"I thought the pity party didn't start until six," Cleft said and feigned looking at his watch.

"Hilarious," Peter said. He came in and sat down on the couch along the wall and put his feet up on a small coffee table. "You have some state of the art security here."

"My clients expect it. Can I get you something to drink? Water, coffee, arsenic?"

"You can't drink arsenic."

"Sure you can. I just invented it. Arsenic with a touch of vermouth. Over ice."

"I prefer my vices in pill form," Peter said and looked down at a book positioned in the center of the coffee table: *Things Men Like Better Than Boobs* by Clea Vage. Peter leaned over and opened the book and flipped through the pages. They were all blank.

"I have a relationship with the publisher and they give them to me to give to potential clients. It costs next to nothing to print them. Get it?" he said and snickered. "They're all blank."

"I get it," Peter said and looked down at Cleft's desk. "What's that?" He pointed at the case of baseball cards. Topps One, 1972, in the originally sealed hobby box.

"My dad collected these when he was a kid. He would buy case packs in the original packaging and then, he kept them. He put them in a box that said, *Don't open for fifty years*."

"He got me one?" Peter asked.

"No, Peter. He bought a bunch of these and when he died he left them to me. I don't care about baseball. I couldn't tell you the difference between Babe Ruth and ... and ..." he stopped.

"Do you know any other baseball players?"

"Bo Jackson?"

"I'll give it to you but only on a technicality."

"This is your box," Cleft said and pushed the box closer to Peter. "Open it or don't open it or auction it off. It could be a winning lottery ticket. Who knows what's in that box, but whatever you do, don't open it, okay?"

"Okay," Peter said. "Thank you. I appreciate it. I'll take good care of it."

"Yes. Please do," he said and leaned back in his chair and put his feet on his desk. "How's the conspiracy business these days?" Cleft flashed a wide smile at him. The whiteness of his teeth was framed by a thick beard. The beard was something new for Cleft. He thought he'd try it out for a while and see what people thought. For him, it portrayed authority and unwavering confidence. Besides, if you could grow a bushy and nicely framed beard, you should. Cleft was a fairly late bloomer, and growing robust facial hair wasn't something everyone could do, so Cleft didn't want it to go to waste. "I had a drink with Hoffa last night. He loves your work."

"I didn't come here to have you laugh at me."

"Yet, here you are."

"I need your help," Peter said as Cleft spread his hands across his virtually empty desk. A small laptop computer sat in the middle next to the oversized red button. No phone, no pictures or acute identifiers that could tie Cleft back to any sort of human existence. "I was hoping you could look something up for me," Peter said. "A website."

"Sure," Cleft said and made a show of punching his fingers down on the keypad of his computer. "I should start putting that in the commercials that I so broadly advertise everywhere: 'Re-identity services featuring high-speed internet.'"

"You're being an asshole," Peter said and started to get up from the couch.

"Easy there, buddy. What is it? What do you want me to look up?" Cleft said as he indicated with his hand for Peter to stay.

"It's called CheaterStation dot com." Cleft lowered his head. "I'm being serious," Peter added.

"Is the angle that they are funded by the Illuminati?"

"Hilarious."

"I'm not going to do your dirty work for you."

"There isn't any dirty work. I want to look something up. That's all. CheaterStation dot com." He let it roll off his tongue as Cleft typed it into his computer.

"Now what?"

"Can you do a search on the site?"

"Sure."

"Type in my name. Peter Richards."

"What?"

"Please."

Cleft looked down at the keyboard and punched the keys slowly and methodically and then jabbed his pinky finger into the enter button. He watched the screen for what seemed like eons until something showed up. "Fuck me," Cleft said.

"What is it?"

7.

Cleft swung the computer screen around and leaned back in his chair.

It was a small monitor but I could see my face clearly on the right side. On the left was the word **_CHEATER_**.

Bold-faced.

Italicized.

Underlined.

Highlighted.

Below that was a list of baseball card-worthy stats: height, weight, date of birth, favorite location for cheating. I like to take my victims to Round Rock Express games and then to the Salt Lick for dessert. It also had a list of my preferred victims. Apparently, I was into medium height Hispanic women who didn't want children and who liked to live life dangerously. It was way off on my height preferences, but made up for it by giving me four out of five penises on the cheater meter.

Not bad, I thought.

"Peter ... I have to ask," Cleft said delicately.

"It's not true. Completely untrue. We're going through some stuff and figuring everything out, but—nope."

"All right. If you say so," he said and raised his hands with resignation.

"I haven't cheated on her. I haven't even thought about doing something so horrible to her."

"If Paula ever found this ... if someone found this and told her about it."

"I know—I know. I would be finished."

"This is some post-truth shit, my friend. You'd never see your children again."

"I'm aware, Cleft."

"You would be publicly circumcised."

"Got it."

"Okay, okay." He waved his hands out over the desk. "Do you know who did this? Do you know who would post this about you?"

"No."

"Any enemies? Anyone who is out to get you?"

"No."

"No?" he asked stifling a snicker under his breath. "I'm sure in your line of work you have managed to make yourself a nice line up of potential enemies."

"There's Kingsman but he's in lockup. Maximum security up north in some Supermax prison where they have continental breakfast and high-speed internet." Cleft pointed an assured finger in my direction. I could hear him think, *Bingo!* deep inside the folds of his dynamic brain. Delinquency solved. Time to roll up the sidewalks and call it a night. "Everyone else who I offended or angered is dead. But why? Why would he even bother?" I said, not believing that someone like Larry Kingsman would do something so clever and cruel to me.

"Why? 'Why *not?*' is what you should be asking yourself, Peter. You, me—we ruined him. Tore down the empire and crumbled the very fabric of his life. Of course it's him. Has to be him. Random people don't go around slandering someone for no reason whatsoever. Isn't that something you always say? The most obvious explanation is usually the correct explanation."

"But why me and not you?"

"Maybe he's just getting started. It's been ten years. He's adjusted to life on the inside and had time to settle. Now is a great time. He probably thinks you forgot about him."

"I didn't."

"It's just a thought. Besides, it's the future. Anything's possible. We live in an interconnected, multiplatform world. There's a multitude of ways he can get to you."

"Maybe no one looks at the site," I said.

Cleft pounded the keys on his keyboard. "Five million unique hits last week," he said. "That's impressive and horrible at the same time. You should forget about it and pretend it didn't happen."

"I still want your help though. Sitting here and talking about who might have done it is great, but I need you to do some actual work for me."

"I digress. You'll need to refresh me on the friend-for-hire guidelines."

"You have connections. Connections that can help me."

"If you'd like to grab a drink one day, I can review my business model with you. Maybe help you understand better what exactly it is that I do here."

"That's precisely the reason why I came to you. You have connections to the other side."

"The other side of what?"

"The dark side," I whispered. "You have access to the deep web."

"What's that?"

"Oh, come on! Don't be shady."

"Never heard of it."

"It's the part of the web that's hidden, not indexed, not connected to the rest of the internet. Bad things can happen there and usually do. Do I really have to explain this to you?" He rolled his shoulders. "You're in a shady line of work and you require shady tools. Tools that protect you from the light. The light of the law."

"It's not like a club. I don't have a username and password that grants me access to the underworld. If only it were that simple," he said.

"You provide your clients with an entirely new identification. New passports, drivers licenses, bank accounts. You have an infrastructure of people and companies who provide you with those assets. You can't possibly do business with them through the regular channels with the Miles Cooperative not finding out about it."

"You have quite the imagination."

"Is there a way to tell who posted false information about me on a notorious website?" I asked.

"I'm sure there is, but you don't need this so-called deep web to do that."

"What do I need? I'm technically inept so you'll have to tell me."

"It's the future, Peter. Half of your heart is a machine and there are transmitters in your body that feed information back to your doctor every second of every day for the rest of your life. You can't afford to be technically challenged."

"Paula, too."

"What?"

"They also feed information back to Paula. We have children together. Two daughters. Maybe you've met them?"

"It's beside the point. The way things are, the interconnectivity of everything these days, the future being what it is, you simply can't afford to be technically inept."

"I don't know what to tell you."

"Let it go. You didn't ask for my advice but I'm giving it to you nonetheless. Maybe one day you'll get lucky and some hacker group will release the usernames and credit card information of all the vapid CheaterStation users. Then you can track down the bozo who did this to you. But that day isn't today, so forget about it."

"I can't."

"You need to find some direction. A goal, maybe. I don't know. Some purpose. Trolling people on the internet isn't purpose, it's a gateway to jail time."

"But they're slandering me, Cleft. Doesn't that count for something?"

"The courts won't see it that way," he said and shrugged. Unbelievable. "I know how you are."

"How's that?"

"You have a tendency to get yourself wrapped up in things. Really wrapped up in things."

"That's what makes me good at my job. That's the key to my success."

"It might benefit you to take a step back every now and then and have a look at the big picture. That's all I'm saying. Take a vacation or something. Do something nice with the girls."

"Just … help," I said. "It's all I'm asking. Humor me. Be a friend, my best friend, and humor me."

"All right. Look, if you want to find out who did this to you, if you absolutely must know, all you need is a username. A key identifier," he said. "It's common sense, really."

"Maybe the person who did this left a name and contact information if anyone had any follow-up questions," I said. "Maybe someone read the profile and wanted to know more about me so they left a phone number." *Questions about Peter Richards, call 800-GET-FACTS.*

"It doesn't work that way," Cleft said and swung the computer around.

This time I got up and took a few steps in the direction of his desk. It was a small office, eight-by-eight feet, so I didn't go far. I leaned over and looked at the screen. He pointed to the bottom: Posted by MASKEDALBINO45, followed by the post date. Below the lynching was a comment: *It's so true. What a total scumbag. I vouch for this 100%.*

"Things keep getting better for you," Cleft said.

Who are these people?

"Can you tell me who that is—MASKEDALBINO45?"

"That's the username of the person who created the post."

"Right. But who is it? That's what I need the deep web for."

"The deep web is only useful if someone hacked the website and was selling user information. A list of users with a secondary list that contained, in real life, names and contact information. That's assuming whoever posted this used his or her real name and contact information. They could have provided fake information with a stolen credit card, especially if they didn't want to get caught."

"Leave a comment and see if they reply," I said. "I'll lure him in."

"Use the good old Peter Richards charm on him?"

"Exactly."

"I have to log in to leave a comment, and in order to do that I need an account and I'm not doing that," Cleft said.

"Come on, man. You can use my credit card. I don't mind." I could see he was getting uncomfortable. He shifted in his chair and was probably thinking about how to get out of this situation. It's fine, I understand. I showed up here and asked for his help and now I'm asking him to log into websites and leave comments for people who might as well be ax murderers. His nervousness was warranted but he was going to have to let it go. "Don't worry about it. You're right. I shouldn't have asked," I said.

"Thanks," he said. A strong flow of air escaped his lungs.

"I'll do it," I said and grabbed his keyboard. "You relax."

"Peter!" he said and leaned forward, but I held my hand out for him to stop. He didn't move. I clicked *Login* and set the keyboard in my lap.

A new screen showed up asking me if I wanted to sign in as NOTCLEFTDV4 or create a new username and password.

"What the fuck, Cleft?" I said as I stared at the series of letters on the screen.

"I can explain," he said.

"Is this your account? '*Not* Cleft'?!"

"I can explain," he repeated and put his hands up in a surrender position, but I didn't want to listen to him. I didn't care to hear whatever nonsense he was going to heave in my direction. I didn't want to hear about how he just bought this computer and what an outrageous coincidence this probably was. People who had CheaterStation accounts were filth. They were filth, and lowlifes with no self-worth. And Cleft, apparently.

"What's your password?" I asked him. "I'm going to login in as you and leave a comment. Weed this fucker out."

"I'm not telling you my password."

"It's fine. I'll guess. Can't be that difficult," I said and started punching the keys. Password: *123456, QWERTY, abc123.*

The username and/or password you entered was incorrect flashed on the screen each time.

StarWars.

IAmGod.

CleftIsGod.

Jaba4Ever.

"I don't know anything about *Star Wars*," he said.

FakeBeard.

"Hey. That's not nice."

ILOVEPETER.

Peterisg0d.

"You think I'm some kind of imbecile?" he said.

"Dammit," I said.

"It will lock you out if you keep trying."

"Once more," I said and jabbed my fingers down on the keys: *F-U-C-K-P-E-T-E-R.*

*The username and/or password
you entered is incorrect.*

"Is that what you think?" he asked.

"Oh, wait—hold on."

F-U-C-K-P-3-T-3-R.

Welcome back, NOTCLEFTDV4.
You have no new messages since your last login.

"I can explain," he said again.

"What shall you start with? The reason why you have the account, or the genesis of your heartfelt and clever password?"

He took a breath and rolled his sleeves up. "When I cheated on Phyllis it nearly ruined us," he started in with his story. A story he kept in his back pocket about how once he was bad and now he was good. A few years ago he entered a long-term perverse affair with his secretary. After a while, and probably when he became sufficiently bored with the whole thing, he decided to tell his wife about it. Needless to say, the confession didn't go smoothly and nearly destroyed their marriage, but they worked through it. Cleft likes to talk about this a lot, mostly to show how he's better now, nicer even, but also to show people that therapy and talking about intangible things for long periods of time actually works. It was a story of redemption through and through but I didn't listen. Instead, I stared at the computer screen and let the letters burn into my cerebral cortex: MASKEDALBINO45.

Who was this alleged masked albino?
What did he want with me?
What was his beef?

"It's work but, it's commitment," Cleft said.

"Do you not trust Phyllis? Is that what this is about?" I asked.

"No. It's not that at all."

"What is it then?"

"It's another way to pass the time. I swear. Some people play *Second Life* or *Minecraft*. Some people stream porn or—whatever. This is entertainment. You should see the shit Avery does online."

"I'll pass. Thank you."

"I'm just saying. You go into the rabbit hole—who knows when you'll come out. It's the other side, Peter."

"What about the password?"

"I thought it would be funny. That's all. I thought it would make for a great anecdote if someone ever asked for my password. 'Oh, let me tell you. Hilarious that you asked because my password is *Fuck Peter*. But with threes instead of E's. Great joke, right?'"

"Brilliant. You should have told me. Now you made it a whole thing."

"Sorry. But I didn't have to tell you, because you guessed it. Like some sort of David Blaine mind game."

"Don't apologize. I shouldn't have intruded. I should know my place. I'm the one who should apologize."

"What are you going to say?"

"What?"

"When you leave a comment? What are you going to write?"

"I'm not sure," I said.

"You need to get his attention."

"I got it," I said and punched a few keys on his computer and turned the computer screen around so he could see it. "What do you think?"

MASKEDALBINO45, *I'm listening -Peter (NOTCLEFTDV4)*.

"Very clever stuff, Peter. Almost as precise as your journalism," he said.

"That's a cheap shot."

"I call it how I see it," he said as his computer beeped. We looked at the screen.

Then you can hear me laughing.

"Shit. That was quick," I said.

"Maybe it's one of those autobots that has a pre-programmed response at the ready once you type something. They have outfits like that in China. Lure you in, steal your social security number and identity. Dangerous stuff. I mean, pure speculation."

"Maybe," I said, but I wasn't so sure. I jabbed my fingers into the keyboard.

What do you want?

I waited a second. I could smell the remains of Cleft's lunch floating through the room. It smelled like fried chicken with a strong curry aftertaste.

"Indian for lunch?"

"Always."

"How was it?"

"Terrific," he said.

"I miss it. So much."

"Oh, come on. You sneak food all the time. Chicken and lemon and black coffee diet for life, my ass, Peter."

"No way," I said as the computer dinged again.

We need your help flashed on the computer screen.

Help with what? I thought to myself. I punched the keys again. *DTF?*

"What is DTF? What does that stand for?" Cleft asked.

"It's an acronym," I said and waited for a response.

"I can see that," he said.

"I might sneak out for a cheeseburger tonight."

"I knew it."

"Don't tell, okay?"

"Sure. Fine. Whatever, Peter," he said.

"Down to fuck," I said.

"Excuse me?"

"DTF. That's what it stands for. Down to fuck."

"Why would you write that?"

"Weed them out. Maybe you're right. About the autobot. Maybe they want to steal my identity," I said. "Need to keep all avenues of possibility open."

Let's meet Saturday. 5 PM. Driskill -MASKEDALBINO45.

"Shit," Cleft said.

"Maybe it's not an autobot."

"Did you sign yourself up for a booty call?"

"Maybe," I said and suddenly began to worry about what Carol got me into. But things are the way they are, and here I was, left to face the consequences and sit down with someone who was going to assuredly blackmail me. *Thanks, Carol.*

8.

When I got home I set the case of baseball cards Cleft gave to me on top of a filing cabinet in my office and went to my desk and opened the file for SolChem.

They wanted me to prove they weren't connected, in any way whatsoever, to a global tragedy.

I didn't have much on them.

MISSING AIRPLANE
HUNDREDS FEARED DEAD

SolChem and Rothschild kept their distance.

Truth was, I couldn't find enough evidence in one direction or another. I couldn't find a single substantial piece of evidence to connect them to the airplane disappearance but, at the same time, I couldn't prove they weren't connected and, unfortunately, that's what they needed from me.

They hired me to prove a negative.

Paula could say what she wanted, but I was making a decent income and could help provide for our family. As far as I was concerned, that's all that mattered, but Paula didn't think I was doing enough to give back. She worked for a bioinformatics firm that developed state-of-the-art tools that helped companies understand biological data. Paula and her team would spend months, or years, developing a single tool and when they were finished, they would sell the tool to a company that could eventually benefit from it. She had years of education, a promising career, and was a real contributor to society. She also sold cosmetics in her free time and helped recruit neighbors to sell them as well.

"That's where the real money is," she told me. "If you do it for however many years they'll buy you a brand new car and send you on fancy cruises."

Then there was me.

I had a degree in journalism and spent the better part of my adult life working as a television investigative journalist. I was pretty good at it too, until the local TV news business cannibalized itself with weather and traffic reports and stations running updates on what viral videos were playing online. The local stations didn't have a desire for the prestige and integrity that investigative journalists brought to the job. It's been a decade since I last did anything in that business and it's refreshing to know that very few things have changed since I left. Weather and traffic still drive the numbers, but stations now hire lifestyle reporters to provide updates on what celebrities and styles are trending. Their job is to sit at the news desk and read stories they found on blogs the night before. Groundbreaking stuff.

The Peter Richards of the world were a dying breed, but I haven't let that discourage me. I've used my experience in the local news business in hopes that I would find another career. I've tried everything from newspaper reporter to on-air radio personality, and even volunteered to be the editor for a local university's alumni magazine.

Nope, nope, and absolutely no way.

I set aside the SolChem file and began to draft a plan for when I would come face-to-face with MASKEDALBINO45.

I made sure the plan wasn't complicated and took into account Cleft's apprehensions. I told myself that I wouldn't let it get out of control and that I only wanted to find out who would post such insidious things about me. The internet is a dangerous place, and if people are free to post anonymous accusations about people they don't know, then they should be held accountable.

I had a little over forty-eight hours before I was scheduled to meet MASKEDALBINO45 at the Driskill Hotel downtown. Cleft offered to go with me, but I told him that wasn't necessary. He was being a good friend, but I could handle this situation on my own. I was going to arrive at the Driskill at four and grab one of those comfy couches in the lobby that's always occupied by important business men waiting for their weekend cocktail before heading home. I would order a white wine to combat the heat, and didn't plan on waiting for more than thirty minutes. I anticipated my rival showing up early and being caught by surprise when they discovered I was already there. That's how I would know who it was: the shock on their face when they saw me sitting in the lobby enjoying a nice glass of wine. I would then go over and introduce myself and ask them to join me for a drink, and I'd get the backstory. I already called a friend at the *Statesman* asking if they would be interested in running a piece on catching local internet predators. They said they were sure they didn't think they were interested, but said they would call me back nonetheless.

I would listen intently as MASKEDALBINO45 gave me a recap of what they posted and then nod my head in disgust as he or she apologized profusely. They would agree to take the post down and issue an apology on the internet, and to take out a half-page advertisement in each of the big Austin newspapers:

Peter Richards, wrongfully accused of adultery, is a good man.

The plan was near perfect, and I was building a list of suspects in my mind when my phone rang. It was Paula.

"I'm waiting on a protein sequence to finish running." Such important work she's been doing. "I wanted to remind you to pick Joyce up from camp today. She has gymnastics and Maya is going to Emma's house for the night."

"It's a Thursday."

"We can't win every argument. Also, Joyce's competition is Saturday, so she has practice every night this week. I thought we'd discussed this."

"That's fine."

"She needs to be there by four on Saturday. You know how ... particular ... they are about showing up on time."

"And then I can leave, right?"

"Why would you leave?" she asked.

"I have an appointment. Something important."

"More important than Joyce's gymnastics competition?"

"Different levels of importance. It's a subjective thing. Can you take her?"

"Depends on how this sodium trial goes. It might be a few late nights for me. Also something we may or may not have discussed. What do you have on Saturday again?"

"Ah—a thing is all."

"Sounds important," she said, but I could sense her attention drifting. Nothing could possibly be as important as a sodium trial.

"Hey," I said. "Did you know someone posted something about me on a website saying I cheated on you?"

"What?" she said and laughed.

"Easy there."

"That's ridiculous."

"What's ridiculous? That someone posted it or that I would do that?"

"Did you do that?" she said. "Did you cheat on me?" A deafening silence floated through the phone line. "Hello?"

"No, of course not, Paula," I said.

"No. It's not 'Of course not, Paula,'" she said. "It happens. It's something people have been known to do. Not you or I, but people in general. People we know, in fact. We've also had some rocky moments, who doesn't really, so I thought I would ask."

"Appreciate it but the answer is still no," I said and meant it. "Not that I don't have options."

"Oh really? Keep me posted on that, Peter."

"Of course," I said.

"Do you know who posted these slanderous things about you?"

"It's not slanderous. It's libel, actually. They wrote it so it's libel. If they went and said that stuff about me in public, on the news for instance, it would be considered slander."

"Seems arbitrary."

"It's not. In fact, it's pretty precise. If it ever got to court, that is, it would be libel. Anyway, that's what I'm doing on Saturday. I'm having a face-to-face."

"Sounds dangerous."

"We don't really know right now. I'll take the proper precautions though. I promise."

"We?"

"Yes. Me and Cleft."

"The dangerous duo, you two."

"Fighting crime one internet creep at a time," I said a little more enthusiastically than intended.

"Did you also find a way to get people to watch local news?" she added and continued to laugh at me.

"Cruel, Paula," I said and lowered my head and examined the dirt on my shoes. "Anyway, that's what I'm doing on Saturday. We're going to the Driskill and we're going to have a drink."

"Maybe it's Betty."

"Betty?"

"Yes. She always had it out for you."

"Out for me?" I asked.

"You always sort of bothered her. Rubbed her the wrong way. She thought you were strange and couldn't quite put her finger on it." Betty was the mother of Maya's friend Emma. Paula and I had dinner with her and her husband, whose name I can't remember, a few times, but we found them to be incredibly boring. I always thought Betty had a thing for me, but apparently, I was incorrect in that assessment. It's possible Betty was saying those things to Paula to deflect from her true feelings. Betty also never bought cosmetics from Paula and I suspected that irritated Paula.

People are complicated.

"I don't know who it is, but I set up a meeting. I'll get it all sorted out."

"It's strange they would post that, especially if it wasn't true."

"I know, and it's not true."

"We've been over this."

"I know," I said and thought about it. *Paula had a point. What was the point of posting reprehensible things about me if they weren't true? What were the odds I would find it?* "They must want something in return."

"Oh, for sure," she said. "Doesn't everyone?"

"Eh," I said and shrugged it off. There was no way to know for sure until I was there. Face-to-face. Man to man or woman to man or auto-bot-in-the-flesh to man. DTF autobot having cocktails at the Driskill.

"I noticed that your heart rate is running a little high," Paula said. "You might want to take a pill before you pick Joyce up."

"Okay."

"Can't have you dying on me twice."

"Three times, actually," I said. "If we're keeping track."

9.

Paula, the girls, and I live in a three-bedroom, two-and-a-half bath fixer-upper in the southwest part of Austin.

It's relatively close to downtown, the zoo and, this part is very important, feeds into a good school district. At least, that's what the realtor said. A good school district means the girls would receive a relatively good education, have a better chance of getting into top tier colleges, and land jobs that would give them enough money to pay for our nursing home. The dollars we saved by not going the route of private education went directly towards our mortgage and property taxes. It was something that would pay dividends later on in life. Again, the realtor. Besides, if most of your income wasn't tied up in a thirty-year mortgage, and a fifteen-year second mortgage, you weren't living the American dream.

Joyce was about to start sixth grade and spends her free time asking questions.

Maya recently turned ten and spends the majority of her time inside a virtual reality headset we got her for Christmas. I think she has freckles on her nose but it's been so long since I've seen it.

Given the school district we were in, Joyce was going to attend Harvard and enjoy a corner office at Goldman Sachs by the time she was twenty-three. Maya was going to attend MIT and become a world-renowned chemical engineer. Given how things were going, she would probably still have the headset on.

Paula and I felt that living in an area with a good school district was an important investment in our daughters' future. In fact, Paula made this decision on her own when we were separated. At the time, I lived in a one-bedroom apartment around the corner from our old house in the north-central part of the city. I was only there for a few weeks when Paula told me that she and girls had decided to move. Paula and I needed space to work through some things, so my moving out temporarily was the best solution. It didn't occur to me at the time that Paula was going to decide that she and the girls needed to be farther away from me.

At least, that's how I saw it.

Paula said it was because the school district was in a better area and they needed to move there while houses were still affordable. They moved, got settled, and a few months later, Paula called me up and said I was welcome to join them. If I was free and didn't have any plans, I was welcome to move back in with my wife and two children.

So inviting.

Paula later told me, in her heavy native Russian accent, that she didn't want to seem eager about it. The door was open and it was up to me to decide whether or not I wanted to come back in.

That accent.

The disappearing reappearing Russian accent.

For the first few years of marriage, Paula feigned a convincing American accent that she picked up from a summer spent at the Moscow Arts Academy. We met on a website that provided charming American men, who didn't like their options, with beautiful and educated Russian women who wanted to move to America and start a family. That sort of union was usually frowned upon and heavily judged, so Paula and I made up a story about how we met and fell in love in college.

The story was good for a few years.

We'd reminisce about spending spring break in Cabo and the last minute trip we took to wine country. Things began to disintegrate when Paula told a group of friends about how we had dinner with President Reagan at Musso & Frank in Los Angeles. She said that she always dreamed of dining with the famous American actor, and how he was shy and nicer than she expected. Needless to say, she wasn't a pro with her American history and the story of our union started to crack.

People asked questions:

"Where in Massachusetts did you grow up?"

"Have you ever been to the Topsfield Fair?"

"What do you mean you never heard of the Topsfield Fair?"

We couldn't hold up to the intense scrutiny.

Apparently, the Topsfield Fair is a very real thing, and if you live in Massachusetts, you've heard of it, and have attended at least once.

We gave the charade a rest and decided to tell people the truth. I met Paula online, paid for her and her daughter, Joyce, to travel to America, and she assumed an American identity. It made for great conversation at dinner parties. Paula embraces the Russian accent now and throws in a good old Texan "y'all" every now and then to keep people on their feet: "Can I have some borscht with that, y'all?" "Can you believe Putin is still in power, y'all?"

"I fucking hate this," Joyce said under her breath.

"Don't say things like that," I said.

We were sitting along the side of the gymnasium and she was pulling off her sweatpants and watching her team do warm-ups on a trampoline.

"They're going to give Abbey the pommel horse routine because I wasn't on time."

We were ten minutes late. My fault. "They can't penalize you because your dad didn't hit all the green lights."

"Sure they can," she said and stood up. "Watch me." She tossed her sweatpants into her gym bag and joined the group mid-stretch. She leaned over to touch her toes. Her coach went over and tapped Joyce on the shoulder and whispered something in her ear and pointed to a pile of sweaty towels steaming in the corner. Joyce excused herself from the group and went over to the towels and started folding them. She looked over at me as the sweat of teenagers wafted under her nose. The squint in her eyes wasn't anger or annoyance.

It was disappointment.

Dad didn't hit the green lights so Joyce is late and has to say goodbye to that Olympic dream her coaches sort of promised her.

Thankfully we were in a good school district and she was receiving a reliable education.

I gave her a shrug to let her know that I felt bad but things would be okay eventually. Things always managed to work out no matter what the circumstances. She would move on. If folding towels and being persona non grata was really the punishment for being late, then maybe gymnastics wasn't the right thing for her.

Sometimes it was good to be persona non grata.

I looked around at the other parents dolefully waiting in the wings. They were armed with a plethora of modern day technology to keep them occupied until they had to drive their kid to the next socially acceptable conformist activity they signed their kid up for to show the world their kid is a) an active participant and b) on the road to success. The parents were all face-down, absorbing unending streams of information.

All except for two of them:

A man and a woman.

Probably my age, maybe a little older. They weren't encumbered with technology. In fact, I couldn't see a phone, watch, tablet, or vision device anywhere near them. This was the future and they weren't taking advantage of it. Did they not get the message? Or did they get the message and willfully chose to ignore it? These Luddites were doing the unimaginable. They were watching their daughter do the pommel horse. Abbey. Joyce's nemesis.

Figures.

They probably showed up fifteen minutes early and brought donuts for the coaches. Everyone has an angle. Mine was being unpredictably irritable and emotionally unattainable. It didn't benefit Joyce much, and I was pure shit at dinner parties, but it had its advantages.

Next to the mom was a boy. Straggly brown hair and a slender face with strong cheek bones. He was also fully engaged, cheering his sister on.

Something was off.

It wasn't the absence of worthwhile technology or the ersatz enthusiasm. It was something else, and a flitting sense of unease passed through my stomach. It wasn't yesterday's skinless chicken breast comingling with this morning's dry toast.

It was something different.

The dad seemed familiar but I couldn't place it. He was leaning against the wall but looked tall. He had short-cropped surfer-blonde hair and a dark eyes. He wasn't the general straight-from-the-cutting-block dad you normally see at these gatherings, indistinguishable from all the other dads. He was on TV. That sitcom people ridicule in social circles—"It's so offensive. That format has been dead for decades."— only to go home and binge watch while sucking down homemade pinot grigio.

That wasn't it.

The woman was also familiar. Maybe a world-renowned athlete

who was siphoning her dreams off on her daughter and holding her son hostage to watch. Greatness in the making.

But that wasn't it either. I didn't recognize them separately. The dad wasn't from TV and the mom wasn't an athlete. It was a collective recognition. All four of them in fact. It was rare I would see a ten-year-old kid who wasn't mine and think I saw him in a past life.

The dad, mom, son, and daughter.

I knew them all and in a single instance, a thought passed through my head, and my stomach was penetrated by a torpedo and sunk.

Cleft told me not to get carried away with things, not to let my imagination and thoughts get the best of me. I needed to buckle down and focus, but this was something I couldn't ignore.

10.

"Joyce, let's go," I said as the coach finished the final routine.

When Joyce was done folding all of the towels, they let her spot Abbey as she did three cartwheels as part of a more elaborate floor exercise. It was good they weren't letting Joyce's talents go completely to waste.

I helped her pack up her stuff and then took her back to the house.

"It smells amazing in here, Mom," Joyce said as she set her bag down on the kitchen table. I went over and turned on the television on the kitchen counter and started to set the table.

"Go wash your hands," Paula said and then looked over at me. "I saw that your sodium levels were off the charts earlier so I made you a salad."

"It gets a bad reading every now and then," I said and went over to Maya who was sitting on the couch in front of the television. But she wasn't watching TV, she was wearing her ReTrak Utopia Virtual Reality Headset.

I lifted up the side of it and gave her a kiss on the cheek. "Learning anything in there?" I asked.

She nodded and waved me away.

"You need to take care of yourself. You've been doing so well," Paula said.

"I might have a little salad and then head out."

"Out?"

"I have to meet with those guys from SolChem," I said and leaned in to give her a kiss but she moved away from me. I turned the volume up on the television.

"You can take the salad with you," she said. "What are you watching?"

"Some story about how someone stole a chemical weapon from a military base in North Carolina."

"Let me guess. Kennedy is somehow involved."

"No, but that would be pretty interesting," I said. "Hey, have you seen this family at gymnastics?"

"I've seen a few families—yes."

"No, it's a specific family. Mom, dad, girl, and boy," I said. "Joyce, what's the name of that girl you don't like?" I shouted down the hall.

"Abbey," she said. "She's the worst."

"Abbey. That's right. Do you know her parents?"

"I don't think so. Why?" Paula asked.

"It's … something about them. I don't know. It's something familiar."

"What do you think it is?"

"You ever heard of the Mandela Effect?"

"Peter. Stop."

"It's when we remember something a certain way but we are actually incorrect the whole time. Like you think you know Abbey and her family and you're used to seeing them around but in fact, you don't know them at all. Actually, it's possible this is the first time Joyce has actually seen them."

"I don't think that's it," Paula said.

"Abbey gets all the praise," Joyce said as she came back in shaking water off her hands. "Everybody loves her but I only think that's because she's new. The love will wear off, once they find something to judge."

"No. I got an uneasy feeling when I saw them. Something doesn't sit right."

"Part of the Skull and Bones, are they?"

"No."

"Maybe they're zombies?" Joyce added and smiled at Paula. "Zombies who want to destroy the world economy."

"It's not funny. I'm serious."

"Of course you are, honey," Paula said as she set a plastic to-go container in front of me. It was stuffed to the brim with state-of-the-art quinoa and spinach. It tasted like sand, but was better for the heart. Supposedly. "Don't be out too late," she said.

"Of course not," I said as I took the food and kissed the girls good-bye.

I went into the garage and got into the car.

I set my dinner on the passenger seat and started the engine and pulled out of the garage.

I cut back through the neighborhood and went to a wine bar that was on the main road outside of the neighborhood. I sat at the bar and ordered a glass of wine and a cheeseburger. One cheeseburger wasn't going to kill me.

At least not this time.

Fine. Hold the mayo.

The television above the bar was running some evening news program hosted by Travis Holt.

"Tonight. We have an update on the Red Mercury that went missing from a military base in North Carolina," Travis said. "Red Mercury is a highly dangerous powder that has the ability to wipe out entire populations. When asked for comment, the head of the NSA said, 'We're working on it and everyone should remain calm.'"

Travis used to be an anchor for KVAN in Austin and then died when he was going a hundred miles an hour on the interstate with a fifth of Fireball in his system. Fireball was popular with fraternity houses, country musicians, and local TV anchors getting over a tough breakup. Travis and his partner of seven years, Doug, were having some problems and Doug decided to call it quits.

Travis didn't take the breakup well, spent a week drowning his sorrows at Stubb's, and then took his F-350 on a joy ride on I-35 in the wrong direction and came face-to-face with a semi-truck carrying fresh produce.

Police said he didn't feel a thing.

The Fireball wiped out any sensation he had left.

Two hours after the accident, the station's parent company showed up at the county morgue and claimed the body, and said it was for research and "the future of television." Travis had no family to dispute the claim so the suits at the network took Travis's body back to New York and put it through a few network mandated upgrades and technological improvements.

Two weeks later Travis was promoted to the evening news.

The network's parent company was also a majority stakeholder in a robotics firm that was developing human-to-robot technology. The technology was light-years ahead of its competitors and made my ∂-zero heart look like it was created for a high school science fair project. The company gave Travis Holt a premium upgrade. They removed all of his vital organs and replaced them with cutting-edge machines that regulated his internal systems. His heart, liver, lungs, and intestines were all made of premium-grade platinum and outfitted with RFID chips that sent information back to the mothership twenty-four hours a day, seven days a week. In fact, it's been suggested that the company wanted to replace Travis with a complete robot altogether, but the network pushed back saying that Travis had a loyal following. Even more so now that the human version, Travis 1.0, died in a horrendous car crash that could only garner additional sympathy.

"It's fucking crazy, isn't it? A robot hosting the evening news. What has this world come to?"

I looked over. Abbey's dad—that guy from gymnastics—was standing behind me. He waved his hand in the general direction of the bartender. "Two more please."

"Part robot. Ten percent human," I corrected.

"That's right. They have to keep the viewers happy."

"The viewers are only part of it. I used to work in the business. People watch stuff out of habit. They don't care who's telling them what. People would listen to the news if a fish wearing spandex was reading it to them."

"That's pretty funny," he said and laughed. "I'm David." He proffered his hand.

"Peter."

"Peter, nice to meet you."

"Don't I know you?" I asked.

"Our daughters do gymnastics together."

"Oh right. That's it." But it wasn't. There was something else.

"That's Darlene over there," he said and pointed across the bar, where a woman with light blonde hair was sitting sipping on a glass of wine. She looked up at us and smiled. Her hair went past her shoulders and framed her face kindly. "Darlene, this is Peter! His daughter—"

"Joyce."

"—is in Abbey's gymnastics class!"

"Nice to finally meet you, Peter! Joyce is such a doll," she said and raised her glass.

"It's peculiar, isn't it?" David said.

"What's that?"

"Your old job being outsourced to a robot. Doesn't that freak you out?" I shook my head. "What use are we if robots can do what we do?"

"It's called innovation and it helps society be more efficient and aspire to loftier goals."

"That's what they want you to think. Between them and the Miles Cooperative having their nose in everybody's business, we might as well call it the end of the world."

"What do you mean having their nose in everybody's business?"

"Are you not familiar with the Miles Cooperative? They're the over-lords of your fine city."

"I'm familiar. Peripherally."

"You should look them up," he said. "They have a big super-secret meeting here next month. Prominent world leaders and elite intellec-tuals will play golf, drink craft cocktails, and discuss the formation of a secret One World Government."

"Oh really?"

"Oh, yes ..."

"I'll see that I do that," I said. "Are you going to this meeting?"

"God no, Peter. I would rather be caught in a back alley with a transvestite. I'm one of the good guys," he said. "What do you do now? If you don't mind me asking. What line of work are you in?"

"I debunk conspiracies. I legitimize people, companies, and events."

"How is that working out for you?"

"I make a living off it, if that's what you're asking."

"If that's what's important to you," he said. *Who was this guy?* "I love it. The top story tonight, from the mouth of Travis Holt, a man among men, is about skyrocketing unemployment. Especially with low wage workers being outsourced by robots and humanoids. The irony."

"I suppose." *Asshole.*

"You're part machine, aren't you?" he asked.

"Excuse me?"

"Your wristband—Ǝ-zero." He looked down at the wristband I was wearing. A thin gray metal bracelet with a backwards *E* in the middle.

Underneath the backwards *E* was a transmitter that sent information back to headquarters and Paula.

"My heart. Part machine."

"With a few upgrades you'll be carrying one of those titanium beasts around inside of you in no time. The bracelet will be an antique and they'll shove the transmitter under the skin on the bottom of your wrist. You won't be able to tell the difference between a few nuts and bolts and your own bones."

"You know a lot about this stuff?"

"I pay attention. It's only inevitable. Everyone is talking about what the future will bring, what promises the future holds, they forget to realize they are living in the future. We should be more concerned about the end."

"Oh," I said and looked down at my bracelet. "The future is not what I imagined."

"It never is. Is that a world you want to live in, Peter? Where you can't tell the difference between yourself and a machine? Did you vote for the Socialist?"

"I haven't given it much thought," I said.

"You should," he said and jerked his finger over his shoulder. "You guys live in the area?"

"About a mile away. You?"

"We're renting a place around the corner. We want to move into the neighborhood—but, shit, those prices."

"Good school district," I said as the cheeseburger tumbled around my stomach.

"Here. Take this," he said and took a cocktail napkin from the bar and wrote something down on it. "It's my number. Give me a call. Maybe the girls can ride together to gymnastics—or whatever."

But my daughter hates your daughter, I thought to myself as I took the napkin. "Thanks," I said and looked down at it. It was a 512 area code. Austin. I crumpled it up and shoved it in my pocket. "Are you sure I don't know you? You look familiar. Familiar outside of gymnastics," I said.

"Don't let your imagination get the better of you, my friend," he said and put a hand on my shoulder. "It was good to see you."

"Good to see you, too."

"See you at practice," he said as he picked up two glasses of wine and walked away.

I turned back to the bar and looked up at the television and took a bite of my burger.

CNN was on with another update about the family that went missing from Florida. They were interviewing a neighbor and then put the pictures of David and Darlene Creed on the screen.

I looked away and then back up at the screen again.

My eyes froze.

The picture of David Creed on the screen was familiar: square-shaped face and blonde hair with a receding hair line. His nose was narrow and made a small point right at the tip. He had dark eyes and small dimples.

My napkin slipped off my knee and floated down to the floor.

I turned around but David was gone.

I stood up and walked past the bar and went into the coffee shop that was connected to the restaurant.

It was empty.

I went back to the bar.

"Did you see where that couple went?"

"What couple?"

"He came over for two glasses of wine."

"No idea," he said. "You need anything else?"

"The check," I said and took my phone out.

"Hello?" Cleft said softly on the other end.

"Did you hear about that family that went missing from Florida?"

"What family? No."

"They went missing in broad daylight. Disappeared. It was weird. TV is saying it's strange."

"Drug mules?"

"I think I just talked to the guy. Their daughter is in gymnastics with Joyce."

"What? Are you seriously calling me about this?"

"What? I'm eating dinner and he comes over and starts talking to me and then I see the picture of David Creed on TV and—same guy. Pretty sure. I haven't seen them before gymnastics."

"Good-bye, Peter." Cleft said and hung up.

The bartender came back and set the check down.

I looked at it and put a fifty down.

I got up and walked outside and was welcomed with the warm humid air of early summer and Detective Skelly standing by a trash can smoking. A lady was standing next to him. "Oh, hey, Skelly. What are you doing here?" I asked.

"Just hanging out."

"Hi. I'm Peter," I said to the lady and proffered my hand.

"She doesn't care," Skelly said. "I saw they have a robot doing the evening news. How you feel about that? Must hurt. Huh, Peter? It must tear into you. Maybe a little bit?"

"Who are you?" the woman said as she looked at me and squinted.

"Don't worry about him," Skelly said. "He's just a ghost. See you on the other side, Richards," he said and flicked his cigarette in the trash and walked away.

11.

Paula and the girls were asleep when I got home.

The temperature in the house was set at a cool sixty-seven degrees, the result of an end-to-end integrated home system that Ɔ-zero grew into perfection over the past decade.

What started out as smart televisions and ubiquitous built-in video surveillance has evolved into motion sensors, automated temperature control, real-time energy consumption, and overall self-awareness. The home is able to take care of itself better than any single human being could. It's a home built for efficiency and modern-day living. When my car is within two hundred feet and its remote sensor connects to the sensor on the front of the house, it triggers the porch lights and opens the garage door for me. That is, of course, if the sensor can tell that I'm not under duress. If I have an elevated heart rate and increased blood pressure it asks me for an audio confirmation. If I provide the correct passcode, it initiates the Welcome Home package. If I provide it with a dummy passcode—*dirigible, Peter Fonda, tuna fish sandwich*—it calls the police.

I took my shoes off in the coat room and went into the kitchen.

The lights were dimmed to my liking and the sound system started playing one of a thousand songs it thought I'd like based on my internet search history divided by my current mood. If I liked what it was playing I could simply hit the buy button on my watch and it would download it to my current yet ever-expanding music library. I listened to a Miles Davis tribute band play "Seven Steps to Heaven" as a Rube Goldberg machine sat on the kitchen counter concocting a cup of sleepy-time tea to my exact preferences. I decided to forego the tea and went upstairs to the home office and shut the door. I would receive a text from the customer satisfaction department at Ə-zero in approximately ten to twelve minutes asking me if I was enjoying the tea or if there was anything that needed to be done differently next time. I needed to remind myself to tell them that I don't like tea and that I didn't need it every time I came home.

If I run out to pick up the girls—tea.

Run out to the gym and come back—tea.

The type of tea was determined by the time of day. The only exception was first thing in the morning when it would give me black coffee. The sugar and milk were reserved for Paula.

The walls of the home office were filled with newspaper clippings of Larry Kingsman, former owner of one of Austin's most-prized television networks. It wasn't him I was so much interested in, but more so the occasional mention I received in conjunction with his ultimate take down: *Peter Richards Foils Criminal Enterprise* or, my favorite—*Peter Richards, Man of the Hour and Former Reporter Takes Down the King!* Paula had a field day with that one. She said that I shouldn't let it get to my head and my best days were ahead of me. She was being kind.

I went over to a filing cabinet that was pressed up against the couch.

I opened the bottom drawer to find two rows of old DVDs. Most of them were copies of stories I did when I was an investigative journalist in Boston and there were a few from my short stint at KVAN in Austin. I reached behind the DVDs and pulled out an old VHS tape. I dusted it off and spun around in my chair to turn on the television. I put the VHS tape into an old Emerson four-head player. After a few minutes a grainy image appeared on the screen and then the word *ZAPRUDER*.

There was a knock at the door and Paula peeked her head in.

"What are you doing?"

"Zapruder," I said and pointed to the screen.

"Again?"

"It's for sure fake. There's a part a few seconds in where it looks like the frame drops. It's a fraction of a second, but I'm sure it's there," I said. "I thought you were asleep."

"Restless," she said and looked at the other tapes in the drawer. "I remember you telling me about those. Undiscovered Austin crime syndicate."

"He never did let me do the story. Those guys—they're still out there. Where's the justice in this world?" I said as Paula came over and sat down next to me and stared at the television with me.

"Maybe they had a sense of remorse and quit? Found a better life," she said.

"That doesn't happen."

"Maybe they took their winnings and went to Monte Carlo. That's what all bad guys do," she added and smiled.

"They aren't called winnings when they're stolen."

"Maybe they should be. Maybe people should actually protect the things they value the most. If they really cared about their money or their valuables it wouldn't have happened."

"I guess. It's only stuff after all. Things. Items of no discernible value. Just applied value."

"They should be more worried about what the government is doing with their tax money. Where is that going? The infrastructure of this country—*our* country—is no better than a dilapidated *Monopoly* board."

"For someone with US citizenship you sure do have a lot of complaints."

"Observations, if you will. Besides, it's our right. We have the freedom to vote for what we think is right. We get to vote for what we think should happen in this country."

"That's presuming you don't think the election system is totally rigged," I said

"Peter Richards loves a good cover-up," she said.

"You know me too well."

"You should put your old stuff online. It might be a little outdated, but you did some good work."

"I'm sure people will love my theory that a gang of crooked cops was behind the burglaries. Meticulously orchestrated from police head-quarters. Some things are better left...undiscussed."

"I wanted to ask you something—tell you something and then ask you a question. I forgot earlier," Paula said and then continued to look at the television.

"Don't bury the lead," I said.

"I spoke with Phyllis this morning. She called me."

"Oh." Phyllis was Cleft's wife. She was always in my business and always concerned about what Peter Richards was up to these days.

"Apparently, Avery is looking to hire someone."

"Avery?" I said incredulously. "He's like twenty-two."

"She. She is twenty-four," Paula corrected me.

Avery was Cleft's son and used to sell prescription drugs on the black market, went to juvie for a while, and came out the other side as some kind of gender nonconformist with a brilliant idea to reform the juvenile justice system. Something about letting criminal kids become gardeners so they could understand the significance and value of life. Sounded like some royal bullshit to me. But that's Avery for you. It's not as if s/he invented gardening. Anyway, some hedge fund manager, whose asshole kid was also in juvie, got wind of this and gave Avery twenty million dollars in seed money. So far, all Avery's done is draft a mission statement and play video games. I'm sure s/he's onto something though, after all, s/he is hiring, apparently. "She's trying to get things up and running," Paula added. "She has cash to spend and needs someone to help her run the day-to-day operations. Someone she trusts."

"You mean someone Phyllis can lure over."

"It's a job, Peter."

"I have a job—things—I'm doing. Besides, I don't see how helping a derelict run a fake company has anything to do with my experience as a journalist. It doesn't seem to fit the mold."

"I think you should be open to the mold changing, and it's a very real company. You'd be great at it."

"Eh," I said and waved my hand at the TV. Let's get back to business and what really matters here. "Will you help me put my stuff on-line?" I finally conceded.

"Have Maya do it."

"I'll ask her next time she comes back to reality. I don't think I've seen her face since she was five."

"That's a little dramatic," Paula said. "Call Avery. We need you. We've been through so much, more than most maybe, so don't become idle and let it all fall apart. I need you to become something—someone. Not a shadow of a man who sits and waits for something to happen."

"Things are happening. I'm going places. Becoming great. Again."

"Be less inert, my half-human husband."

"Very funny."

"Lots of comedy clubs in Moscow," she said and let the door close behind her.

12.

Skelly pressed his back against the cold wall inside Exam Room 1 inside the Medical Examiner's office.

The office is located inside a three-story free-standing building.

The first floor houses investigations, the morgue, and the body coolers. The second floor houses the toxicology department and histology laboratory, while the third floor is home to the administrative offices and doctors' offices. Histology is the study of microscopic anatomy of cells and tissues of plants and animals. Skelly had to look it up a few times before he could retain it.

Despite the morgue being hermetically sealed off from the rest of the building and a chilly sixty-two degrees, Skelly could still feel the heat and humidity from outside. It lurked under the doors and through the air vents and caked the bodies of the deceased.

"You doing okay over there, Skelly?" a voice said from the other end of the room. It was Nicole Matter, Chief Medical Examiner.

She was leaning over a body. A rare sight given the state of affairs these days.

She only came in twice a week. Monday mornings were reserved for general housekeeping and Thursday afternoons were for cleaning and routine maintenance. On occasion, Nicole would be called in to make an assessment on a corpse before it's shipped off to the Miles Cooperative for research and development.

The Medical Examiner's office has five medical examiner positions, including the Chief Medical Examiner, the Deputy Chief Medical Examiner, and three Deputy Medical Examiners.

Nicole probably wasn't even thirty, but had held the top spot for the last two years. She graduated top of her class from the University of

California and took her medical degree straight to Austin and the Medical Examiner's office. In addition to being the Chief Medical Examiner, she was also the Deputy Chief Medical Examiner and, depending on her mood, the Travis County toxicology expert.

It was all the city could afford.

The other two medical examiners were reassigned to administrative positions downtown and had to sign lengthy nondisclosure agreements. If people asked, they told people they felt like they needed a change of scenery. Being around the dead isn't what it used to be. Besides, with the increased amount of safety and oversight from Miles, investigating deaths wasn't a thriving business.

Today was different.

"You look like you need some fresh air," Skelly said.

"Don't worry about me," Nicole said and looked back at him and smiled. Skelly couldn't help but notice that he spent most of his work day surrounded by young highly-educated women who, possibly, expressed some interest in him. He didn't mind that. "Come over here when you're done being weird. I want to show you something."

Skelly pushed his body off the wall and moved over to Nicole's side. She was standing over Molly Cooper's body.

Molly's body was covered with a white sheet from the chest down and she stared up at the ceiling. Eyes open.

"There's some small bruising around her torso and traces of skin under her fingernails," Nicole said.

"Strangulation?"

"Doubtful. If she was strangled it would create ligature marks or a dark bruise around her neck. Not the torso, Skelly."

"Right."

"Where was she?"

"She was found dead at two a.m. behind the Blue Bonnet on Guadalupe."

"Who found her?"

"Anonymous call into the non-emergency line."

"Was it Miles?"

"Miles is here to observe and collect information. They aren't here to interfere and report crimes."

"How helpful."

"You're telling me," Skelly said. "Do you think it could be a heart attack? Did you run a medical profile on her?"

"I did and it's clean too, buddy. Her heart was fine along with everything else."

"Drugs?"

"Clean for those too, even the tricky synthetic ones."

"Maybe she's sleeping one off. Did you try and wake her?"

"You learn that at cop school?"

"It's the first thing they teach you at cop school."

"I'd like to hold on to her for another twenty-four hours," she said.

"Probably a good idea, but I don't think it's going to happen," Skelly responded. "There's a system in place. Procedures and processes we need to follow. As much as I hate to say it, we need to stick to what's expected."

"You got a drum lesson to get to or something?"

"I'm supposed to do a television interview with the Chief of Police."

"Assert how safe everyone is because they're investing our tax dollars in state-of-the-art police technology?"

"Pretty much."

"Bought and paid for, if you ask me," she said and waved her hand elegantly across the room. "You should check Bales for a pulse when you see him. Long overdue."

"I can't get close enough. He stinks like bureaucracy."

"Day-old mixed grill?"

"You know it."

"Anyway, I got something here for you. I think it might be … relevant," Nicole said as she pulled a folder from underneath the cadaver table.

The front of it had a picture of a white ghost on it.

"Scary ghost," Skelly said as Nicole set the folder on top of Molly Cooper's torso and opened it up. On the left-hand side was a picture of a middle-aged man with thinning hair, light stubble and puffy cheeks. "Who's that?"

"Donald Smolder. Forty-two, divorced, no kids. Works at a software company in the Domain. Found dead outside his office two weeks ago."

"News to me," Skelly said. The Domain was an outdoor mall in the north part of the city that catered to a transitioning middle class. "What happened to him?"

"I don't know. I only had a few hours to run some tests on him before Miles took him."

"Maybe you need to go back to forensics school. This guy looks like he's about two drinks away from a coma. Looks like he couldn't get to the bar fast enough so his heart gave out. What's your theory?"

"Cause of death is inconclusive. His heart just stopped, but his health screen is above normal. If someone drops dead, there's usually an underlying condition they didn't know about, but not with this guy. You didn't hear about this?"

"It was never on the board. If it's not on the board it doesn't exist," he said, referring to the murder board at police headquarters that listed all open homicide investigations. Skelly knew it wasn't on there because the murder board has been empty for the past two years. The same two years since Darren Bales was appointed Chief of Police and the Miles Cooperative took over.

"You think something is amiss?" Nicole asked and looked at a microphone that was dangling from the ceiling. Skelly nodded. "Murders?" she asked.

"I don't know for sure. But the similarities between Donald Smolder and Molly Cooper are alarming to say the least," he said. "Homicides."

"They're technically not homicides. Smolder was classified as something of interest, or found body, but that's it. You want to murder someone you go out to Burnet or up to Dallas where they allow that sort of thing."

"This one is my case, and I'm calling it a homicide," Skelly said.

"I don't see how you'll be able to do that based on how Miles re-coded everything."

"I don't care about the codes. I'm going by my intuition."

"No, no. You can't do that."

"Damn well I can," Skelly retorted.

"See, it's not on the list," she said and pulled a clipboard from the side of the cadaver table. She pointed down at a list, the top of which said, *Cause of Death: natural, accident, suicide* and *undetermined.*

"Homicide isn't even on the list so you can't choose it, Skelly. The system doesn't work that way."

"Write it in."

"It will create an error in the system and I'll have to redo all the paperwork and you know how much I hate redoing things."

"Fuck me," Skelly said and looked at Molly Cooper's body.

Helpless.

Deceased.

"This isn't anything new, Skelly. Can't you just play along?" she asked. "We'll put 'undetermined' and I'll release the body to Miles for research and development and everyone will go on their way. You can go back downtown and continue doing whatever it is you do down there. Take your drum lessons and slowly fade into retirement."

"Nope. I'm not going to do that. I'm going to go back to headquarters and put it on the board."

"Based on what? We don't have anything here, Skelly. They'll call you reckless. You'll be branded a fearmonger and they'll put you through so much red tape your head will literally implode and you'll end up here and I'll classify it as 'undetermined'."

"I'll handle the red tape. I need you to bury yourself here and come up with something. Twenty-year-old girls don't drop dead for no apparent reason. If her heart gave out I want to know why."

"Why don't you put in a request with Miles and look at the video feed?"

"Erin is downtown right now doing that."

"How is Erin these days?"

"Fine," Skelly said.

"Maybe once you take a look at the feed this will all be moot. Miles hears and sees everything," she said and pointed up at the microphone hanging from the ceiling.

"Maybe," Skelly said. "But do the due diligence on this, will you? I don't care where it ends up. Even if I'm wrong on this—*which I'm not*—I can handle it."

"Whatever you say," she said.

When Darren Bales took office he gave the Miles Cooperative the keys to the city. Miles implemented a new system of video surveillance and monitoring that swept through the city like a rabid dog. Every street corner, shopping mall, restaurant, and gas station was equipped with video cameras that recorded people's every move and sent it back to a digital warehouse that processes the data. Once processed, the data goes over to Miles's corporate office. At any point in time, with a limited amount of paperwork, a police officer could request day-to-day activity on any one of Austin's citizens. The requesting officer will then receive a data package that includes video surveillance images along with aggregated data and locations from third-party sources. The third-party sources range from fitness tracking and apparel companies, phone and watch makers, and automobile companies. Any company, essentially, that has the ability to track the whereabouts of someone at any given time. The result of this has been an almost nonexistent homicide rate and a steep decrease in crime overall in Travis County. If someone wants to murder someone, they could drive them out to Williamson County and do it, since Williamson County wasn't monitoring and collecting information on its residents. At least not yet.

This wasn't all Darren Bales idea either. He wasn't much of a yes-man and he lacked any sort of entrepreneurial spirit. Crime fighting by data gathering was the brain child of the Miles Cooperative, who courted Darren Bales from the very beginning, and generously financed over ninety percent of his campaign to become Chief of Police.

"You okay, sir?" Skelly said as he sat down next to Darren in Studio 3. He looked like he was about to puke his brains out.

13.

"I think I had a bad taco for lunch," Bales said.

He was more man-child than anything else.

They were sitting on opposite sides of the news desk inside the KVAN studio.

An inert Travis Holt sat between them while a makeup artist messed with his hair. "I fucking hate tacos," Bales added. His voice was muffled because he was wearing a HTC Vive headset.

"I'm sorry to hear that, especially since you're not going to like what I have to tell you," Skelly said as he looked at his reflection in the faceplate of the headset. "Can you take that ludicrous thing off for a second? I'm trying to talk to you."

"What's that?" Bales said holding back some air in his chest.

"You have two minutes," a producer yelled at them from the production booth. "Can someone please turn Travis on?"

"Got it, sir," a voice said.

"Bales, take off your headset. You can't wear that when we go live."

"I'm finishing this game. Give me two more minutes! BAM! BAM! BAM!"

"You don't have two more minutes."

"Give me a break," Skelly said and reached over and pulled the headset off and pressed it against Bales's chest. "Pay attention!"

"Watch yourself, Skelly." Bales said. "I was this—this—close. You ruined it for me," he said and wiped a pool of stagnant sweat from his forehead.

Bales hated doing interviews.

Two misplaced words could obliterate years of training and department policy.

Why did your officer decide to murder the suspect instead of shooting out his kneecaps?

Why does the booking process at the central jail take five hours?

Who do we have to call around here to make a formal complaint?

Why do we need the police department when we have Miles?

Bales wanted to be loved and admired by the people and not seen as the pawn for a large omnipresent corporation.

He let the thoughts simmer inside his head for a few seconds. He was a man and could make his own choices, and could walk away whenever he wanted. Besides, he thought, he was in this business because he cared about law and justice. He wasn't the pawn people thought he was. He looked at Skelly. "You have a lot of personal issues you need to resolve, Skelly. Issues that, unfortunately, can't be solved by drum lessons," he said shouting past Travis.

"After this I'm going to go down to the station and log a homicide on the board," Skelly said.

"You're going to do what?" Bales didn't seem like a person who had ever received a piece of good news in his life.

"I'm going to put one up on the board."

"What board?"

"The big white board in headquarters that we used to call the 'murder board,' but you forced us to change the name of it."

"Why would you go and do a thing like that?"

"Because people are getting murdered in this city and it's going to make you look bad."

"Go ahead and do it," Bales said as a smiled crossed his face. "You'll spend most of the afternoon looking for the right forms."

"I don't need any forms. I'm going to walk right up to the board and write it on there with a Sharpie. *Homicide* in big fat red letters and you won't be able to do anything about it. You understand?"

"But … that's not even possible. I threw all the Sharpies away!"

"I have my own."

"The red tape will make your head explode."

"You're the Chief of Police, Bales. You do the red tape."

"Five seconds, everyone," the producer said.

Travis Holt's eyes came to life and the lights on the stage got brighter.

"Actually, two homicides," Skelly corrected.

"Four," the producer said.

"You're really out of your senses these days, Skelly," Bales said as his face started to redden.

"Three."

"That guy in the Domain, he fits the profile too. They were both murdered."

"What guy?"

"I didn't know about it until recently."

"How?"

"Two."

"I don't know. That's my job—to find out. To detect things."

"You're a maniac," Bales said as the producer pointed his finger at the stage.

Travis Holt's head rotated towards the camera.

"Good afternoon, Austin. I'm Travis Holt and this is your midday update," the post-robotic-transformation silicone around his mouth expanded as he smiled. "Joining me today is Austin Chief of Police Darren Bales and a seasoned detective on the brink of retirement. Welcome to the show, Detective Skelly." The sound of pre-recorded applause echoed throughout the studio and quickly dissipated.

Travis was still mostly flesh and bone, but there was a distance to him. Something Skelly couldn't put his finger on. He thought maybe if he leaned in close enough he could smell the Fireball on Travis's breath.

"Police Chief Bales is celebrating two years of zero homicides in Travis County," Travis said. "How does that make you feel, Chief Bales?" His entire body rotated so he faced Bales.

"I'd like to acknowledge the officers who put their lives on the line day and night in this fine city. Without them Austin wouldn't be one of the safest cities in the country. Also, considerable mention should go out to the Miles Cooperative, who furnished this city with a wide array of surveillance equipment and technology that helps keep our citizens safe day and night."

"You mean by monitoring people," Skelly said under his breath.

"Excuse me?"

"Watching what they do and collecting information about them."

"Crime is going down and is almost gone entirely. That's the important part."

"The Miles Cooperative collects data about the city and our residents and then they go and sell that data."

"The first-degree murder rate in Austin has been zero for the last twenty-two months," Bales stated as he looked across the news desk at Skelly. He held his arms up and made the shape of a zero. "Big fat nothing."

"Wow," Travis said. "That's incredible."

"That's right. There has also been a sharp decline in class-A and -B misdemeanors. We are safer than we've ever been. It's not only in Austin either. The Miles Cooperative is also in Houston and a dozen other cities across America. In fact, Travis, I bet if you put that brain of yours to work, you could aggregate the crime data for the entire United States. You'll see a significant decline in the cities where the Miles Cooperative is."

"Great idea, Bales," Travis said as his eyes momentarily closed.

"What's happening?" Skelly said.

"He's pulling data from the United States crime database, you bone head," Bales said.

"Twelve," Travis said as he opened his eyes.

"Excuse me?" Bales asked.

"Twelve homicides this year in the United States."

"And how many in the cities protected by the Miles Cooperative?"

"Zero," Travis said.

"See," Bales said as he looked over at Skelly.

"I think it's fair to say that the Miles Cooperative has made it impossible for us to do our job. With your assistance, they have essentially circumcised the department. The reason why there are no class-A or -B misdemeanors is because the violent crimes in those categories have been re-categorized as class-D misdemeanors, which means the accused will pay a small fine and receive no jail time. So while there are still crimes, shoplifting and assault for instance, they've be re-allocated to a less scary category."

"Police work is evolving and Skelly is having a hard time keeping up. Technological advancements."

"Will these technological advancements help eliminate the recent homicides?" Skelly asked.

"Excuse me?"

"That's ... that's nothing," Bales said.

"What recent homicides?" Travis asked. "That sounds scary."

"We have two pending homicides right now."

"Two?" Travis said. "That's sixteen point six six six percent of the national average."

"They aren't pending. They aren't anything. I don't think we even have a category for homicide because we don't need one. Skelly, you're a beat cop looking to rationalize your existence. We don't need a homicide detective anymore."

"Can you tell us about these homicides?" Travis asked.

"We don't know much right now except that the citizens of Austin need to be extra careful."

"This is unbelievable," Bales said under his breath.

Skelly looked at the camera. "A young girl, Molly Cooper, was found dead two nights ago behind the Blue Bonnet Court motel. We need your help finding out who did this."

"Everyone is safe, Skelly. Found dead doesn't mean she was murdered," Bales said and turned towards the camera. "Citizens of Austin, you have my word that you're all safe."

"It's the illusion of safety."

"Will you shut up? You're a fearmonger. People will panic and do things they regret because of your senseless logic."

"We'll be right back after this commercial break," Travis said to the camera. "Wow. That was some exciting stuff, you guys," he said as the crew started to clap. "When can you come back?"

"You're out of your mind, Skelly. I hope you know that. You know that we continue to receive funding and donations from the Miles Cooperative because we have no crime? The nonsense you're talking about could put this whole city in jeopardy."

"I didn't kill those people. I'm telling people they need to be careful."

"When I get back to my office I'm going to write you up. Put you behind a desk for a few years until that pension kicks in. That's why we're keeping you, isn't it?"

"You're out of line, Bales."

"Damn right I am, you indignant piece of shit. I wouldn't be surprised if you're creating job security for yourself."

"What does that mean?"

"You know damn well what I mean," Bales said and ripped his microphone off and stood up.

"Don't forget your helmet," Skelly said. Bales grabbed his headset, put it on, and walked out.

Travis tilted his head towards Skelly. Fireball wafted under Skelly's nose. "What is it, Travis?" Skelly asked.

"You guys want to come back tomorrow?"

14.

Sometimes I get a feeling in my chest.

It's not the sensation of the Ə-zero working overtime, but more of an ever-growing concern and worry that manifests itself through gas and various pressure points in my chest and upper body. An occasional reminder that despite all else, I'm alive. A reminder that I'm human and require food, sleep, exercise, and love, and that I need to take care of myself despite all else. Sometimes these feelings show up in an unusually aggressive manner, pressing and prodding my body, telling me that I'm living on borrowed time and it's only a matter of days or weeks before my time is officially up. When I go to the other side there will be no option to come back. These feelings, these reminders of my mortality, make me wish that I was dead again.

Not that I don't appreciate my life or my family or the overall benefits of living in general. Eating, drinking, and sleeping.

Exercise.

Sex.

Lunch.

Repeat.

The things that make us uniquely human. It's that sometimes, on occasion, I find myself dreaming about the afterlife. Not how I imagine it or how one thinks it might be, but rather how I saw it even if it was just for a moment. The memory of it and the feeling I had when I was there. The feeling that life was over and I didn't have to worry about, or be responsible for, anything. Any responsibilities I had as a living and breathing human being. A person. A father. A citizen of humanity. Those feelings, that manifest themselves as pressure, were absent from the afterlife. Sure, there was confusion coupled with awe and a certain disbelief. But the heaviness and slowly growing madness from life was gone. It was a relief, an all-expense paid trip to Tahiti. Somewhere I didn't have to fight for anything or fear anything or wait until something went wrong. I was dead and that, after all, was what people ultimately fear: death, not existing, and having no value. It was the stresses of everyday life that brought us down but the realization that we couldn't withstand those stresses and that would, in the end, make us expendable.

I was weak.

I had glimpses of strength, but at my core I was reticent and afraid. My inert state was apprehension. A state of waiting for something, or someone, else to find the solution. Not me. Couldn't be me. I was waiting for someone else to do what I simply could not. I don't know what this was a result of or why I was this way. Maybe it was genetics or maybe it was a history of being perpetually disappointed with myself. I came to expect this from myself. Sure. I was a fine person. I made overall good decisions. I married correctly and had good offspring, but that could be luck. It's not because I willed great children and an outstanding spouse into my life. I didn't imagine them and then they came to be. Those things, the tangible stuff, were coincidence and good fortune. I had a history of experimental prescription drug use. This was by my own doing. I liked how it made me feel. I liked how it helped me break out of the mold and feel like I was living—doing something— even though I wasn't. In fact, my decision-making led to my ultimate downfall and ultimately death. I chose the lifestyle of drugs and that led me to lose my job, my house, and my family and then death. It's so clear when I look back on it now. Death was the only option for me and I brought it upon myself. Don't get me wrong, everyone dies, but I accelerated the process.

Here I am now. Death rejected me and told me to come back at a later point in time so I'm living as best as I can.

Half-human and half Corporate America machine-man.

I was sitting on a dark blue mud-stained cushion watching my eldest daughter do cartwheels across a spring-loaded floor. For what? A hundred dollars a week and bi-monthly potluck with neighbors who you run into at the grocery store on occasion and catch up:

"It's been forever, Peter. How are you?"

"Good, Teddy, just living for the weekend."

"Fantastic. Let's play golf some time and talk about how difficult our families are."

"Deal, fucker."

But that wasn't me. I didn't get my fulfillment from meaningless interactions or from watching my daughter maybe become an Olympic gymnast. The coaches were certainly blowing that smoke in my direction. Joyce needed to find her place in the world on her own. I could advise, share experiences, encourage, and support her in perpetuity, but she was ultimately going to decide where and how she wanted to end up. I wanted the best for her; what parent wouldn't? So I decided, in this very moment, that I was going to start living my life the way it should be lived. The way my children and my wife expected me to. With strength. With pride and with total unfaltering conviction. I was going to shut down the fear and forge ahead with living. Life, our existence, is an intangible and fluttering thought in some distant universe. It only has the value we give it, so I was going to give it my all no matter what. Show my family that this life we have is worth living no matter what happens and no matter what anyone says about it.

"Dad? Hey, Dad! I'm talking to you." I looked up. Joyce was standing in front of me. "You there? You're staring at the floor," she said.

"What is it? I'm thinking about something. Mulling things over in my head."

"What?"

"Work stuff. Dad stuff."

"Ha! That's believable."

"What does that mean?"

"It means ... nothing. Don't worry about it. Can you try and not be a weirdo here? It's fine at home, but people notice you when you're staring off thinking about dad stuff."

"Are you ready to go?"

"I need you to sign this," she said and proffered a piece of paper. "It's a parental consent form for the competition this weekend."

"Consent for what?"

"It basically says the gym isn't responsible if I fall and break my neck and you understand that and won't sue them."

"I'm not sure if I would be okay with that, actually."

"Can you just sign it? I'm not going to die," she said and glared at me. I took the paper and pen from her and looked down at the sheet and scribbled my name on it and handed it back to her. "Thanks." Behind her—on the other side of the gym, David and Darlene stood with their daughter, Joyce's presumed nemesis, Abbey. "See. You're doing it again. Stop looking weird."

"Do you recognize those people?" I said and nodded towards Abbey's parents.

"Ugh, yes, those are Abbey parents. She's the worst."

"I know that but do you recognize them? Other than being her parents, do they look familiar to you? Do they look suspicious?"

"What? No. What kind of question is that?" she said, and she was right. I was asking a twelve year old if her friend's parents looked suspicious. "Besides, Abbey is an asshole," she added. "We've been over this."

"Joyce, you can't use that word to describe everyone you don't like."

"I can't help it if I'm surrounded by a bunch of assholes, Dad."

"You don't have to use such harsh language to describe people."

"What language would you like me to use?"

"You aren't surrounded by a bunch of assholes, Joyce. People can be ... assholes and make asshole choices. That doesn't make them assholes. People are inherently good, but have the ability to do things that aren't so good."

"Like Abbey, for instance? Born good but making bad choices?"

"Sure."

"Therefore, an asshole," she said and spread out her arms in adolescent victory.

"Forget it," I said and pulled out my phone.

"Who are you calling?"

"Hold on," I said and held up a finger to silence her while I watched David and Darlene praise Abbey for no reason whatsoever. "What's Abbey's last name?" I asked Joyce as Cleft picked up on the other end.

"I'm about to go into a meeting. What do you want?" Cleft said.

"I need you to run a background check for me," I said into the phone and covered my mouth.

"Is this about that family that disappeared in Florida? If so, I'm not doing it. I'm not giving into your wild theories."

"It's for a new project I'm working on. Actually, I'm helping Joyce with a thing."

"What thing?" Cleft asked.

"Don't bring me into this, Dad," she said.

"A school thing. Super-secret project."

"It's a total abuse of my power if I let you do this," Cleft said.

"Never stopped you before," I said and I was right. "Aren't you selling that detective info on your clients?"

"That's totally different."

"How much does he pay you?"

"I'm not doing it, Peter, and you can't threaten me."

"I haven't even told you what it's for yet."

"I know what it's for and I'm not doing it. I'm not here to help you snoop on people."

"Are they a client of yours? Are you protecting them? That's why you can't help me. It's a conflict of interest for you."

"What?! That's insane, Peter. They aren't a client of mine."

"Easy for you to say. I can't dispute it. Your entire business is structured around subterfuge so I would never know."

"They aren't my clients. I didn't help the Creed family find a new identity and tell them to move to Austin. You're off your hook, dude."

"But you've been dishonest with me before, right? So it's not implausible," I said and looked at Joyce. "What is Abbey's last name?"

"I don't know," she said.

"If you're so damn curious, why don't you ask them? Maybe they'll tell you," Cleft said.

"What's the fun in that?"

"Good-bye, Peter," Cleft said and hung up the phone.

"If you don't help me, I'll tell everyone about your beard," I said assuredly, but Cleft was gone. I slid the phone back in my pocket and took one last look at David and Darlene. They seemed happy and well-balanced. Something was off.

"What about his beard?"

"Let's go," I said, ignoring her question.

"Where are we going?" Joyce asked.

"We're going home, but I have to make a stop first."

"I think you're the suspicious one, Dad," she said as we walked out of the gymnasium and towards the car.

I opened the door for Joyce, and put her gear in the trunk, and then got in the car and watched as David and Darlene got in their car.

It was a black SUV, at least ten years old, with a white piece of paper where the rear license plate should be.

"Dammit."

"What?" Joyce asked.

"Temporary plates," I said. "The car is old, but the plates are new."

15.

Skelly was accustomed to waiting for people.

His job required him to be a patient man. It took time to solve crimes and catch criminals. Even the stupid, below-the-line criminals took a certain amount of patience and due diligence to apprehend.

Skelly didn't want to invest paid police time to arrest someone only to have it thrown out on a technicality by some subpar attorney.

In the twenty years that Skelly's been investigating homicides for the city of Austin, it's only happened to him once. Most officers and detectives attribute it to collateral damage of police work: "We bring people in. It's not up to us what happens to them afterwards." But Skelly didn't play that way. He felt a certain civil responsibility to do his job the best he could and give accurate and actionable evidence and information. This caused him to be a bit obsessive-compulsive and manic about his job, but he felt that it ultimately benefitted the people of Austin.

Fifteen years ago, a man by the name of Vincent LePearl called 911 to request a courtesy call on his neighbor, Nancy Garcia. Nancy was recently divorced and moved in next door to Mr. LePearl a month earlier. Late one night, LePearl heard commotion coming from Nancy Garcia's house. Naturally, he was curious. LePearl was well into his eighties and spent his time inert in front of the television. A noise coming from next door, a suspicious noise, was a diversion from the ordinary. Unable to check out the commotion on his own, and not knowing his neighbor's telephone number, he picked up the phone and requested that a police officer come by and check on Nancy Garcia. Ten minutes later, a cruiser pulled up in front of Nancy Garcia's house. While approaching the house, the responding officer discovered a smear of blood by the

91

front door. Assuming that the blood was enough for probable cause, the responding officer entered Nancy Garcia's house and performed a cursory search from room to room. Two minutes into the search he found her body in the upstairs bathtub. Her limbs and head were severed from her torso and soaking in a mixture of bleach and battery acid. Following department protocol, the responding officer called it in. Dispatch told the responding officer to sit tight, *absolutely under no circumstances whatsoever should you fucking touch a thing*, while it sent out additional officers, a forensics team, and two detectives: Detective Pierce and his protégée, Detective Skelly. Skelly and Pierce had been working together for a few years at this point and Pierce was becoming more confident with Skelly's judgment and decision-making skills when it came to homicide cases and crime scenes in general. Skelly had a knack for breaking a scene down piece by piece. It was a gift. Pierce was also a few years away from retirement and a hefty department-issued, and department-promised, benefits package was waiting for him on the other side.

He told Skelly to take the lead.

The first thing Skelly did was a quick walk-through of the house. He surveyed the bathroom, and then went outside and talked to the responding officer. The responding officer recounted the events and mentioned how the blood was suspicious and that gave him probable cause to enter the house. Everything was fine and dandy until he hung up the phone with dispatch. The *absolutely under no circumstances whatsoever should you fucking touch a thing* warning was heard loud and clear, but he had been driving around for an hour before he received the call, so he desperately had to pee. In fact, being closer to a toilet made him have to pee even more. He knew he wasn't supposed to touch anything— *HANDS OFF*—but he figured it was better to use the toilet for a quick second rather than make his way downstairs and outside with the risk of peeing all over himself and the victim's lovely plush carpeting. It was a judgment call and he told Skelly about it. Skelly slapped him over the wrist a few times but understood the complications of the situation and told the officer not to worry about it. The next day, with the help of some hard policing and common sense, Skelly tracked down Richard Pears, Nancy Garcia's ex-husband. Apparently, Richard went on a last-minute vacation to Port Aransas and rented a house in the well-to-do Cinnamon Shores neighborhood with his girlfriend's credit card. His girlfriend was visiting her ailing father in Florida and wasn't aware of her boyfriend's quick trip to the popular-yet-dilapidated Texas coast. Skelly brought Richard back to Austin and to the forensics lab downtown. Forensics found traces of bleach and battery acid on Richard's hands and forearms. The evidence persuaded Richard Pears to confess to the murder of Nancy Garcia. Apparently, and this is how Richard remembers it, she was trying to extort money from him and was going to use secrets about his sexual fantasies as leverage. If Richard didn't pay up she was going to tell his girlfriend, sister, and parents everything he liked and desired in the bedroom. Richard went to her house in attempt to reason with her, things got heated, and he decided the only solution was to chop her up and let her body decompose while he went to Port Aransas. He didn't strike Skelly as a very rational man. Skelly did wonder though, what could Richard have wanted in the bedroom that was so horrible that he couldn't bear another person knowing about it.

Nonetheless, Skelly was pretty happy with the work he did and carried that confidence all the way to the District Attorney's office when he presented his findings. The DA's office did their due diligence, which included interviewing the responding officer and reviewing the forensic data. When they sat down with the responding officer he said that he thought Skelly was a "top-of-his-class" detective, but was unnecessarily harsh with him when he told him he used the restroom before exiting the crime scene. The DA noted that in their records and those records were eventually shared with Richard Pears's court-appointed defense attorney, who then had the entire case thrown out. The responding officer's willingness to use the restroom at a crime scene—in the same room as the victim—showed incredible lack of judgment and character. Also, Skelly left this detail out of his recounting of the story and it raised flags as to what else Skelly could possibly be omitting.

It was a huge blow to Skelly and ultimately Nancy Garcia.

The case was dismissed on a technicality and Nancy Garcia's alleged killer never saw his day in court. That being said, Skelly was as thorough as they come and is immensely patient when it comes to catching his man. He leaves no room for error.

But today his patience was about to run out.

He'd been standing outside the Capitol Grill for the past thirty minutes. He was waiting to eat lunch with Liam Reynolds, trusted adviser and supposed pawn for the Miles Cooperative and everyman to many of the political elite in Texas. Truth be told, Skelly didn't know and didn't much care what Liam Reynolds did. Reynolds called him. Reynolds asked him to lunch and told Skelly that it would be worth his while. Skelly put it off for a while, dodged all of the calls, but eventually gave in because Liam Reynolds wouldn't leave him alone and Reynolds offered to pay for Skelly's lunch. The Capitol Grill was downtown inside the Texas State Capitol and served a wide variety of food that appealed to the political masses.

Skelly didn't care. Rubbing elbows with the political elite was of no interest to him.

"Skelly," Reynolds said as he floated effortlessly towards the entrance of the restaurant. "We had some important donors show up at the very last minute. You know how it goes. They want to see all the puts and takes." He stopped inches from Skelly's face and reached out and shook Skelly's hand.

"Unfortunately, I'm not sure how it goes. But that's okay with me," Skelly said as the scent of burnt coffee and soggy pastries drifted under his nose.

"Quite a performance on the news."

"Let's go eat. I only have a few minutes," Skelly said as he released his hand from Reynolds's grasp and headed inside. He opted for the salad bar and watched as Reynolds helped himself to the wide array of pastas they had out. He was coupling penne with grilled chicken and garlic. Anything to wash out the pastry scent currently lingering in his mouth, Skelly thought.

"I'd like for you to think of it as a natural progression. A next step sort of thing," Reynolds said. "Austin is the city of the future—we're currently living in the future and—we need a leader for the future," he continued. They were sitting across from each other at a small table at one end of the pasta bar. If Reynolds so desired he could simply reach his hand out and grab an additional batch of garlic.

"I'm kind of into my drum lessons now and figuring out the ... next phase." Skelly didn't want to say "retirement" as if he were giving up.

"You can't be serious."

"Bales seems to be doing a perfectly fine job," Skelly said.

"But his ticket is up and the city needs somebody new. Bales is just a body in a room, if you ask me, serving someone else's political agenda. The city needs a hero to stand up to the face of evil."

"What's the evil? I keep forgetting."

"I think you know the answer to that."

"You saw us, we were on TV—"

"With that robot."

"Right, with that robot. Crime has been nonexistent for the past twenty-two months, with the exception of the recent occurrences."

"That's a statistic. You can run those numbers all sort of ways. You pretty much said so yourself. Bales will stand by those numbers, but you're different. You're smart."

"The point is: We're safe. The people of this city are safe. Love it or hate it, Bales and the Miles Cooperative are protecting this city."

"You too?"

"Sure."

"I want you to run for Chief of Police."

"It's not for me."

"But it's what the people need. They need a good guy in office who they know is protecting them. Not some political stool. These recent murders indicate there might be a serial killer on the loose."

"It's not that," Skelly said. "We aren't working with a serial killer here."

"But we could be. Whether it's a serial killer or not is secondary to whether or not people think there's a serial killer. I'll throw it over to the guys in the PR office and see what they come up with. City of Austin fears ... the White Ghost. Or, City of Austin on alert because of ... Ted Bundy reincarnate. It's a very real and very tangible fear and"—he shifted closer to Skelly and lowered his voice—"whether people admit it or not, that's what they need."

"Ted Bundy?"

"A bad guy. A definite thing to be afraid of. Nowadays people don't know who the good guys are and the bad guys are. The news media will pick at anything these days. It's been like that for a while. It used to be us against Russia, plain and simple. Western Bloc against the Eastern Bloc. We had one hand patiently waiting on the trigger while the other hand diligently flipped through the nuclear codes. But then the Cold War ended, Russia got its shit together—sort of—and people didn't know what to do with themselves. After that we had Osama bin

Laden for a while. He died about ten years before we killed him but the government didn't tell anyone because it gave our country a mission, a goal. We needed him to be alive so we could kill him."

"Whoa, whoa, Reynolds," Skelly interrupted. "I think you've gone a little too far with that one."

"Fine, but my point is that people need a motivation. Fear. Death."

"Fear is an easy button to push."

"Because we all have it. Every accomplishment in life is motivated by the thought of not existing. You understand that? Intro to psychology right there. All we have now is the uncertain uneasiness of what Miles is doing with the data it collects about us, and that's the people who actually open their eyes and think about what's going on. Ninety-eight percent of the population have no idea. They're idle."

"What do you think they're doing with the data?"

"Nothing really. Well, selling it for sure, but that's all Miles is concerned about. Profit. My concern is what the governments and organizations they sell it to are doing with it. My money is on thought control." He paused. "You stay awake at night, right?" he asked.

"Not really."

"Bullshit," he countered. "Everyone lies awake in bed in the middle of the night. Maybe not most nights, but some nights. Unless said person is heavily drugged, but point proven right there. What do you think about when you lie awake in the middle of the night?"

"I don't know," Skelly said and ran his fork through his food.

"I'll tell you what I lie awake at night and think about: my kids, the second mortgage on my big-ass house. My job. Security. Losing all of it. It's really an all-encompassing thought process. One day it might all go away. What then? That's what my mind tries to comprehend at night. Then I wake up in the morning and I have a purpose, a drive. Those fears. They're my bad guys."

"Good for you."

"You're a strange one, Skelly. Anyone ever tell you that?"

"Not lately."

"My point is you're not heroic if you don't fight anything. You're not going to get into office with a slogan like *Everything's fine and continues to be. Vote for Skelly if you like boring.* Average is death."

"Who said I wanted to run?"

"You will, eventually. Everyone always does. Your ego will catch up to you and reason with you. I saw you on TV. We need that."

Skelly took a bite of his food and squinted to show Reynolds that he heard him. He wasn't interested but he heard him nonetheless. "The future of fighting crime, or policing as you call it, in this city isn't technology and mass surveillance for some corporate overlord. The future of policing is hard-nosed police work. The future of policing is working with the people, for the people. You can understand that, I'm sure." Reynolds stopped and took a bite of food. "It's why people still buy records. Nostalgia. You're next, Skelly."

"What did you say?"

"You're next, Skelly," Reynolds said and pointed at him.

Skelly thought about the note that he saw at Blue Bonnet Court.

"I think you're right in the fact that it's not about surveillance, but rather actual police work. But let's not romanticize what I do. It's incredibly hard work and the rewards are few and far between," Skelly said, but Reynolds wasn't listening. He removed two phones, one from each pocket.

"Excuse me for a second. It's incredibly rude, I know," Reynolds said as he took a call on one of them and typed an email on the other.

Skelly thought about what Reynolds was proposing. Reynolds knew how to appeal to Skelly's work ethic and passion for the job. But, Skelly wasn't interested in becoming the next Police Chief. No matter what Reynolds said. He was a detective, an investigator. It's all he knew and it's all he cared about it. Sitting in an office downtown, playing the game of politics, in search of some intangible bad guy, wasn't what Skelly was cut out for.

"Think of it this way, you could eviscerate Bales," Reynolds said to him, with his phone pressed up against his face. Skelly didn't know whether he was talking to him or not but he did have a point. Bales was going to have to go at some point, but Skelly didn't think he was going to be the one to replace him. "Plus, your salary will quadruple. If not more," Reynolds said and then said something into the phone and hung up.

"Quadruple?" Skelly asked.

"At least. What do you make now? Fifty? Sixty?"

I wish, Skelly thought to himself. "What's the catch?" he asked.

"I'm not agreeing to this in any way whatsoever, but I'm curious as to what's in it for you."

"I want to watch Miles burn to the ground," Reynolds said quietly and looked around. "But, unfortunately, there isn't anything I can do about that. They're ubiquitous. They're an all-knowing, all-seeing pain in my ass."

"Miles? You're their biggest advocate. You helped them get started here."

"Let me ask you something, Skelly," Reynolds said as he set down one of the phones and took another bite of food. "Where do you want to be? Not in five years or ten years, but where do you envision your life going? Are you happy with where you are now?"

Skelly started to say something, but Reynolds continued.

"I got my undergraduate degree in Houston and then moved here for law school. When I graduated I had a mountain of student debt and a job offer to work in the county clerk's office. I took the job and spent fifty hours a week on my ass stuffing pieces of paper into a filing cabinet. After about two months, I said 'fuck it' and went and found a new job working for the mayor. Why? Because that's what I envisioned for myself."

"Working for the mayor?"

"No, where I am now. Helping people realize their dreams and their potential. Working for the mayor was one step in that process. One step towards the bigger picture, Skelly."

"I see. You had dreams and aspirations. That sort of stuff."

"Exactly. And I want to help you realize your dreams and aspirations. Don't you ever dream, Skelly?"

"No," he said and pushed his salad aside. "Can't a job just be a job? Can't I be good at this one thing and have that be okay?"

"There's more to you than that. I know it. You're not human if you don't evolve. You aren't some robot programmed to perform one task after another and then call it a day."

"What I do is a little more intricate than that. I think you're selling it short."

"Of course it is, but when you've been doing something for so long it becomes rote. Yes, your job requires an immense amount of skill and talent but you aren't challenging yourself. You aren't pressing the limits of what you can become."

"What if I aspire to move to Australia and start a farm? Can you help me with that? For example."

"I want to help you become Chief of Police, Skelly. That's what you're meant to do," Reynolds said as he pointed his finger aggressively towards Skelly. "Skelly and to-be-determined serial killer. Double ticket."

"It's not going to say that."

"Of course not. But that's what it is. People need the enemy. They crave the enemy. Without the enemy, the fear, they're lost. You know how great you feel after riding on a rollercoaster? Watching a scary movie?"

"I hate that shit."

"Fine, but it doesn't negate the point. The decisions you make to-day will affect what you do tomorrow. Let's make some good decisions together, okay? If you say no, I'm going to ask Travis Holt. People love him," Reynolds said as Skelly's phone buzzed in his pocket. It was over a hundred degrees outside and the air conditioner inside was working overtime to accommodate the swarm of people in the restaurant.

Skelly needed to get out.

He pulled his phone out of his pocket and looked down at it. It was dispatch. "I need to take this," he said and picked up. "Hello?" he said. He listened and then hung up and set the phone down on the table and wiped a surplus of salad dressing from his chin.

"Everything okay?" Reynolds asked.

"I need to go," Skelly said. "I'm needed at headquarters. It's an emergency."

16.

Joyce and I sat in the car for a few minutes.

We were outside a pale brick office building watching the sun set. The air conditioner in the car was turned off and I could feel the heat and humidity slowly creeping through the cracked windows. It was uncomfortable and Joyce told me, on a few occasions, that if we have a luxury like air conditioning, we should use it. We aren't cavemen, she liked to point out. Also, I wasn't proving anything to anyone by turning it off and suffering through the sweltering heat and dreary humidity. But I liked how it made me feel despite Joyce's incessant objections.

"What are we doing, Dad?" Joyce asked me.

"Waiting," I said, deliberately leaving out the true purpose for our visit.

"It's hot in here."

"Yes, that's the idea."

"Are we just going to hang out?"

"For a minute. Then I'm going inside. You can wait out here and listen to your music if you like."

"Good," she said. "My music is better than whatever you and Mom listen to," she said as she rolled her window down. She stopped it half-way. A few seconds went by and she added, "Are you going to go inside and see him?" she asked. I could sense her impatience.

"One more minute," I said.

We were across the street from Cleft's office building. I could see the light on in his office on the second floor and I was waiting for him to turn off the light and leave.

Once I knew he was gone, I would go inside and let Joyce sit out here and turn on the air conditioner and play her music. Based on what

Cleft said in our conversation, I suspected that David and Darlene were clients of his. I needed to get inside his office and prove it.

"Tick tock, Dad," she said as I saw Cleft's shadow walk across the window and then his office went dark.

"Ten more seconds, honey," I said.

"Jeeze. Mom is much more interesting than you," she huffed and looked down at her phone. The back door to the office building opened and Cleft came out. I flicked the visor down to cover my face as he walked towards his car. Joyce was too busy scrolling through her music catalogue, so she missed him when he got in his car, blasted the air conditioner, and pulled away.

"Sit tight and I'll be back in a few minutes." I kissed her forehead and reached for the door handle.

"Can I come with you?"

"Okay," I said and thought about the possible repercussions. "But this has to be our secret, understand? You can't tell Mom or your sister, got it?"

"Can't tell them what?"

"That we came to Cleft's office. It simply didn't happen. We went and got smoothies."

"They are going to be so pissed we didn't get them a smoothie."

"It's the way of the world, Joyce. We forgot to get them smoothies. It happens and they'll learn to be okay with that, but under no circumstance did we come here. Got it?"

"Got it," she said and nodded.

We got out of the car and went around to the front of the building. There was an alpha-numeric keypad on the door. I jabbed my fingers into the keypad: F-U-C-K-P-3-T-3-R

The door unlocked.

What a jerk, I thought to myself.

"After you," I said and let Joyce go in first.

We headed up the staircase and reached the door to his office, which also had an alpha-numeric keypad. It was a small two-story building designed to hold a few small businesses, but Cleft rented out the entire place to himself. He chose a small office on the second floor and used the remaining offices for storage. He did put nameplates on the doors though. He liked to keep up appearances. When clients would come in he would sometimes talk about Jakob in accounting or bring up Selena in marketing and how she would always bring in breakfast tacos on Monday morning.

Everyone loved tacos.

It was a fabrication to give clients some context and comfort when they met with Cleft. He wanted to sell the idea that they were visiting a full-service business with people who cared about their needs and desires. Clients loved the fact that Selena brought breakfast tacos.

Steak, egg, and cheese pressed between the folds of a warm flour tortilla with a splash of spicy red sauce. Or migas with Jack cheese, queso, and pico de gallo on a homemade corn tortilla.

Cleft said it was good for business.

You weren't human if you didn't love a good breakfast taco.

I wondered if he said goodnight to Jakob and Selena when he left for the night.

"Can I guess this one?" Joyce said to me looking at the keypad on Cleft's door.

"What's your guess?"

"Avery-three-thirteen," she said. "Avery and his birthday."

"Very smart," I said as I leaned down and rotated my body so I was between Joyce and the keypad.

I punched the keypad. F-U-C-K-P-3-T-3-R

Click.

"Great work, honey," I said and smiled at her as we went into the office.

As expected, Cleft wasn't there and the lights were off.

"He's not here," she said as I flicked on the desk lamp and sat down.

"He left something for me," I said and ran my fingers over his computer keyboard.

"Do you know his password or do I need to solve it for you?" Joyce asked. She was standing behind me.

"As a matter of fact, I do," I said. "Cleft is a pretty predictable guy. Why don't you go and have a seat over there while I take care of this," I said and pointed to the couch.

Joyce went over and sat down on the couch and took a book off the coffee table and flipped through it. "Why are the pages all blank?"

I pressed my finger against the monitor's touchscreen and an image of the computer's desktop came up.

No password required.

I ran my finger over the various files and stopped when I found a file sitting on his desktop:

client_list_v_39

"Holy cow," I said and pressed my finger down on the file icon so it would open up.

"What did you find, Dad?" Joyce asked, but before I could answer, the phone on Cleft's desk started ringing.

I looked down at the caller ID: Cleft Duvall.

What the?

"Who is it?" Joyce asked.

I pressed my finger down on the speaker button. "Cleft Duvall's office," I said and winked at Joyce.

"Peter, what the hell do you think you're doing in my office?" His voice boomed over the microphone.

"I'm sorry. Who are you looking for?" I said.

"Very funny, you piece of shit," Cleft said.

"Cover your ears, honey," I said to Joyce.

"What are you doing in my office?"

"It's a long story," I said. "How did you know?"

"This is the future, Peter. I get a notification as soon as someone steps within ten feet of my office and then a goddam homing pigeon craps on my shoe when someone enters. Don't even get me started on what happens when you start printing items from my computer."

"Now I'm curious …"

"The paper erupts into flames if you print it. The ink is made from holy water."

"I would do no such thing," I said and looked back at the printer that was spewing out page after page of Cleft's client list.

"It doesn't matter anyway. It's encrypted," he said. "You don't have a chance in hell."

"What's encrypted?"

"The client list, you idiot," he said. "I hired some KGB defects to encode it. Phyllis and I put our house on HomeAway last winter and a Russian family rented it. Turns out they were on the run from the Putin regime. Nice people, actually. I think Paula sold her some lash extenders."

"Joyce and I were actually running out to get smoothies and I needed to pee."

"Peter, these people from gymnastics aren't my clients. How many times do I have to tell you that?"

"It's suspicious is all, Cleft. You know me, I have to do my due diligence. Explore all the angles. It's part of who I am."

"That's rubbish and you know it."

"Abbey's family?" she asked.

"It's nothing," I said as I waved my hand towards her.

"Damn right it's nothing, Peter," Cleft said. "I don't know who you are. You're headed down a road you shouldn't even be on," he said as Joyce continued to look over at me. "Peter. Don't touch anything and get out of my office. We'll talk about this tomorrow."

"As you wish," I said.

"Joyce," he continued, "I'm going to hang-up. Please make sure you and your dad leave immediately. You could be in some serious trouble snooping around like this."

"Whatever you say, sir," Joyce said. "Say hi to Avery for me."

"All right," Cleft said. "Good-bye, Peter." But before he could hang up I felt a few taps on the top of my wrist.

I looked down at my wristband.

It was glowing red.

"Shit," I said. "Cleft, the power on my heart is drained. Can I stay awhile and refuel?"

"Don't you have patches for that sort of stuff? Use those."

"I didn't bring any with me."

"Joyce?" Cleft asked. I held up my wrist so she could see the red light.

"It's legit," she said.

"There's a backup in the top left drawer. Five minutes. That's all you have and then leave."

"Thanks."

"Joyce, keep an eye on him, will you?"

"You got it."

"And don't take the client list!" Cleft said and hung up.

"Dad, what's he talking about? Abbey's family?" she asked. "I told you not to bring me into this."

I shrugged lightly and opened the top left drawer of Cleft's desk and pulled out a small silicone white patch. It fit in the palm of my hand and had a small cord sticking out of the corner. I put the patch over my heart and pulled the cord out and plugged it into the outlet behind the desk. I wasn't sure how to respond to her. It was a mistake taking her here. I was too eager to find out about the Creed family and wasn't being careful. Now I've exposed her to things I wasn't ready to explain and didn't fully understand myself.

I reached over to the printer and grabbed the client list and set it on the desk in front of me. It was split up into multiple columns and was an indecipherable series of random letters and numbers, going in all sorts of directions. Joyce came over and stood next to me and looked down at it.

"It's nonsense," I said.

"It's good. He's protecting his clients," she said and set her hand on my shoulder.

"But what about me? What about what I want?"

"It's not about what you want. Besides, do you really want to know what's in there?" she said.

"I think something's up with them and I'd like to know what. The list is just a way to get more information about them."

"But they aren't on the list. Cleft said so himself."

"It's his job to say that and to protect his clients," I said. She'll understand how it works one day.

"Right but, Dad, listen to me: There are people who aren't going to be on that list. It's a fact. So it's not impossible for him to say someone isn't on the list when, in fact, there are millions and millions of people not on that list."

"What's your point?" I asked.

"If you don't see it, then it doesn't exist. You could walk away and everything will be fine. No change," she said.

"They're either on the list or they aren't."

"But that's not right," Joyce said. "There's a version of the story where they are on that list and there's a version where they aren't, understand?" *Understand?* My own genetic makeup telling me how it goes. "It's up to you which version of the story you want," she added.

"What about the version where I look at the list and they aren't on it?"

"There's that too but I don't think you want that version of the story."

"Why not?"

"It's quantum suicide."

"Excuse me?" I asked. "You're twelve, Joyce."

"Almost thirteen. Besides, it was in some book Mom was listening too. *Life Decisions or Life Is Short: Make It Count.* Something like that. I can't remember. They talked about something called quantum suicide and how the universe splits in two every time you make a choice."

"What does that mean?" I asked.

"Like how Mom likes Splenda in her coffee. Every morning she puts one Splenda in her coffee. There's a timeline where the rest of her life plays out if she decides to put sugar in her coffee instead of Splenda. There is also a version of events where she puts two Splenda in her coffee or no Splenda, and so on."

"Wow," I said.

"My point is: it's entirely up to you. Your life. Your choices."

"Is there a version of the story where she puts a hundred Splenda in her coffee?"

"Uh—no. A hundred Splenda wouldn't fit in the coffee cup. Obviously."

"Touché," I said and held the list up so she could see it. "It's encrypted." Jumbled letters ran across the page. Fifty letters to a line and at least forty lines on the page. It would put the Enigma Code to shame. Maybe Cleft Duvall is the Zodiac.

"There must be another way to find out," she said.

"You're smart, like Mom."

"You too, but a different kind of smart."

"Gee, thanks, Joyce," I said. "I'm going to borrow the list and think about it for a few days. Put it under my pillow while I sleep and maybe the code will come to me. How does that sound?"

"Whatever you think is the best choice, Dad. I think looking at that list is going to create more problems for you than you could ever possibly imagine."

"Maybe. But, what's the point of living if you don't take a risk every now and then?"

"Oh, such a bore," she exclaimed.

I heard a light beeping sound.

I looked down and the patch over my heart was green. I turned around and unplugged the device and put it back in Cleft's drawer.

"Let's go home," I said and grabbed the pages of the client list and stacked them together and got up.

Joyce followed me out of the office and down to the parking lot.

The humidity outside was strong and our faces were immediately drenched in sweat. We got in the car and I turned the air conditioner on. It was mostly for Joyce's benefit. Kids these days.

"You're going to take me to my competition tomorrow?" she asked.

Shit.

"Yes, of course, honey," I said. I forgot about the competition and the meeting that I'm supposed to have with *someone* at the Driskill downtown. "We'll figure it out," I said.

"Okay, good," she said. "When we're there, you can pull a registration list from the admin office. The office will be empty and you can get their address and phone number from the list."

"It doesn't seem like enough. It's easy to find out where people live."

"It's the best chance you have, until you figure out how to decipher Cleft's list."

"Huh," I said, thinking about it.

"Or you could invite yourself over."

"Maybe," I said.

"It's not stealing anyway, right? Research? That's what you do for a living, right? Research and investigate?"

"Pretty much."

"Then that's what we'll call this. Research. What you do after you get their info is totally up to you. Maybe it's nothing and you can move on."

"Okay," I said and kissed her forehead. "Thanks, honey."

I slowly pulled the car out of the parking lot and thought about the complications of tomorrow. I didn't have enough time to take Joyce to her competition and meet with my suitor at the Driskill, but she did bring up a good point about the registration list. The registration list would have their address and phone number and that was enough information for me to start with. The only thing Cleft's list would have is undeniable proof that they changed their identity. I would have to steal the admin list and find someone to decode Cleft's list.

"Is Abbey in the competition?" I asked as a brilliant thought crossed my mind.

"Yes," she said and glared at me. "Why? What are you thinking?"

"Someone owes me a favor."

"Who?" she asked as I punched the screen on my watch.

A ringtone blasted through the Bluetooth speakers followed by a soft "Hello?"

"David?"

"Yes. Who is this?"

"It's Peter. Richards."

"Oh, hey Peter. What's up?" he asked. "How did you get this number?"

"You gave it to me, remember?"

"Oh, right. Of course."

"Look, I need a favor, buddy."

"Dad, what are you doing?" Joyce whispered to me.

"Uh, sure. What is it?" David asked.

"I was wondering if Joyce could ride with you to the competition tomorrow. I have a meeting and Paula is working."

"Dad!" Joyce yelled at me.

"Stop, Joyce. I'm on the phone."

"You're insane," she tacked on at the end.

"Sure, Peter. I think that would be fine. Send me your address and we can pick her up on the way. We'll have to leave a little early but it shouldn't be a problem."

"How about I drop her off at your house before my meeting?"

"Nah. We'll be out. We'll pick her up if that's cool with you."

"Thanks. I owe you one."

"Have a good night, Peter," he said and hung up.

I looked over at Joyce. She was still staring at me. "After the competition tell them I'm going to pick you up at their house. That's our in," I said.

"You're not coming to my competition?"

"I have another meeting. It's important," I said. She huffed lightly and crossed her arms. It was a half-hearted protest but I got the message nonetheless. "If it wasn't important I would be at the competition. You'll understand one day." Of course she would, we all do. Eventually. She didn't even like gymnastics anyway.

There was another soft tap on my wrist. I looked down at my heart monitor. It was glowing red again.

"Dammit," I said.

"What's wrong?" Joyce asked.

"My battery is almost dead," I said.

"Didn't you just charge it?"

"Yup."

"How long do you have?"

"A few minutes maybe," I said. "It's like a low gas tank. You think you're in imminent danger but then you find out that you can go for miles without refueling."

"We can go back in," she suggested.

"No, let's go home," I said and cranked the air conditioner up a few more degrees and pressed down on the gas pedal.

The smoothies would have to wait.

17.

"What was the emergency?" Skelly said as he set his keys and badge down on his bare and sterile desk. He was almost out of breath.

Erin was sitting in his chair wearing a VR helmet.

"It's not an emergency. I told you not to rush," she said through the helmet. She put her feet up and flexed her toes towards a framed pictured pinned to the cheap cubicle divider that separated Skelly's desk from the rest of the room. It was a picture of a younger and more vibrant Skelly.

"No problem at all," Skelly said and looked down at her. "You comfortable?" he asked as he let his breathing regulate itself. "Those stairs. They get steeper every time I come in here."

"You need to get yourself a standing desk. Better for your back … your life," she said as she moved her head from left to right.

"It's a waste. I'm hardly ever here."

"All the more reason."

Skelly waved his hand in front of the helmet. "Hellllo?"

"Stop it, Skelly. You're distracting me."

"Oh, you can see me."

"I feel you hovering over me."

Erin removed the helmet and looked up at him. She had big round brown eyes.

"You called me."

"Oh, right," she said and set the helmet down on Skelly's desk and pulled her phone out from her pocket.

"From one distraction to the next." Skelly said.

"Look at it," she said and tilted the phone so Skelly could see the screen.

When he looked down, the video on the screen started to play.

The video was from a closed circuit camera in a new apartment complex on the other side of Guadalupe from the Blue Bonnet. The footage was grainy and unclear but Skelly could see Molly Cooper talking to a few kids who were standing in front of a small compact car. A few words were exchanged and then Molly gave them the finger. A few seconds later a door to one of the rooms opened and a tall slender figure emerged from the room. It was late and dark outside so Skelly had a tough time making anything out, but he could see what resembled a thin figure grabbing Molly from behind and pulling her into a hotel room.

"Did you see it?" Erin asked.

"It's not very clear. I thought this stuff was state of the art. Miles was supposed to see and hear everything."

"Miles didn't tag this camera yet. It was put there to catch people sneaking into the parking garage, not to catch rapists at a motel across the street."

"Is that what we're calling it now?"

"I'm saying we need to work with what we have. It's a blessing we got this much."

"Did Miles get us anything?"

"Nah. They're still processing the paperwork. I know you're short staffed so I'm helping you out."

"Did your supervisor approve that?"

"I was hoping you would approve it. Is that okay?"

Skelly thought about how much he liked working alone but he also needed the help. "Sure," he said. "What's on his head?" he asked and pointed at the screen. "The image looks like she was snatched by a bobble-head."

"Why does it have to be a him? Couldn't it just as easily be a woman?"

"It was a … saying. 'What's on his head' is easier to say than 'What's on his or her head,' and saying 'their head' is grammatically incorrect and unclear. Simply a saying, Erin."

"From an initial glance it looked like a motorcycle helmet," Erin said. "You can see an almost insignificant glare over the faceplate and there is a smoothness to indicate that the hair is being covered by something."

"Makes sense."

"But I can't see anything through the faceplate. Not in that light at least."

"Did you check any of the other cameras to see if any motorcycles were in the area? If it's a helmet, there must be a motorcycle somewhere that goes it with it."

"Miles gave me a list of every vehicle in a five mile radius. There was one motorcycle a few blocks away." She put her phone away and looked up at Skelly. He was looking at her, waiting for her to finish her thought. "It was registered to a local university student and he had an alibi."

"Was it a good alibi? Did he look like the type?"

"The alibi checked out if that's what you mean, and no—he didn't look like the type," she said.

It's so hard to know what people are really up to these days, Skelly thought.

"Okay," Skelly said and let it roll around his head for a few seconds and then let it go. "I suppose I'll go out there and do some actual police work. Care to join me?" he asked.

"I think you should start here," Erin said and set a business card down on Skelly's desk. Skelly looked down at it.

Head Room
High-End Headsets for a Luxurious & Integrated Experience

"Head Room?" he asked.

"They design headsets," she said and tapped her finger on hers.

"Oh," Skelly said.

"VR," she added.

"Right," Skelly responded assuredly.

"Virtual reality," she said, but she could sense he wasn't catching on. "You follow me, Skelly? Virtual reality. Computer-generated games and experiences. It's not really a new thing."

"I follow," he said as he continued to stare at the business card that had a hologram of a person's head on it.

"They have an office and a show room in the Domain. The office is mostly sales managers and reps who work with larger corporate clients on experiential, VR-driven events. The sales floor is for your everyday consumer. People who have heard of VR, but don't know much about it and want to have … an experience."

"Why am I checking this out?" Skelly asked.

"Because Donald Smolder worked there. He was in charge of outside sales and global accounts." Skelly looked at her. "I made a few calls," she added.

"Good for you."

"He was down in the showroom during his lunch break the day he died."

"But that's his job, right? What's your point?"

"He wasn't down there to see customers. He was using the equipment. He was playing. He goes down there every day during lunch and plays," Erin said and held up her phone again. Skelly looked down at it. It was a screenshot from the surveillance video. Donald Smolder was standing on a raised platform that had an eight or nine foot circumference. It was surrounded by a padded railing. "It's called a containment area," Erin added. "So players can get the full experience without hurting themselves. Headsets, might I point out, they look an awful like motorcycle helmets."

"Got it," Skelly said and leaned in to look at the picture. The figure was wearing what appeared to be a black motorcycle helmet. "Are you sure that's him?" he asked.

"You better believe it," she said. "Every day from noon until one thirty or two."

"If he's down there every day, what was different about the day he died?"

"The difference is that when he died he was still wearing the helmet. He left the showroom. Better—he ran out of the showroom."

"How? Isn't the helmet connected to something? Power supply? That would have stopped him."

"Not everything needs wires anymore," she said. "We aren't all like you."

She had a point.

"Where was he running?" Skelly asked and she shrugged. "Was he running back to his office?"

"The guy on the sales floor said it looked like he was running away from something. He was scared. Something happened in the game that set him off. That's what they think, at least."

"Huh," Skelly said and set the business card down on his desk. It didn't add up in his head and he didn't see the connection between Smolder and Molly Cooper.

"And the helmet?"

"It's the HR-3030. Their latest technology. It gives the user a fully integrated experience. To call it 'mind blowing' would be an understatement."

"I don't see the connection," Skelly said.

"What? Are you serious?"

"I don't see how you connect this guy to the dead girl on Guadalupe."

"The helmet, Skelly! It's clear as day."

"It's not. A motorcycle helmet is a pretty ubiquitous thing and you can't prove that the headset is the same thing the suspect in Molly Cooper's death was wearing. Even if you could prove that, it doesn't necessarily prove anything except they both had on a headset. Besides, so what? Donald Smolder just died. His heart gave out. We don't know what happened to Molly Cooper. Two totally different things, Erin."

"They aren't two totally different things," she said.

"Yes, they are. Trust me," Skelly said. "There is stuff you can't tell from dusting for prints, Erin."

"That's a cheap shot and you know it."

"I'm sorry but you haven't seen everything. If you had, you would understand."

"It's a game."

"No shit, it's a game. Our entire existence is a game."

"You're not following me, Skelly. It's a literal game. It's called *SP 3.0*. It's the game Donald Smolder was playing they day he died."

"Miles tell you that?"

"No. One of his coworkers mentioned it. It's in the file, the thing you used to call a murder book."

"That's a terrible name for a game."

"Stands for *Stolen Planet*. It's an online, VR-driven game. MMORPG, if you will," she said and smiled at him. "MMORPG stands for massively multiplayer online role-playing game, in case you were wondering."

"Of course it does, and I wasn't wondering. I knew that already. Everybody does."

"Players create avatars and are able to interact with other avatars, places, or objects. They can explore, meet other residents, socialize, build, create, shop, and trade virtual property. You get the idea. Donald Smolder apparently had a profile and would play every day."

"Good for him."

"Also, and this is according to the salesman who worked in the showroom, SP 3.0 apparently has a very big student following. High school and college students. They see it as an escape from the trials and tribulations of their everyday life," she said as Skelly nodded. "I called a friend at campus police. He said that the university has at least two user groups. One of them meets every Sunday night off campus and the other—"

"Can't Miles tell us what they were playing?"

"Miles can't access the interface. At least not yet."

"Isn't that convenient," Skelly said.

"It's kind of the point."

"What's the other user group?" Skelly asked.

"It's not as popular as the off-campus one but it meets every Saturday night at the Blue Bonnet."

"Doing some actual detective work there, are you?"

"Appears that way."

"That was the night Molly Copper was killed, right? A Saturday?" Skelly asked. Erin nodded. "Blue Bonnet Court Motel," he said and shook his head. It only has eleven rooms. Decrepit, unassuming, and small. Not an obvious choice.

"It was a small group."

"Did they pay for the room?"

"It's cheap and if they pooled their money it would be negligible."

"Maybe."

"So, you think there's a connection?" Erin asked.

"Any idea what's in this game? What it's about?"

"No, but you're going to find out," Erin said. "I created an avatar for you. You can thank me later. It will take you out of your comfort zone."

"I'm good. I'll probably visit the motel again and ask some questions. Maybe one of them knew the owner or the manager and got a deal. Besides, I'm waiting for the Medical Examiner's results to come back."

"Don't worry about it. I'll go to the motel and find out who was renting the room and I can talk to Nicole. I am a forensics officer after all. Unless you prefer to speak with her?"

"Nope. I'm good," he said after a brief pause.

"Then there's no issue," Erin said. "You can pick up your headset any time after four today. You can sync it to your phone or computer—whatever you prefer—they'll walk through everything with you and show you how it's done," she said, and spun around in his chair without a care in the world.

Didn't she understand that people were dying out there?

"I need to get out of here," he said. "Go to Vegas for a few days and knock a few back. Maybe play some blackjack."

"By all means go, Skelly. Enjoy Vegas and for God's sake—live!" she said as she threw her arms up in the air. "I can handle this stuff. I might dust for prints and swab blood, but I'm capable of so much more. Just you wait and see, partner."

"We'll see. What time did you say I could pick up my headset?"

"After four."

"After four it is then," he said as he opened the desk drawer and pulled out some business cards. He put his jacket on and walked away from his desk.

"Hey, Skelly," Erin said as she stopped spinning. "Watch your back."

"Always," he said and turned and walked out.

Erin watched him until he went through the door into the lobby.

18.

"I'll have the Texas Wagyu sliders and a Manhattan with some of the Japanese whiskey that people have been talking about," I said as I sat down on one of the leather couches in the lobby of the Driskill Hotel.

I was an hour early.

"We can't serve you out here, sir," said a woman wearing Driskill-issued black slacks and white dress shirt. Her name tag had a large coffee stain on it so it was virtually impossible to make out her full name. The *A* and the *M* were legible, but I couldn't make out the rest.

Amber.

Amy.

Amelia.

The possibilities were endless.

"I'm meeting someone here," I said defiantly.

She took an irritated breath and looked back at the bar. It was opulence at its finest. Dark leather couches and leather-back club chairs. There was also a bull's head resting above the fireplace watching the few stragglers at the bar intently. It was four in the afternoon and people were slowly trickling in.

"Sliders and a Manhattan?" she asked.

"That would be lovely," I said as I watched an older gentleman enter the lobby. "But with the fancy Japanese whiskey that I've been hearing about lately."

"What's it called?" she asked.

"I don't believe I recall," I said. "Excuse me, but do you know that man? Does he look familiar to you?" I said and pointed to the older gentleman who was now standing in the middle of the lobby. He was wearing an unseasonal brown trench coat and had on a brown top hat to match. He was categorically out of place and looked like he was waiting for someone. Possibly me.

"No, sir. I certainly do not," she said and rubbed her finger over the coffee stain on her name tag. "Dammit, I'm always spilling stuff," she said. *AM-A.*

"In fact, put any type of Japanese whiskey in there. Whatever the bartender recommends," I said as I reached my arm out and gently pushed her aside. She was blocking my view.

"Excuse me. Am I in your way?" she asked abruptly.

"I'm trying to get a better view," I said. "It's strange that someone would wear a trench coat in this type of weather? It feels like the Apocalypse outside."

"We get all sorts of strange people in here. Look at yourself for instance."

"You don't know anything about me."

"I know you don't take good care of your body and you have a natural inclination to think things are suspicious."

"Why is that?"

"Usually people who thinks things are fishy or strange are the strange ones and—I can see your wristband. Ə-zero. My brother has one. His is purely recreational. He uses it to track steps, meals, mood swings—and boy does he have 'em. Yours—yours is two grades above his. Some serious medical-grade doctor-issued stuff you got going on there. But yet, here you are, on a nice hot Saturday afternoon ordering red meat and liquor. Some weird death wish you have," she said and pushed the hair off her forehead. "Are you worried about the Red Mercury that went missing? Figured you'd go balls out."

"Look who's being the dramatic one now, huh?" I said and looked up at her.

"Suit yourself, buddy," she said and walked towards the bar.

I looked back towards the lobby.

The older gentleman was gone.

"Dammit," I said.

"There's a weird-looking one in the bar you might want to check out," Cleft said as he walked towards me. He was holding an ice cold martini in his hand and wearing his vintage afternoon jacket.

"Cleft, go back to the bar. I don't want anyone to see us together."

"Relax, dude," Cleft said and took a sip of his cocktail. "There's a washed-up business man and a Willie Nelson impersonator on the peak of his lost weekend up there."

"You just visiting?" I asked.

"Actually, there's a reason I came out here. There's something you should know."

"Oh and what's that?"

"No matter what happens here—today—I want you to know that I'm still your friend. Or, you're still my friend. Whichever way it goes."

"What exactly do you think will happen here today?"

"No idea actually. It is pretty strange, though, you have to admit that at least. You pawned your daughter off on some neighborhood stranger so you could come face-to-face with someone who wrote some bad shit about you on the internet. Couldn't let that one go, could ya? Had to save face. That being said, you're an overall good guy. You make choices with good intentions. So, keep your head up and feet planted, okay?"

"Okay?"

"Okay," he said as AM-A came out with a plate of food in one hand and a cocktail in the other.

"Your Wagyu sliders and Manhattan with the fancy whiskey," she said and set the food down.

I could feel Cleft's eyes burning into the side of my skull and could smell the scent of salty gin wafting under my nose.

"You're such a hypocrite," he said.

"Oh, this isn't mine," I said and put my hand up as she offered the cocktail in my general direction.

"Excuse me?" she said.

"I didn't order this," I said and held up my wristband and waved it in front of her. "Doctor-issued. No carb, no fat, no love diet. Fake heart and living on borrowed timed here, lady. I've already died once."

"Don't call me lady, sir. You literally just ordered this and then you asked about some guy you thought was strange looking. Do you remember that?"

"Peter," Cleft said.

"It's fine, Cleft. I'm sure this isn't the first time this has happened to her."

"I'll take that, actually," a voice said and reached out for the Manhattan.

It was the older gentleman in the unseasonable trench coat.

"A little warm out for a trench coat," I said.

"It is, isn't it?" he said and took a sip of the Manhattan. "That's pretty good. What's in it?" he said and looked at AM-A.

"Nikka. Japanese whiskey," she said.

"*That's* the name of it," I said.

"We seriously do not mess around at the Driskill, sir," she said.

"Peter, do you know this man?" Cleft said and pointed at the older gentlemen in the trench coat.

"Do I know you?" I asked.

"Would you excuse us?" he said and looked at AM-A and adjusted his gazed towards Cleft. He was over six feet tall, trim, and in relatively good shape for a man of his age. He had a slender face and pointed nose, and his voice had a certain authority to it. A power gained from years of instructing people on what to do.

Jump off this bridge.

Jump of this tall building.

Whatever the task at hand was, people surely listened.

"Me too?" Cleft asked tentatively.

"Yes, you too. You can go back to your perch at the bar. Keep an eye out for anything suspicious, will you?"

"Always happy to help," Cleft said and pouted his way back towards the bar on the tail of AM-A.

"May I sit?" the older gentleman asked.

"By all means," I said and moved down on the couch so there was enough room.

He flipped the back of the trench coat up and sat down next to me.

"Thanks for meeting me," he said.

"Of course," I said with an unexpected amount of deference in my voice. Where did the take-action and hold-no-prisoners Peter Richards go? I memorized the script and went out on stage and was choking. *How dare you slander me, asshole?! I requested the meeting. You are meeting with me!*

"Maybe when she comes back I'll order another one of those," he said. "Do you mind?" he asked and leaned forward and grabbed a slider. "These days I find it harder and harder to tell who's a robot and who isn't. Do you find yourself having the same problem?"

"I know what I am."

"Oh, but do you?" he said. "Let me start off by saying sorry for writing that stuff about you. On the internet," he said and took a bite of the slider.

"It happens," I said. Be a good soldier, Peter. Respect the authority figure and show your gratitude.

"Truth is, we needed to get your attention."

We?

"It's not something where I could have called you up and asked you to drinks and explained myself. You're a popular guy, a local celebrity, if you will, and we didn't think you would have taken it seriously. We all have a lot going on, things that keep us busy. I needed to get your attention, grab you by the neck, and make you focus. You see what I'm saying?"

"Sure," I said. "But how did you know I would see it? Websites for serial adulterers seems like a niche market."

"We put lots of stuff out there about you. We had a whole team working on it. Lots of rubbish on you, sir."

"Oh," I said and looked down at the plate of sliders.

"But don't worry about it. It's virtually impossible for people tell the difference between what's true and what isn't. I'm sure you understand, especially in your line of work. Information needs to be vetted and confirmed before it's considered fact."

"Right, but Joe Public doesn't do that. Joe Public sees one piece of information and runs it into the ground as gospel." My appetite was slowly waning. This guy, he could be fifty, he could by eighty, I seriously couldn't tell. "Why me?" I finally asked.

"Listen to me," he said and leaned in closer to me. He was still watching the lobby. I could smell ketchup on his breath. "We need someone like you. A proficient, top-of-his-class and grade-A professional."

"Professional what?"

"You're adept and observant, able to keep an even keel and not jump to conclusions. You hear things out and look at all sides. That's what we need. We need a thorough, balanced, and rational third-party perspective."

"Who are you again?"

"Me? I'm nobody really. But the collective we, our organization, we run a company that develops cities of the future and for the future."

"Future? But this is the future. We're living in the future right now. Did you not get the memo?"

"What I'm talking about is post-future. Future's future, if you will. Our organization has been under some close and misallocated scrutiny lately and we want you to help correct it."

"How so?"

"We want to hire you—pay you cash—to come to our annual meeting and do a story on it. How does that sound?"

"When is the meeting?"

"Next month. It's here in Austin."

"What does your organization do again? I missed that part."

"We want to create a new-world civilization."

"Of course. Right."

"I hope you are able to remain objective."

"Naturally."

"I'll lay it out for you and you tell me what you think," he said, and I nodded politely. "We want people to live off a resource-based economy where they are able to utilize natural resources and have sustainable development. There will be no war, and homelessness will be obsolete. That's the goal at least. Big thinking here, you follow?"

"I'm with you so far," I said and began wondering if Cleft was behind this. Maybe this was some sort of put on.

I looked back towards the bar. Cleft was chatting it up with the Willie Nelson impersonator.

"There would be a socioeconomic system that would bring creativity, beauty, and happiness and people wouldn't be driven by the accumulation of material possessions. Shit jobs would be outsourced to robots. We're seeing that already. Travis Holt, he's a superstar. Also, we'll make buildings in factories, and cities would be pre-designed in order to conserve resources. There would be no police, no army, and no prisons. The idea is to not shame people. Resources would be distributed among people based on a scientific methodology. Elitism would be extinct. Crime would be extinct and the monetary system we know today would be obsolete. Money would no longer motivate people. They would be motivated by love and passion. Like I said, future's future."

"How do you expect to do this? Where would you start?"

"We've already started. We need to expand."

"And this is your idea?"

"Me and a handful of notable scholars and thought leaders in politics, banking, and education around the world. It's a truly global initiative and we have pedigree."

"So what's the problem?"

"Some of our biggest opponents think we're trying to create a One World Technological Government. I'm sure you've heard of it, or versions of it."

"Sure. It's pretty common in my field. It's the idea that the government and world elite are here to take our money and condemn us to some remote island as slaves. Very logical scenario."

"More or less," he said. "We need you to do a story. Debunk that thinking and legitimize our initiative. Use your channels to help our image."

"But are you trying to do that? Are you trying to create a one-world government?"

"Does it matter?"

"It's good to see all the angles."

"Of course we're not trying to do that, and if we were, why would I ever tell you?"

Point taken.

"Let me think about it," I said.

"You have twenty-four hours and then the offer expires," he said and turned towards me and handed me a small white business card. Heavy stock.

"Wait," I said. He leaned closer to me and tilted his head. "I didn't get your name."

"Of course you did," he said and stood up and walked away. I flipped the business card around.

"What was that about?" Cleft said as he hustled over.

"Not sure," I said and looked down at the business card. There wasn't much on it. No contact information and no fancy font. There was only a single word in the center in large black letters:

MILES.

19.

"I'm here to pick something up," Skelly said cautiously. "A headset."

"What's your name?" a teenager said. She was standing behind a wide glass counter looking at pictures of different VR headsets on a tablet. She had a headset pushed up above her forehead.

"Skelly," he said and looked at the collection of energy drinks lined up underneath the counter.

"We've been expecting you," she said evenly. "If you'll head over to station number two someone will be right with you," she said and gestured towards the center of the store where there were three raised circular platforms. They each had an eight-foot circumference and were surrounded by a metal fence with a gate for easy access.

And the end of mankind as we know it is all around me, Skelly thought to himself as he walked over to the center of the store and opened the gate to the only empty platform.

He hesitated, suddenly unsure of what he was doing.

"He who hesitates dies, am I right?" a voice said behind him.

Skelly turned around.

A short older woman was standing directly behind him. She was wearing a second-hand Ann Taylor peacoat and seasonal stretch pants. Both were off-white to fend off the imposing summer sun. Skelly could smell her lunch. Sushi burrito dipped in whipped wasabi.

"I'm Detective Skelly."

"I know. I have your viewfinder right here," she said and held up a black headset. "It's charged and ready to go."

"Go where?"

"Wherever you want," she said and motioned her hand towards the platform. The floors were high-end laminate and the walls were painted an off-white color, to match the pants and peacoat. Everything else was nondescript.

Skelly wanted to turn around and slowly walk out. He wasn't accustomed to state-of-the-art things. He didn't care for things that were more advanced than he was, and found them to be uninteresting and against human nature and the way he thought things should be. He especially didn't understand being immersed in a virtual world where anything was possible.

"Which game would you like, Detective Skelly?" the woman asked as her head appeared to float in midair. The off-white of the walls and her outfit clashed perfectly.

"Which game?"

"We have several for you to choose from," she said, but could sense his hesitation. "A popular one is *White Fall*, where you team up with a group of New Zealand explorers to search for a missing climber on Everest. Why they put the word fall in the title I'll never know. There's also *Mr. Ruble*, where you parade around New York City as a real estate developer only to come to realize that you're actually a sleeper agent for the KGB. Don't worry though. You find that out early on so I'm not ruining anything for you." She wasn't getting the response she wanted. "How about *Jiro Ono*, where you get to play famous sushi chef Jiro Ono as he prepares a meal for the G8 Summit? Our hand sensors are so advanced that people actually scream when they cut a finger off. One person even called 911."

"What can you tell me about Donald Smolder?"

"Oh," she said. She was caught off guard. "Not much. He worked upstairs and would come down and play. It's a shame what happened to him."

"Did he say anything when he came down here?"

"He came to play. He didn't say much."

"Do you know what he played when he came down here?"

"It's confidential," she said.

"*Stolen Planet?*"

"I ... shouldn't really ... you wouldn't want me telling people what you go around doing."

"Can I play it?"

"There are so many games, you shouldn't start with that one."

"Is there a problem?"

"No problem."

"I'll try that one."

"There are so many other options though."

"I heard it's very popular with college students. There must be something to it."

"Honestly, if you want my opinion, I think it's dangerous."

"Why is that?"

"It is popular, but with a very niche audience. The developer is new to the market and hasn't given the Miles Cooperative access to the interface and that makes people nervous. Some people find that aspect appealing but most people feel like they are aren't safe if Miles isn't watching over."

"Can I play it?"

"If you insist," she said. "If you could please step onto the platform. I'll get you all set up," she said and waved her hand out to formally present the playing space. Skelly took a few steps forward until he was in the middle of the platform. She handed him his helmet and went over to a control panel on the outside of the platform. Skelly suddenly felt trapped. "Can you tell me the nine digit code on the inside of your helmet?"

"Sure," Skelly said looked down at the inside of his helmet. "Q7s23Ev3i."

"Thank you," she said and punched the code into the control panel. "What was the last—?"

"An *i*."

"Thank you," she said and firmly pushed one last button. "You can put the helmet on now. Your partner took the liberty of picking a username for you and designing your avatar that you can use in hundreds of games. I hope you don't mind. I think she did a pretty good job. Erin was her name, right?"

"Right," Skelly said and looked down at the helmet. He shifted his feet towards the platform's exit. He was sure they got walkouts all the time.

He cautiously raised the helmet over his head. There was a small metal piece that went over his nose and two buds that went into his ears.

"Do you dream, Skelly?"

"No," he said as he watched the darkness on the inside of the helmet.

"Adjust the chin strap so you're comfortable and I'm going to press the power button. The game you selected is *Stolen Planet*," she said loud enough for others to hear. This made Skelly self-aware and uncomfortable. "Once the game starts you'll see a soft blue light."

"A blue light?" Skelly asked inquisitively.

"Yes. It's the sky. Blue sky. Everyone is always so concerned about the light but it's really nothing. It's totally innocuous. Blue light and then nice fluffy clouds show up and you hear some music with a nice soothing voiceover by a recognizable but often forgotten about celebrity."

"Don Johnson?"

"How did you guess?"

"It's my job."

"It feels like a movie and you're right in the middle of it."

"Okay," he said as he felt her press the power button.

A soft blue light slowly emerged from the center of the darkness. The essence of sushi burrito faded and Skelly smelled fresh open air. It was the smell of promise and expectation.

A title card appeared in front of the blue sky:

WELCOME TO *STOLEN PLANET*
The journey starts here

"Hello," a voice said. "I'm Don Johnson and welcome to *Stolen Planet*."

The title card faded and white cumulus clouds came into view. The various clicks, bumps, and hisses from the showroom drifted away.

Skelly was immersed.

The concerns of everyday police work no longer bothered him. It was just him, and the voice of Don Johnson, floating through the sky.

"*Stolen Planet* is a first-person game where you are on a quest to save your homeland from an unknown enemy," Don Johnson said. "Right now we're floating over the District of Columbia. You may have heard of it. Home to the Washington Monument and the Lincoln Memorial. Look down and you'll see it." Skelly shifted his body around and tilted his head until he could see the Lincoln Memorial below him. He was getting closer to the ground. "I also have a house here," Don Johnson continued. "Which is probably surprising to you. What is famous Hollywood actor Don Johnson doing in the heartland of American politics? Funny you should ask because I'm also the President of the

130

United States of America. That's right. There's my house over there on the left." Skelly rotated his body. "No, go a little farther," Don Johnson said. Skelly turned a little bit more until he could see the White House. "That's right. Why don't you come down and we can have a little chat and then you can be on your way. I'm sure you're anxious to start playing *Stolen Planet* and I don't blame you. It's an amazing game."

Skelly reached his arms out to steady himself as his body slowly started to descend on the White House lawn.

He was greeted by two Secret Service agents who led him into a side door. They ushered him down a long brightly lit hallway. Before he knew it they were showing him into the Oval Office.

The one and only Don Johnson was standing in the middle of the Oval Office eating a cheeseburger. His silver hair was slicked back and there was a reflection of the room in his soft blue eyes.

"I'm sorry," he said and crammed the last bit of burger into his mouth. "I didn't expect you so soon." A bit of mustard shot out of his mouth and landed on the Presidential Seal. "That's a damn shame." Skelly didn't say anything. "You can talk, you know. You have a microphone."

"No problem?" Skelly said into a small microphone that was positioned discreetly on the side of his headset. "Can you hear me?" The echo and gravitas of his own voice was startling.

"Have a seat," Don Johnson said as he proffered his hand out towards the couch. Skelly walked over and sat down. "Comfy, isn't it?"

"Sure," Skelly said.

"Why don't you touch it? Run your fingers on it and see how it feels."

"Excuse me?"

"The couch," Don Johnson said. "Put your fingers on the couch and see how it feels. The technology is better than anything you have ever seen." Skelly looked at the couch and slowly reached his fingers out and ran them over the soft fabric of the couch. He could feel the fibers tingle against his fingertips. It felt like cashmere and smelled liked a fresh load of laundry. "And that's just the beginning. You'll be amazed at what's possible in *Stolen Planet*."

"Do you know Donald Smolder?"

"I'm sure that I don't," Don Johnson said. "We need to review some ground rules before you get started. Do you understand?"

131

Skelly nodded his head to show that he understood. He was still massaging the couch and was starting to get used to the headset and enjoyed looking around even though he knew everything was entirely fictional.

"Actually, I need you to say yes or no to that question," Don Johnson said. "For legal reasons."

"Yes. I understand," Skelly said and looked up from the couch.

"Great. Are you over the age of 18?"

"Yes."

"Have you reviewed, and do you understand, the *Stolen Planet* rules of operation?"

"I'm not familiar with them."

"They state that you, and only you, are responsible for your actions in the game and that you will be held accountable in a court of law if you disclose, knowingly or unknowingly, any of *Stolen Planet*'s trade secrets. That's it. Everything else is allowed."

"Everything?"

"It is a game, Skelly, and we aren't monsters."

"Court of law? This place is fictional," Skelly said with a faint edge of disbelief in his voice.

"Here we have a court of law and lawyers who will happily represent you. The world and place may be fictional, but the choices you make and the consequences are real."

"I don't think you can prosecute me in court for something I do in a game," Skelly said.

"You can have your doubts, but this is how it is. Now before you get started are you clear on your objective?"

"At the beginning you said something about protecting the homeland from an unknown enemy."

"Precisely. There is a secret organization that we need you to infiltrate and dismantle from the inside. Become one of them, get to know them, and then exterminate them by any means necessary."

"Secret organization? Like the Freemasons? Knights Templar?"

"All things you will need to find out for yourself as you play. What I can tell you is the total gameplay is anywhere between two weeks and six months. It's not continuous though, that would be absolutely ridiculous."

"Right, of course," Skelly said as he looked past Don Johnson and out the window as Marine One landed on the White House lawn. He wondered if there was any connection between the game and Molly Cooper's murder.

"Come with me," Don Johnson said as he stood up from the couch. A Secret Service agent opened the double doors that led to the White House lawn and Skelly followed Don Johnson out towards the helicopter.

"Where are we going?"

"I'm going to take you to a fancy hotel in London where you'll go through a brief orientation before gameplay will officially start," he said as he stepped onto Marine One. He motioned for Skelly to join him. "If at any point you want to pause gameplay, say your safe word three times fast."

"What's my safe word?"

"What do you want it to be?" Don Johnson said as he took a seat and pulled out a bottle of bourbon from a secret compartment.

"Why don't I just take the headset off?"

"Sure. You could do that. Why don't you try that now and let me know how it goes."

Skelly reached his hands up to pull off the headset but quickly realized that he was pushing on air.

"It's the technology. You can't tell the difference between your game hands and your real hands. So, what would you like your safe word to be? If you can't provide me with a safe word one will be given to you automatically."

"Uh—" Skelly hesitated.

"Nash Bridges."

"Excuse me?"

"That's your safe word. 'Nash Bridges.' I know it's a little self-serving, but I can't help myself."

"That's a name not a word."

"Touché. Safe phrase, if you will. Say it three times fast and gameplay will be paused. Got it?"

"Nash Bridges, Nash—"

"No, no. Not now, you fool," Don Johnson said and put his hand up to stop Skelly.

Skelly nodded and looked outside as the helicopter slowly ascended as Don Johnson poured a glass of bourbon and handed it to Skelly.

Skelly rotated the glass between his fingers. It felt real. "Try it."

Skelly held the glass up to his nose and took a sniff. It smelled oaky. He took a small sip. It was good. "It's a trick. Obviously you aren't drinking bourbon, but it feels like you are. Have enough of those bad boys and things will start to get a little fuzzy."

"Wow."

"Everything that happens in the game occurs in real time. One hour in *Stolen Planet* is one hour in real time. We understand the total immersion effect of the game so every fifteen minutes you'll receive a little update at the bottom of the screen." Don Johnson pointed his finger down as a small window showed up on Skelly's screen. "It will give you a brief health update and any nutritional deficiencies you may have. It will literally tell you if you're thirsty or not."

"I don't feel thirsty. I had some bourbon."

"But that wasn't real," Don Jonson said. "Are you ready to get started?"

"I'm ready," Skelly said as he looked out the window.

"Fantastic. Can you tell me who referred you to *Stolen Planet?*"

"Excuse me?" Skelly asked.

"Who referred you to the game?"

"Uh … Erin …"

"Erin who?"

"I don't know," Skelly said and tried to think. How did he not know her last name? "She signed me up. That's all I know," he said.

"A simple sign-up will give you access to the bar and recreational area. That's where we are headed now but we need to do a double-authentication in order for you to go anywhere else in *Stolen Planet*. Top secret stuff, and we can't have you wandering around if we don't trust you."

"What else is there?" Skelly asked.

"You'll soon find out," Don Johnson said. "If you can provide me with the names of two users who referred you, or the name of one user and then answer five questions correctly about how the Digital Revolution was the ultimate downfall of mankind. That is if you really want to play. Otherwise you can hang out with the unmotivated common folk in the bar and recreational area."

"What can I do in the bar and recreational area?"

"There's a water cooler if you're thirsty."

"How was the Digital Revolution the downfall of mankind?" Skelly asked.

"Is that the option you're going with?"

"Nash Bridges, Nash Bridges, Nash Bridges."

20.

"Where are you, friend?" David's voice bellowed from the other end of the phone.

"I'm finishing this meeting," I said. "Are you at your house? I haven't heard from Joyce yet, but I'm happy to stop by."

"We're not at home. We were going to drop her off at your house, but Paula's not home and we didn't know how long you would be. We didn't feel comfortable leaving her there all by herself."

"She's twelve and it's a safe neighborhood, but you make the decision that you think is best."

"Every neighborhood is safe until it isn't," he said.

I shrugged and flipped the recently acquired business card around. There was one word printed in Veranda font, sixteen point:

MILES.

"I'll be back in fifteen, depending on traffic," I said and flicked my wrist and looked at my tracker. "Why don't I come and pick her up at your house?" I said thinking that this small inconvenience could work to my advantage. If I could find out where they lived and get into their house I wouldn't need Cleft's client list. At least not yet. And clearly, suspicious people keep suspicious things in their houses. Maybe I would be fortunate enough to come across a recent issue of *The Daily Doings of Shady Neighbors*, or better yet, a handwritten list of all the shady stuff David and Darlene did and subsequently had misgivings about. That's how this scenario was playing out in my head. That is, if they in fact had misgivings about their bad deeds.

Maybe they live in a guilt-free world.

"No, no. That won't work," he said abruptly. "We stopped and got the girls ice cream. Come meet us. It's that new place on 620, north of the Galleria."

Jesus. "You're in Lakeway?"

"That's what I said, isn't it?"

"You live all the way out in Lakeway now? I'm confused."

"No. We like the ice cream place that recently opened in Lakeway. It's some liquid nitrogen shit. It'll freeze you're fingers off."

"Fine. I'll be there in a little bit," I said.

He was nice enough to offer to pick Joyce up and bring her to the gymnastics meet, but apparently I was expecting too much when I asked him to bring her back to our house afterwards. And God forbid I suggest we meet at their house. How intrusive of me to propose such a thing. I could always follow them home or put a transmitter on their suspicious car.

Events at the Driskill were running long and strange and I couldn't find a reasonable enough excuse to step away. I found myself with at least a thirty-minute commute out to Lakeway, a small suburb on the outskirts of Austin that catered to an ever-growing middle class. I tried calling Paula on the way out there to see if she heard how Maya's sleepover was going, but she didn't pick up. I'm sure the sodium trial she was working on was going smoothly. Maybe she was cornering her new best friend about multi-function eye cream.

I reached Lakeway in twenty minutes and parked in front of the ice cream shop, which was located in a strip mall between a vision center and some trendy pizza parlor. I hadn't been out here in a few years and little had changed. Lakeway was an island unto itself. It was an oasis stuck between liberal downtown Austin and the deer head-toting roughage of the boonies. People who lived in Lakeway tended to stay in Lakeway and the rest of Austin was OK with that.

"Hey there, stranger," David said as I walked into the ice cream shop.

He was sitting at a table near the front window next to Darlene. Joyce and his two children were sitting at a table behind them.

Joyce looked tired and irritated.

"Can we get you something?" Darlene asked me. "The mocha chip is amazing."

"I'm good," I said and smiled at her. Joyce got up and ran over to me and gave me a hug. "How did the competition go?"

"It was fine."

"Fine?"

"You heard me," she said and then looked at Darlene. "Can I have my phone back now?"

"As long as your dad says you can have your phone back," she said in a tone that made my skin crawl.

Joyce looked up at me.

"Sure," I said. "I think that's fine." Darlene reached into her purse and took out Joyce's phone and handed it to her.

Joyce went back to her table to finish her ice cream.

"What happened?" I whispered.

"Nothing. What do you mean?"

"Why did you take her phone away? Did she do something wrong?"

"No. We don't allow our kids to be around ... that sort of stuff."

"Oh, you have certain windows of time when they can use their phones and whatnot?"

"No," Darlene said.

I looked in David's direction for some sort of guidance, clarity in this sea of noise, but they were both staring at me.

"Whatever works best, I guess. We parent in our own way."

"What Darlene is trying to say is that we don't believe in advanced technology."

"Mennonites?"

"I think you're thinking about Luddites."

"What are those?"

"People who don't believe in technology."

"Actually, the Luddites were a group of English laborers who destroyed machines because they saw machines as a threat to their jobs," Darlene corrected.

"What are Mennonites then?"

"How am I supposed to know?" she said. I'll have to remember to look that up later.

"A Mennonite is someone who is part of the Protestant cult that emphasizes adult baptism and rejects the church organization, military service, and public office." Joyce said from the other table. She was on her phone. Abbey and her brother were leaning over her shoulder watching intently.

"Cult is a rather strong word, isn't it, honey? I think you meant to say church."

"I don't think so," she said.

"There you have it. Kids these days, right?"

"Don't get too close to that, kids," Darlene said as she watched her kids leering over Joyce's shoulder.

This woman is certifiable, I thought.

"Seriously, Abbey," David chimed in. "Listen to your mother." *Him too?* David looked up at me. "We feel that technology imposes on natural human development."

"It's just a phone. Some apps and moving pictures. What could the harm be in that?"

"It hinders our potential as human beings."

"Didn't I call you on a phone?" I said.

"Yes, as a matter of fact you did," David said and pulled out a gray Motorola phone. It had three buttons on it: *Police, Fire, 911.* "The essentials. We're aren't robots after all. Isn't that right, Peter?" he said and gave me a smile.

"Technology offers promise and hope for the future."

"I'm afraid you're wrong on that one, friend," Darlene said. "Technology is a threat to our very existence. The games and platforms are so advanced, people aren't able to tell the difference between the game and this"— she waved her hands around, indicating—"the real world."

"Surely, that's a matter of opinion," I said. "You drive a car. That's technology."

"Let me offer you this example," David said. "In the late seventeen hundreds, workers at a wool factory in northern England issued a protest against the growing use of scribbling machines, which were taking over a majority of the labor the workers were performing."

"Excuse me, what's a scribbling machine?"

"It's a textile thing—not important," David said. "The protests were ignored and the workers were eventually laid off because their jobs were being outsourced to these machines."

"Maybe they were fired because they were whining about their jobs?" I said and smiled at him.

"You're missing the point," Darlene said.

"Lay it on me," I said and spread my arms out in deference.

"The question is: how are those workers, the ones with a learned skill who are now out of work, supposed to provide for their family?"

"Can't they get a new job?" I asked. "If their company outsourced their job to a machine they should go somewhere else and find a new job—adapt."

"But who will provide for their families when they are looking for a new job or learning a new skill, Peter?" Darlene asked.

"I don't know," I said.

"And if one company is outsourcing their job, what's to say another company, and another company won't start doing the same thing?"

"People need to be flexible. My job is being outsourced to an alcoholic robot and I figured out how to survive," I said.

"We're going to start seeing an increase in software and machines doing the very things that used to be done by people with a college degree," David said. "Advanced robotics could reduce employment in manufacturing, medicine, accounting, and even education."

"We're already seeing it. It's all around us," Darlene interjected. "What happens when your job is outsourced and you're out of work and have to pay for training for a new job?" she asked. I shrugged. These people were out of their minds. "You go into debt and then you get a job that helps pay the bills, if you're lucky, and then you spend the next ten or twenty years trying to pay off the debt you acquired from learning a new profession and then all of a sudden the gap between those who have—the capitalists—and those who don't—the laborers and workers—is vast and wide."

"So, what you're telling me is that I should start building robots?"

"He's part robot," David said and pointed to me. "He has one of those hearts."

"Interesting," Darlene said and looked me up and down. The look of judgment on her face wasn't lost on me.

"He could be useful," David said to her under his breath and with a partially covered mouth but I still heard it.

"Useful for what?" I asked.

"Excuse me?"

"You just told her that you thought I could be useful."

"No I didn't," he said and scoffed at me and then looked down at his empty ice cream dish.

"Yes—you just said, 'He could be useful.'"

"You must have misheard me."

"Oh, okay. My bad. I'm making shit up as I go along apparently," I said. "You guys are so strange. You know that? I don't know what it is with you guys, but it's something. Ever since I first saw you in gymnastics something bugged me about you guys. I'm not sure what it is though. Where did you guys say you were from?"

"Uh, I'm from here—Austin—born and raised. Hook 'em!" David said.

"Where did you go to high school?" I asked.

"In this neighborhood, actually. My buddies and I used to come here and eat ice cream after school. Oh, the good old days."

"This place is new—you said so yourself. You're so full of crap," I said. "I don't know what it is about you two but I'll figure it out. I usually do."

"Listen, buddy," David said. "We're simply telling you what we think, okay? Take it or leave it. We are who we are and you're you." *But who are you?* "I'll tell you what. Why don't you and Paula come over later? We have a beautiful patio in the backyard and I can make us a few drinks and we can smooth things over. How does that sound?"

"He's got a heavy hand, but makes a great Manhattan."

"Sure," I said apprehensively. "I'll ask her."

"Come by. We'll be waiting."

"If you insist," I said. Now I had a way into the house.

"Deal, dude," he said and put his hand out to give me a fist bump. I reciprocated but he took it too far and let his hand explode on retreat.

Joyce was already halfway to the door. I followed her out and got into the car.

"That was strange," she said. She set her gym bag down.

"We need to learn to accept people despite our differences."

"Bunch of wackos, if you ask me," she said quietly.

"You should hear what they have to say about you," I said and smiled at her.

"That's not nice!" she said and swatted my arm playfully.

"How was the meet?"

"The competition was fine. You didn't miss anything."

"I'm sorry."

"It's fine. I'm glad it's done," she said and leaned over and pulled out a stack of paper from her bag and handed it to me. "I got you something."

"What is it?" I said and flipped the pages around in my hands.

"I did it," she said and let out a small smile.

"You did what?" I asked and watched as her smile got bigger. "You didn't?" I asked.

"Oh, I totally did," she said.

"You stole the registration list?" I said, not sure if I should be proud of or disappointed in her.

"No. Why would I take that risk? It's easy to find out where people live. If you really wanted to know you could follow them or look it up online."

"Oh."

"It's Cleft's client list."

"But, we have that, Joyce, and we can't make sense of it."

"This one is decoded, Dad," she said as I looked down at it and flipped the pages over to see hundreds of names, phone numbers, and addresses. "The names on the left are—"

"Wait, how did you do this?"

"I took Cleft's encrypted list and scanned it and ran it through a program that runs a billion lines of code per second. His code was pretty sophisticated but ultimately breakable. Everything is. The program I used said Cleft was using some old KGB code," she said. "Alan Turing is rolling in his grave, am I right?"

"Shit," I said and looked down at it.

"The names on the left are the clients' original names. The names on the right are the new identities that Cleft provided them with."

"What is Abbey's last name?" I asked.

"I think you know how to find that out," Joyce said and she was right.

I flipped through the pages and looked at the client names on the left.

There were hundreds of them.

I stopped.

CREED. David and Darlene
(+ two minors: 1 boy, 1 girl), Fort Myers, FL.

"That asshole," I said and ran my finger across the page and stopped.

PIKE, David & Darlene
(+ two minors: 1 boy, 1 girl)
1219 Johnny Miller Trail, Austin, TX.

"Good work, honey," I said and paused while an ulcer formed in my stomach.

There was a soft beep on my wrist, which meant my blood pressure was rising.

I pulled out my phone and called Cleft.

"What is it, Peter? I'm busy."

"Why is your client list in some weird KGB code?"

"Why don't you ask your Commie wife?" he said and laughed.

"I'm asking for my friends. Maybe you know them. David and Darlene Pike and family."

"I can explain."

"I bet you can," I said and hung up the phone. I looked over at Joyce. "Let's go get some dinner."

21.

"Get me a Bulleit on the rocks, Bev," Erin said as she sat down at the end of the bar at the Cloak Room, an unassuming bar across the street, and down a flight of stairs, from the Capitol.

It smelled like crushed peanuts and stale Scotch and was a favorite amongst the Capitol elite and lawyers from the numerous nearby law firms. Erin liked how low-key it was. She also liked how police didn't come here, at least not often, as they didn't like to mingle with the lawyers and politicians. This wasn't TV after all.

"You cops think you're so clever," Bev said.

Of course her name is Bev. What else would it be? Erin thought to herself every time she came here. Bev has been behind the bar here for more than thirty years and has probably seen her fair share of unsavory activities and under-the-table political dealings. It's been rumored that she has a rather heavy hand. Erin didn't seem to notice.

"Make that two actually, Bev," a man said as he sat down next to Erin. Erin looked at him in his tan JoS. A. Bank linen suit.

The bar was empty.

He didn't have to sit right next to her.

"Do I know you?" she asked.

"Liam Reynolds," he said and stuck his hand out towards her.

"Never heard of you."

"I work over there," he said and motioned towards the door, beyond which was the Capitol.

"That means nothing to me," Erin said and took a sip of her drink.

"Trusted adviser to many of the political elite in Austin."

"How do you say 'scumbag' in French, Erin?" Bev said and laughed as she set a drink down in front of Reynolds. She may not like everyone who came in here, but she didn't discriminate.

"Everything I do is above the table, Bev. You know that."

"That's not what it looked like last night."

"Do you think you could put some Tom Petty on in here, Bev?" Liam asked.

"You bet your ass I won't," Bev said and turned around.

"She's always such a delight, isn't she?" he asked.

"I'm actually meeting someone. They should be here in a few minutes," Erin said and turned her body away from him and focused her attention on a wall of photographs behind the bar.

Ever since the Cloak Room opened, they'd been collecting pictures of customers. There were at least a thousand behind the bar and another thousand or so on the stairway that led up to the bathrooms.

"I know Skelly is supposed to be here in a few minutes. That's why I'm here," he said.

"It's a creepy thing. Normal people don't do that sort of stuff. Normal people call and make arrangements. They don't just show up in a bar and impose themselves. You do understand that, right?"

"This is a different sort of matter. I'm a friend and want to ask for your help. I didn't want to handle this through the proper channels," Reynolds said and finished his drink. He was quick, efficient, and boring. Bev was nearby with a quick refill. "This requires special handling," he said.

"I bet it does."

"I want Skelly to run for Chief of Police," Reynolds said. "I have a whole team of people who are onboard with this. He's the guy. This is just between you and me, of course. Bev too, I suppose."

"That's right, honey," Bev said.

"He's into drumming right now," Erin said. "He's really busy."

"You can't be serious."

Erin thought for a second and took and sip of her drink and slowly set it down and looked Reynolds square in the eyes. "He's not the guy."

"Sure he is. He's the only guy, as far as I'm concerned."

"Have you met Detective Skelly?"

"I've known him for a while and we had lunch recently."

"It's not possible. He doesn't eat."

"I explained it to him."

"Then you should know he would never do it."

"How long have you been his partner?"

"I'm not his partner. I'm a forensics officer," she said pointedly. "Helping him out with a case or two."

"What do you know about him anyway? In my opinion, and I've known him for a while, I think he can be persuaded. He's reluctant and that's understandable. He needs a nudge. That's all," Reynolds said and raised his glass. "Will you nudge him for me, Erin?"

"You're gross."

"I'm pointing out what's so obvious to everyone else."

"Don't cramp her style, Reynolds. She'll put you away for life. And I don't mean prison," a voice said.

It was Skelly.

He was standing behind Reynolds.

"Skelly, we've been waiting for you," Reynolds said and turned around with a smile on his face. He put his hand on Skelly's shoulder and moved over to create space between him and Erin. "Have a seat."

"I like standing," Skelly said. "Hey Erin."

"Hey yourself. How did it go?"

"How did what go?" Reynolds asked and craned his neck between them like a pterodactyl.

"It was … different," Skelly said. "Could you excuse us for a second?"

"Sure. I need to use the pisser anyway. Oh, I forgot we were around lady folk. Pardon my language and get me another, Bev," he said and walked towards the staircase at the back of the bar.

"What's he doing here?" Skelly asked.

"I was going to ask you the same thing. Apparently he knew we were meeting. He wants to talk to you about being Chief of Police."

"He's a broken record."

"He seems to think you'd be perfect for it," she said. "Skelly's moving on up!" she said and held her glass up.

Skelly didn't reciprocate.

"He needs someone who is less of a stool than Bales is."

"Do it and you can get rid of Miles."

"He's ridiculous," Skelly said. "I need your help, Erin."

"What is it?"

"The game—*Stolen Planet*—it requires that I authenticate myself."

"What does that mean?"

"It only gave me access to one very small piece of the game. The introduction. But in order for me to play the actual game I need to tell them who verified me."

"I did."

"No. You didn't. You just signed me up and told me about it. Some-one, actually two people, have to vouch for me."

"I'll vouch for you any day."

"No, Erin, no, people who are currently playing the game need to vouch for me. Security."

"What happens if they don't vouch for you?"

"Then you hang out at the water cooler with Don Johnson."

"What does he have to do with anything?"

"I've been asking myself the same question."

"I can ask around."

"What did I miss out here?" Skelly asked. "Did you hear back from the Medical Examiner's office?"

"No," Erin said and grimaced at him. "I thought you were still doing that, right? Since you and Nicole are best buds or whatever it is you two are."

"We're nothing, Erin," Skelly said. "Not that it's any of your busi-ness anyway."

"You're right, Skelly. I'll stay out of it," she said and pursed her lips. She reached into her pocket and pulled out a slip of paper and slid it across the bar towards Skelly.

"What is this?"

"The handwriting sample on the note found on Molly Cooper's body came back."

"Oh." Skelly said and looked down at the slip of paper.

"Surprised?"

"I can't say that I am," Skelly said and crumpled the paper up.

"What do you want to do about it?"

"I'll handle it," he said. "Did you have any luck with the motel?" he asked. "You know, since you're helping out and all?"

"As a matter of fact, I did," she said and reached into her pocket and pulled out a small notecard. She slid it across the bar towards Skelly.

He picked it up and looked at it.

BARRY FOSTER

"Who's that?"

"He's the person who was renting the room that night," she said. "He's a student at the university."

"Did you talk to him?"

"Nope."

"I can do it."

"It's not that. He wouldn't talk to me," Erin said and waved her finger so Bev could get her another drink. "I met him outside after one of his classes and explained to him what happened and showed him my badge. He confirmed he rented a room that night with his friends but he said he didn't see anything, and he and his friends were high as kites, so even if he did see something it wouldn't be reliable. He said a lawyer would shoot holes through his testimony in court, so don't bother. Now might be a good time to mention that he's a law student."

"Dammit," Skelly said. "Why do all the kids want to be lawyers these days?"

"Maybe there's still some glory in it?"

"Doubtful. Thanks for trying though."

"I should also mention that he was freaked out when I asked him about the motel."

"What do you mean? Freaked out that a cop was asking him questions?" Skelly asked.

"No. Oddly enough he seemed okay and comfortable with that part of it. But when I brought up the motel, his disposition changed. He became fidgety and different."

"You think he did it?"

"Maybe or he's protecting someone in that room who did it. It's hard to tell."

"Can we bring him in for questioning? Maybe even get a lawyer to talk some sense into him. You okay doing that?"

"Doing what? Bringing him in for questioning? That seems like something you should do," Erin said.

"Normally I would, but I need to get back to this *Stolen Planet* thing."

"Seriously?"

"Seriously. I think there might be something there and I need to see it through."

149

"I knew you'd be into it," Erin said and patted him on the shoulder. "What lawyer should I use?"

"I'll introduce you to one," Skelly said as Bev came over and topped off Erin's drink.

"Hey, Skelly."

"What's new, Bev?"

"Oh, you know, just catering to the political elite. Status quo. You?"

"People are getting murdered, so …" he said and raised his shoulders slightly.

"Oh, really?" Bev said and Skelly gave her a slight nod. "It's about time something happened around here. The one thing Miles didn't promise: excitement."

Reynolds came back and sat down next to Skelly. "Sorry about that. I didn't realize the Browns were going to the Super Bowl."

"Oh my goodness, that's disgusting," Erin said.

"I don't get it," Skelly said and looked at Erin and Bev. "I don't watch football."

"It's okay, honey," Bev said. "You keep fighting the good fight."

"I'm glad I found you two here," Reynolds said.

"I don't recall mentioning this to you," Skelly said. "Did you, Erin?"

"I've never seen this man before in my life."

"Lucky you," Bev said from the far side of the bar.

"Do you mind, Bev?" Reynolds said. "I'm trying to have a meeting here."

"As you wish," she said and put her arms up in resignation.

"Look, Skelly. I wanted to finish our conversation from the other day. I know you weren't too keen on the idea and all, but I thought you might need some time to think things over and let the idea digest. I also want you to know that the Miles Cooperative is very much in your court. They think a guy like you would do wonders for this city."

"The Miles Cooperative?" Erin asked. "Jesus, Skelly."

"Reynolds is on their payroll. He might be a little disenfranchised, but they still pay his bills. He thinks if I run I'll remind the city what real police work is."

"Truth is they're seriously considering backing out of the city if you don't run."

"Good. Let them."

"What does that mean? Backing out?"

Reynolds started to speak but Skelly held his hand up. "I'll take this one," Skelly said. "The Miles Cooperative has certain investments and interests in our fine city. Things that Bales was a big supporter of."

"What sort of interests?"

"All the fine surveillance equipment we have, for one. Also, that new forensics kit you recently asked for."

"What about it?"

"The Miles Cooperative donated it to the city and the best part is, Bales let them."

"I think you're giving Bales too much credit," Erin said and shifted her gaze between Skelly and Reynolds. Reynolds pointed his finger at her and winked. "Besides, I need those to do my job."

"The point is," Skelly said, "the Miles Cooperative is collecting information and data about you and your every move."

"Right. It helps keep us safe."

"That's one part of it."

"What's the other?"

"So they can sell it."

"To who?"

"The government. Probably. Maybe they sell some of it to Russia or North Korea. They come in and sell big data to us as some Godsend and then use the data they collect to monetize us. Miles made four billion dollars last year in profit."

"Whoa, whoa," Reynolds interrupted. "I'd like to point out that is Skelly's opinion. There is absolutely no proven evidence that the Miles Cooperative is doing anything with your data except using it to create a better overall user experience."

"How do they make money?"

"I don't know. Why are there twenty year olds buying million dollar homes in Rollingwood? Some things I simply cannot explain."

"Say what you want, Reynolds, but all of this has been possible because of Bales."

"See, that's why we need you, Skelly," Reynolds pleaded with him. "You aren't Bales. You're the opposite of Bales."

"I may be a has-been detective set in my ways, I'll give you that, but I know what's going on. I pay attention. That's my job. You thought you'd offer me a high salary and I'd leap at the chance to get out of a dying industry, didn't you?" Reynolds stared at his glass and rotated it between his fingers. "It's okay. You don't have to answer. I know that I'm smarter than you. Always have been and always will be."

"Come on, Skelly," Erin said.

"No. He knows. He can handle it," Skelly said. "You thought I would be so blinded by opportunity that I wouldn't see the reality of it."

"Whatever, Skelly," Reynolds said and signaled for another drink.

"Not whatever you, little shit," Skelly said and put up his hand to stop Bev. "You thought I didn't know what was going on."

"No, that's not—"

"It wasn't a question," Skelly said. "You thought I was so out of touch that I didn't know what Miles was doing and that I would be so eager to take the job I wouldn't give it a second thought. You walk around pretending Miles is horrible so we can be buddies and you lure me in. It doesn't work that way. We aren't buddies."

"You got me, Skelly," Reynolds said and raised his hands in surrender. "You're right. I thought you were a has-been and a total burnout with no direction. That's why I picked you. No promise and no potential. That would be the perfect candidate for Chief of Police, right? You have it all wrong, Skelly."

"Right, actually," Skelly said.

"And it's not only Austin and it's not just Bales or the Miles Cooperative. If Bales wasn't going to toe the line with Miles they'd find someone else. They'd drive him off a cliff and find a talking head who was willing to regurgitate their nonsense. But Miles isn't the bad guy here. There's a dozen other companies that do the same thing. If the Miles Cooperative left Austin there would be a line out the door to fill their place, but we want you. You're smart, and the police and Miles working together will give us mileage. Mileage the city needs."

"I got things going on. I'm learning to play the drums."

"So I heard."

"Tell him about the handwriting," Erin said. "The note."

"What note?" Reynolds said innocently.

"There was a note on Molly Cooper's body. I'm sure you heard about it," Skelly said.

"No. What did it say?"

"The handwriting matched yours."

"Oh, well. That must be—"

"Stop, Reynolds. I know you put the note there."

"Why would he do that?" Erin asked and looked at Reynolds.

"I'm just messing around with you," Reynolds said and laughed.

"You can't mess around with a crime scene."

"Why do you have to be so serious about everything?"

"That's my job!" Skelly shouted and slammed his hand down on the bar. "I don't want to be Chief of Police."

"Maybe you're underestimating yourself."

"That's not possible," Skelly said.

"Erin, help me out here. Raise your hand if you think that Skelly, on occasion, tends to be rather hard on himself."

"Uh ..." Erin said and raised her hand.

"It's okay. We're in a judgment-free zone here."

"The hell we are, Reynolds," Skelly said.

"He can be pretty hard on himself," Erin said. "You're right about that."

"See, Skelly. She said it herself," Reynolds said and jabbed his finger into Skelly's chest. "Go easy on yourself, man. You can do this."

"You know what? I'll think about it. I'll take a day or two and really think about whether I want to run for Chief of Police."

"Seriously?"

"Yes, but only if you do me a favor."

"You name it."

"Erin is going to bring a suspect in downtown. Connected—possibly—to the murder at the Blue Bonnet. I need you to be there to represent him."

"What? I'm not a lawyer. I haven't practiced law in at least ten years."

"You don't have to do any actual lawyering. You need to tell the kid that it's in his best interest to talk to Erin and tell her what he knows, okay? Can you do that for us?"

"Sure, if you'll think about being Chief of Police, I'll do it."

"I told you I'd think about it," Skelly said. "Also, I need you to get him to tell you the name of someone else who was in that motel room with him."

"Why?"

"I'm not going to tell you, but it's part of the investigation."

"How am I supposed to get him to tell me that?" Reynolds said.

"Say yes, Reynolds, and make it happen. Get the name and call me in an hour."

"You're being ridiculous, Skelly," Reynolds said and looked at Erin. "He's out of his mind, right?"

"Better get to it, boy," Erin said and tipped her glass in his direction.

"And then you'll think about it?" Reynolds asked.

"A little bit," Skelly said and squeezed his fingers together to create an insignificant amount of space between his thumb and index finger.

"All you have to do is empower yourself and live in a world of yes."

"Miles is corrupt and I don't want to be involved with them, but I'll think it over."

"Unfortunately, you don't have a choice in the matter. Miles is everywhere whether you like it or not. They want someone who will advocate for them and push their agenda on the city. That's all you need to do. Take the job and be a yes-man, man. Saying no will create more problems for you. Give in or someone else will."

"I've been okay so far."

"If you are having a hard time deciding, put your mind at ease," Reynolds said and reached into his jacket pocket and pulled out an envelope. "Two tickets to Vegas. Six days and seven nights. The vacation you always wanted, Skelly."

"How did you …?" Erin started to say.

"Vegas, you said?" Skelly interrupted.

"Yes. The one and only. For you and a … guest?" Reynolds said and smiled at Erin.

"How did you know?" Skelly said as he let out a small smile.

"Skelly? Seriously? You and I go way back. I know what you like, what you need. That's what friends are for."

"It's funny," Skelly said and started to laugh. He laughed so hard he started slapping his hand on the edge of the bar.

 Bev also started laughing. Bev was always there when you needed her.

"What's so funny?" Reynolds asked.

"Yeah, Skelly. What's going on?" Erin chimed in.

"It's just that … that … Bev, why don't you tell him?"

"He hates Vegas."

"What?"

"I absolutely fucking hate Vegas," Skelly said as he stopped laughing.

"Sure you do—you love it. You said so yourself."

"I did? When did I say that, Reynolds? When we had lunch the other day or all the other times I was in your periphery, discussing my favorite things?"

"We're buddies, Skelly. Don't do this."

"The other day you did say that you wanted to go to Vegas. Not for retirement but for a break," Erin said and looked at Reynolds. "He said that."

"And then you went and told Reynolds about our conversation?" Skelly asked.

"No."

"Your love for Vegas is ubiquitous."

"I told Erin I wanted to go to Vegas because I thought you were listening," Skelly said and pointed his finger at Reynolds. "The Miles Cooperative is always listening, aren't they Reynolds?"

"I don't work for Miles, at least not exclusively. I'm my own man."

"Sure you are."

"And how exactly are they listening?" Erin asked.

"That app you downloaded to your phone—your watch, your whatever—that aggregates all of your forensic data? When you uploaded your first data set you gave it access to your microphone, right?"

"Yes," Erin said apprehensively.

"So, in case your hands were too full to type in the data you could dictate it into the microphone, right?"

"Sure. It's a matter of convenience."

"Convenience, yes, but it also gave the Miles Cooperative the right to access your microphone whenever it wanted, especially that time I told you how I really, really wanted to go Vegas."

"You're a nutcase," Reynolds said.

"You didn't seem like someone who liked Vegas until you mentioned how much you liked Vegas and then I was like well, 'He must really like Vegas,'" Erin said. "And I thought that was weird yet awesome at the same time."

"Sorry to disappoint. That's not me."

"But this place has a Club Lyon," Reynolds said.

"What's that?" Erin asked.

"It's a ... a sex club ... a swinger's club. I got you a two-day all-access pass," he said and pulled out two tickets. The tickets were black with gold lettering. There was a barcode at the bottom."

"Oh—wow!" Erin said.

"Think about it. No one at Club Lyon says no and everyone says yes. Everything you ever imaged and dreamed about—yes. All the things you didn't think you could have, or didn't think you deserved—yes!"

"Get out of here," Skelly said and put his hand on Reynolds's shoulder. He spun his body around and gave him a firm but gentle push towards the door.

"I'll leave these here for you and you can think about it," Reynolds said as he set the tickets on the bar top.

"Bye, dirt bag," Erin said as Reynolds left. "Wow."

"He'll be back."

"Thanks, Bev," Skelly said as he sat back down and finished off Reynolds's drink.

"What was that about?" Erin asked rhetorically. She put her hand down on the tickets and spun them around on the bar top. "Crazy place, huh?" she said and listened to the silence that quickly filled the room. "What are you going to do with the tickets?"

"You can have them," Skelly said. "I need to go back."

"Back where?"

"*SP.*"

22.

"I thought you were going to send the report over this weekend?" the voice boomed over the speaker phone in my car.

It was Sly Stallone's younger brother from the coffee shop.

He was the Chief Operating Officer of SolChem. I was supposed to send him my report on Rothschild and SolChem, but I forgot. I was too busy trying to figure out who David and Darlene really were.

"I sent it Saturday morning. Is there a problem?" I asked with a slight hint of frustration in my voice.

"I never got it, Peter," he said. He sounded distracted and irritated.

"Check with your office. I hand delivered it to the reception desk around ten on Saturday," I said as I sat in my car across the street from David and Darlene's house. It was almost eight in the morning and I was waiting for the Pike family to leave for the day. I had it on good authority that Abbey got on the bus two stops before Joyce, so they should be walking out of the house any minute. I wasn't sure about David and Darlene, though. I know Cleft offered clients packages that included temporary employment so I was hoping that David and Darlene were about to leave for whatever jobs they may have. Since they had children, I was counting on Cleft not giving them jobs with a night shift. But, given the recent development, Cleft was a different man than I thought he was.

"Seriously? They're always losing stuff. Can you email it to me?"

"I'm afraid not. I even typed it up on my dad's old Remington typewriter."

"You typed it?" he asked as David came out the front door wearing some sort of athletic gear. He leaned over and in a rather deliberate manner and adjusted his shoelaces. He wasn't wearing any sort of smart watch or device and he didn't appear to have any earphones to listen to music. It was, almost certainly, going to be a very boring jog.

"It's all for your protection," I said. "If someone hacks through your firewall and finds it and puts it on the internet, it will be a public media disaster. I can literally see the headlines in my mind right now."

"No one will hack our firewall, Peter."

"Not yet. It's only a matter of time before the person who has the desire to infiltrate your firewall comes into contact with the person or persons who have the skills and knowledge to penetrate your firewall. The convergence of those two forces will ultimately result in some sort of demise or misery for your company and Rothschild. I can't let that happen."

"Thanks for the wonderful analogy, Peter. I thought we hired you to give us confidence and make us feel good."

"How you feel is entirely up to you. I'm looking out for your best interests and the interests of your company," I said as I looked out my rearview mirror.

The school bus was approaching.

I looked back at the house as the front door opened and Abbey stepped out. Darlene stood at the precipice of the door with their son with the straggly brown hair and slender face. She waved to Abbey and shut the door quickly. "If you want, I can start retyping it for you today."

"Ah, fine. You're right," he said. "Can you give me the highlights?"

"Sure. Two key findings. The first is that Carol Corker did in fact file a change in ownership on the patent. The change was requested about a week ago and makes Rothschild and SolChem the sole owners on patent *US7230568.*"

"Crap," he said and started typing. "I'll have to let the board know about this. They aren't going to be happy, Peter. We've already lost two investors this week alone. Apparently hedge fund managers have spare time to listen to Alex Jones."

"I wouldn't worry too much about it. If you have a good crisis PR firm they can spin it and say that the change in ownership was done to protect the interests of SolChem and the interests of the patent. Something along those lines. Throw in some mumbo jumbo about intellectual property law and the media won't touch it."

"What's the next one?"

"The United Nations has spent over fifty million dollars to find the wreckage of the alleged crash and so far they've found at least a dozen pieces in the Mediterranean. All of which have partial or entire serial numbers that tie back to the airplane, which is a good thing."

"Why is that a good thing?"

"It means that the plane did in fact crash and that Rothschild isn't holding it hostage in some bunker on one of his remote islands."

"But it isn't conclusive."

"It doesn't have to be conclusive. It's only a matter of time before the media blames Russia," I said as the garage door to David and Darlene's house opened. Their SUV slowly backed out of the garage and went down the street. Now was my only chance. "Normally, I would conclude that there isn't a conspiracy here worth shaking a fist at. People can say what they want, but ultimately there isn't any evidence that holds up to support the theory that Rothschild is behind this catastrophe."

"Normally?"

"There is one thing," I said. "Rothschild bought a warehouse."

"So what?"

"The warehouse is located on a small remote island about a hundred miles from the suspected crash site."

"What can you tell me about it?"

"It was purchased a few months before the incident, through one of the holding companies."

"Shit."

"Just letting you know."

"Okay. Thanks, Peter. I appreciate your work on this."

"You know where to wire the money," I said as he hung up.

I looked out my car window and politely waved at a woman who was walking her dog.

After Joyce decoded Cleft's client list for me, I took her to one of her favorite burger joints to celebrate. Even though I'm on a consistently strict diet, I did myself a courtesy and spoiled myself: Double bacon cheeseburger with jalapeños and a side of mayonnaise. If you're going to indulge you should go all out. Besides, I felt great and all my vitals were looking good. Maybe indulging every now and then wasn't a bad thing. Maybe my doctor wasn't the smartest person in the world, and maybe having mayonnaise and red meat once in a blue moon wasn't going to kill me or my mechanical heart. Maybe the tingling in my left hand was because I slept on it funny. The technology was new and expanding so maybe they didn't know everything. Besides, with the recent issues I've been having with my tracker it was possible my Electro-Flux wasn't the most reliable tool. I would go home and eat a jar of mayonnaise later to test this theory out.

When Joyce and I got home, I told Paula about Cleft's client list and explained to her that David and Darlene were in fact not who they said they were.

"I was right," I told her, but she appeared to be disinterested. For the sake of argument, and to spare Joyce the burden of having to defend her less than moral actions, I told Paula that I simply went into Cleft's office and asked him about David and Darlene. I knew the type of business Cleft had and my journalistic intuition told me that Cleft might be involved, directly or indirectly, with them. Maybe he went to the re-identity annual conference and somehow got wind of David and Darlene Creed. I told her that Cleft was initially reluctant but finally came clean about them being his clients. I told Paula that I was planning to go by David and Darlene's house to investigate the matter further. When she asked me why, I told her it was a side effect of my job and it was very hard for me to not be nosy. That point was true. I seriously had no business getting involved in the life of David and Darlene Pike, but I was bothered by the fact that they upended their life in Florida for no apparent reason whatsoever. I also wanted time to myself to think over Miles's offer.

"You don't know everything about everyone," Paula had said to me, and that was also true. She also said that she was sure lots of people went missing all over the world for no apparent reason. I told her that a lot of the time it had to do with drug trafficking, but she didn't think that was a good argument. A successful middle-class white couple with two kids in school doesn't decide to up and leave their life for no reason whatsoever. They didn't win the lottery—I checked—so what was the reason?

There had to be an explanation. Surely Paula could understand that.

Once the lady with the dog was gone, I quickly got out of the car and made my way across the street and went up the walkway to David and Darlene's house. It was a modest one-story house with a limestone facade, which was common for homes built in Austin in the mid-eighties.

I gently knocked on the front door and rang the doorbell. When I released my finger from the doorbell, an infrared sensor above the doorbell turned on and scanned the immediate area. It was a security feature that allowed the home owner to unlock the home using a retina scanner. I closed my eyes as the sensor went back and forth.

After a few seconds it finally stopped.

I opened my eyes and looked at the scanner.

HOME OWNER NOT DETECTED.

Right then and there, I knew it had sent some sort of notification, either to the police or the home owner.

The sensor turned on again and went back and forth. This time I kept my eyes open and let the infrared scan my retina. The device was either a deterrent or I needed to gouge someone's eye out and hold it up in front of the sensor. It went back and forth a few times and then stopped. A red light illuminated on the sensor and started to flash. It was then that I finally turned around and walked back towards the street. I turned towards my car as David rounded the corner and headed back to the house. He saw me and waved politely. "What's going on, Peter?" he said as he got closer to me.

He had on a form-fitting athletic shirt and I could tell that he was in pretty good shape. My initial thought was to suck in my gut, but I was put off by his demeanor. He was friendly and welcoming, and that was bizarre, given our last interaction and the fact I was trying to get into his house. "What are you doing here?" he asked. It was then I realized that he wasn't wearing any sort of device where it was possible for him to receive a notification about me trying to enter his house.

He must have come back for something else.

"Joyce told me she wanted to ride the bus with Abbey this morning, so I was dropping her off at your stop but we missed it."

"That's too bad. Where is she?"

"Where's who?" I asked and then realized what he was asking. "Joyce?"

"Oh, she chased after the bus and flagged it down."

"Is that even allowed?"

"The bus stopped. So, good for her, right?" I said putting an end to this conversation.

"Smart kid," he said. "Since you're here, why don't you come inside?" He gestured his hand towards the front door and started up the walkway. "I need a drink after that workout," he said as he approached the front door and shifted his head so his eyes were in front of the retinal scanner. "That's strange," he said and tapped his finger on the scanner. "The scanner is in Police Mode."

"What does that mean?"

"It means that it couldn't identify a subject so it contacted the police. Must be a solicitor," he said and turned his head to look up and down the street.

"And here I was thinking you were all anti-technology."

"We're renting. The owners installed it. Besides, let's not be ridiculous, Peter. Most houses come with this type of security, and who are we to not protect our children? With all the dangers out there in the world these days," he said as the scanner went back and forth over his eyeball.

"The internet is more dangerous than the neighborhood."

"Our children have never been online," he said as a green light appeared below the sensor and was followed by a soft clicking sound to indicate that the front door was unlocked. "Are you a gin or vodka guy?" he asked as we went inside.

"Black coffee in the morning kind of guy, actually," I said as I stepped inside the house and looked around.

"Make yourself comfortable," he said and disappeared towards the back of the house and left me alone in the living room.

I was standing near a beige couch and black IKEA coffee table with a single book on it: *Things Men Like Better than Boobs*. "Cleft," I muttered.

There was no sign of a television.

I turned and looked at the dozen or so picture frames that were hanging in the entryway near the staircase. The pictures were of handful of people, different ages and varying ethnicities and none of them looked like David and Darlene.

I looked closer at one of the frames and saw a logo for a department store printed on the bottom. This was clearly the work of Cleft Duvall giving people new identities and a pre-fab place to live. I went past the stairs into the kitchen where David was rummaging through the freezer. "I thought I had a bottle of vodka in here," he said.

"I'm okay, really," I said.

"I have some molly."

"Eh," I said. "I don't do that ... stuff ... anymore."

"Good for you, pal. But what about me? Between work and the kids, I can't seem to get a proper day off."

"What sort of work do you do?"

"I thought I told you," he looked at me as I shook my head. "I'm sure I did. At the bar that night."

"Nope. I'm pretty sure you didn't mention it."

"I'm a real estate agent," he said and flashed a smile.

"That's the job he set you up with?" I said to myself and then realized that I said it out loud.

"Excuse me?" he asked and then reached his arm back and shut the door to the freezer. I didn't answer. I pursed my lips and looked out the window over the sink into the backyard. The grass was overgrown and the yard was desolate. There were no play things, no toys, and no residual mess left from kids running wild out back. I knew we were in the heat of the summer but even then there would still be something: a sprinkler, an inflatable pool, anything to curb the oppressive heat of central Texas, but the only thing out there was a shed; a small rundown wood shack that could barely hold a lawn mower. "What did you say?" he asked.

"How long have you lived in this house?" I asked.

"No. What did you say? About my job," he took a step closer to me. "That *who* set me up with it?"

"I'm asking because there isn't anything in the backyard," I pointed out back. "What about Abbey and what's-his-name—?"

"Bryn."

"Right, okay. What about Abbey and Bryn? Don't they like to play outside? I'm confused, that's all." I would just keeping moving, talking about other stuff, keep him on his feet. He didn't hear me correctly. "You know, as a matter of fact, today feels like a gin day. There's some salt in the air. Let's do it."

"We're out of gin," he said.

"I'll bring some next time."

"Who set me up with my job?" he said and took his hand and

slammed it against my shoulder. I tumbled back and caught myself on the counter. He kept moving towards me. "Did you not hear me?"

"Cleft," I said as I let the tension leave my body. "He's my friend. Sometimes he's my best friend; it's purely circumstantial." I put my hands up in self-defense. At least, that's what I would tell the investigators later on.

"Keep talking," he said.

"I saw you on TV. You and Darlene. You were on CNN. 'Florida family vanishes in broad daylight.' I didn't think anything of it until I saw you and your family at gymnastics a few days later. You looked familiar, but I couldn't quite place where you were familiar from. Then I put it together."

"You put what together?"

"Nothing really. You were familiar and maybe I thought you were the family that disappeared from Florida. But what family does that? Who gets up and leaves for no reason whatsoever?"

"Maybe you don't know the full picture."

"Maybe, but it's still pretty strange, right? A lot of people who use his service are trying to escape Miles and recreate themselves under mass surveillance. Anyway, I stole Cleft's client list and ... there you were. Just. Like. That."

"Client list?"

"Yes," I said and pulled my wallet out of my back pocket and opened it.

The piles of credit cards and grocery store receipts fell out and spread across the floor. I looked down and felt overwhelmed with embarrassment.

"What's that?" he said and reached down.

"It's nothing," I said and put my hand out to stop him. "I can do it."

He grabbed the card closest to him. It had one word on it in bold-face letters:

MILES.

My shoulders sank and a knot formed in my stomach.

"What is this, Peter?" he asked and flipped the card around in his fingers. I didn't respond. "You seem to know so much about me, yet I don't really know much about you. This seems like a good place to start."

"It's a … a job opportunity."

"But we talked about this, didn't we? Maybe I'm misremembering. We had a discussion the other night about how bad Miles was."

"That was mostly you talking and me listening. You seem to have a chip on your shoulder about them," I said, but he didn't respond. He stared at me. I wasn't sure what to think, so I continued. "Miles invited me to a meeting. He wants to hire me to … legitimize them."

"The secret meeting?"

"You familiar?"

"There have been rumors."

"Apparently, there are people out there, yourself included, who think they have less than sincere intentions. There's a conference in a few days—this so-called secret meeting—they want me to go and, you know. I can't really talk about it. I'm sure you can understand."

"Sure, Peter," he said and kept his eyes locked on me. I thought I saw him smirk but I couldn't tell for sure. "Peter, I think you and I will become great friends."

"That's a strange thing to say. Why did you and Darlene decide to up and leave Florida, especially with two kids? Let's start with that."

"We won the lottery," he said to me, stone-faced. I don't think he blinked in the last sixty seconds.

"No you didn't," I said as I regained my footing. "I looked into that. The Florida Lottery—the only one that matters, let's be honest—hasn't had a significant payout in the last few months, and before that when there was a considerable payout, all the winners came forward. They did the press conference, held the big check and walked the walk. So, no, you didn't win the lottery," I said pointedly and watched as the air left his shoulders and he relaxed. "It's okay. Whatever it is, I'm sure it's totally fine, but I want to understand why," I said. "People who contact Cleft Duval aren't doing it for recreational reasons."

"Like you said, we wanted to avoid Miles."

"Maybe, but not likely. You could have gone somewhere more remote. There are cities that aren't occupied by Miles. He could have set you up with a nice job and house in Wichita."

"Gah—Wichita."

"That's a city Miles won't even go near. So, sorry, I'm not buying it."

"But the schools here are amazing," David said.

"The neighborhood does have some pretty good schools."

"You seem lost, Peter. You seem like you need some direction."

"Don't put this back on me."

"You know what the biggest problem with Americans is these days?" he asked. "The biggest problem is that they don't have enough ambition. Americans don't have enough drive, and the ambition and drive they do have is misdirected and mostly without any true purpose. They feel like they need to work sixty hours a week and take home a biweekly paycheck so they can pay for the things they can't afford. Bigger houses with super-technology and devices they connect to their bodies so they feel like they have more information about what's going on inside their own bodies and their own minds. But they don't. Not really."

"What did you do in your past life?" I asked. "You were a pool cleaner? Something like that?"

"I owned and operated a pool maintenance company. It's a very intricate process."

"Right, sorry. Why did you choose that profession? Was it for the love and passion you had for cleaning pools, or was it for the money and you rationalized the choice?"

"If everything was for money we'd all become hedge fund managers."

"Touché, but some people aren't afforded the luxury to make that choice. Did you have a prosperous education that offered you endless possibilities when you graduated? I didn't have that luxury. It was either go work at this network and do this job for this amount of money or go back and sleep on your parents' couch and figure it all out again. Maybe cough up two hundred thousand dollars for eight years in graduate school. You know, to realign the focus."

He was about to say something, but the phone on the wall next to the sink rang. It was an outdated landline.

"Hold on a second," he said and held a finger up in my direction. He stepped over to the sink and lifted the phone off the wall. "Hello?" he said into the receiver. "I got back from my run early, yes." He listened for a second. "No. Everything is okay. Peter is here actually," he said and looked back at me. "Yes, it is rather funny. He was telling me about the World Cup and how he loves Pelé and how he went to São Paulo to eat some Cinnamon Toast Crunch," he said and laughed and gave me a thumbs up. These people were clearly on drugs. "Yes, of course, honey. Hurry home," he said and blew a kiss into the phone and hung up.

"Everything okay?" I asked.

"Do you have any plans today, Peter?"

"No. Why?"

"I want to show you something. I think someone like you would appreciate it. Maybe it can even help you find direction," he said and put his hand out with the palm facing the ceiling. "Come on, trust me on this. Give me your phone and your watch, Peter."

"Why?"

"Give it to me already, and spare me the charade."

"Sure," I said and reached into my pocket and pulled out my phone and set it and my watch gently into his palm. "What are you going to do with it?" I asked as he turned around towards the island in the center of the kitchen.

He reached down and opened one of the cabinets and pulled out a medium sized cardboard box.

He set the box on the counter and opened the top and carefully set the phone inside.

I craned my neck to watch.

The inside of the box was lined with what appeared to be aluminum foil and plastic wrap. It was a Faraday box and it was used to block electrical currents. It was obvious that whatever was about to happen, he didn't want the people on the other end of my phone to know about it. "Follow me," he said and walked out of the kitchen.

I followed him to a small den adjacent to the kitchen that contained a small desk and office chair. I didn't see any television in this room either.

No wonder they didn't know who I was.

"This way," he said as he opened a screen door to the backyard. I followed him across the yard to the shed. "Can you hold this for a second?" he asked and handed me the Faraday box and pulled open the door to the shed, which revealed a four-by-four room with walls that were covered with what appeared to be layers and layers of aluminum foil. It was another, larger Faraday box.

"Paranoid?" I asked.

"Being careful," he said and took the box from me and set it inside. He shut the door to the shed and walked back towards the house.

Once we were back inside he pulled out a bottle of gin from underneath the sink and poured me a small glass.

"I thought you were out."

"You ever think about going back to being a journalist?" he asked.

"I'd rather slit my wrists," I said and took a sip of the gin and let the saltiness linger in my mouth.

"What do you think your purpose in life is, Peter?"

"I don't know. What's your purpose? What's anyone's purpose for that matter? Isn't it just what we make of it? People—we, you, me, us— are so dead-set on figuring out what it all means. We desperately want to figure out what the meaning of life is, that maybe, in the pursuit of the meaning of life, we actually lose sight of the meaning of life."

"Purpose? That's important?"

"Yes, and living and saying yes to things. I want to live in a world of yes, David. Purpose and living. Let's have both, shall we?" I asked as the gin slowly settled in my stomach.

"It's up to you whether or not you want to live or die in the Robo-Motel."

"That's right," I said. "Wait. What does that mean?"

"Do you want to live or die in the Robo-Motel, Peter?" he asked.

"I heard you but … what does that even mean?"

"I'll show you," he said and motioned with his arm. I followed him out of the kitchen back towards the front door.

When we reached the entryway he took a sharp left turn and went up the stairs. I followed him and soon found myself in a narrow hallway at the top of the stairs. There was a small bathroom in the center and a bedroom on either side. The door to the bedroom on the left was open and I could see two bunk beds. The first bunk bed was neat and tidy and had a nightstand next to it with a few books. The second bunk bed was messy and both levels were covered with kid's clothes and toys.

"Do you all sleep in here?" I asked as I turned and looked into the bedroom on the right. It was empty.

"Follow me," he said as he entered the bedroom.

The room appeared to be more spacious than the other bedroom and had two windows that were both covered with dark sheets to prevent any excess light from getting in. The floors had new plush carpet and the walls were painted a dark gray color, which must be recent, since I could still smell the paint fumes. In the middle of the room a shiny silver headset dangled from the ceiling. It looked like a gas mask without the breathing apparatus. The face mask was the size of a brick and was connected to an adjustable head strap. I'd seen things like this before but never used one.

"I thought you didn't like technology."

"This isn't technology, Peter. This is a gateway to another world," he said and gestured towards the headset. "Give it a try." I took a step forward and could tell the headset was connected to a thin cable that went up into the ceiling. "It's okay. You can disconnect the cable," David said. I pulled the cable out of the side of the headset and put the headset on. "Press the button on the left," he said and I followed his lead. When I released my finger from the button, the screen on the headset flashed a bright white light and then I found myself standing on a city street. It was dark outside. "Can you tell where you are?" David asked.

"Outside somewhere. In a city. New York, maybe."

"It's London," he said. His voice sounded different. He seemed farther away. "If you move your head from left to right you can see more," he said, and I started to move my head around so I could see more of where I was.

It was amazing.

"I smell French fries."

"Fish and chips," he said. "Each city and each neighborhood has its own smell."

"What am I supposed to do?" I asked.

"It's a game. Your objective is to the find the secret organization and dismantle it," David said. "When they asked you who referred you, tell them it was us," he said as I moved my whole body around and stopped when I saw a sign for the Robo-Motel. "Go in. Everything that happens in the Robo-Motel stays in the Robo-Motel. If you want to eat ten pounds of pasta or drink a fifth of whiskey while you're there, you can. Your tracker won't pick up on it, Miles will never know and, better yet, it won't have any effect on your overall health."

"What's the catch?"

"There's no catch, Peter," he said. "Here, you are no longer hindered by the restrictions that life puts on you," he said as I reached the entrance to the hotel.

A doorman with epaulettes and white gloves opened the front door for me and I stepped inside.

"Welcome to the Robo-Motel. London's finest in luxury service and amenities. The service here is second to none," a voice said. It sounded familiar but I couldn't place it. "Inside the Robo-Motel everything you ever imagined is now possible," the voice said as I stood in the middle of an expansive lobby with sweeping fluid forms with multiple perspective points. The fragmented geometry evoked the chaos and flux of modern life. Lush green trees were in the center of the lobby and there was a waterfall between the elevators that fell into a small stream that ran across the lobby and stopped at a mahogany staircase that went up to the second floor.

"Hi, Peter," a woman said as she walked past me in the lobby.

"Hey," I said and waved at her. I went up to the front desk.

"Welcome to the Robo-Motel, Peter," a man said. He had light gray hair and was shorter than me. He had a nice tan.

"Thanks," I said and looked down at his name tag: Don Johnson. "I thought you looked familiar," I said as he leaned closer to me. "What is it?" I asked.

"Everything that happens in the game occurs in real time," he whispered. "One hour in *Stolen Planet* is one hour in real time."

"What's *Stolen Planet?*" I asked.

"This is *Stolen Planet!*" he said triumphantly as he reached his arms out and then quickly pulled them back in. "We understand the total immersion effect the game has on a person's body and their mind, so every fifteen minutes you'll receive an update at the bottom of the screen." Don Johnson pointed his finger down as a small window showed up on the screen inside my headset. "It will give you a brief health update and any nutritional deficiencies you may have. It will literally tell you if you're thirsty or not."

"I thought whatever I did here didn't affect me."

"It doesn't, but this is so you can monitor your body on the outside," he said. "Can you provide me with the name of two people who referred you to the game?"

"Excuse me?"

"It's part of the verification process. Two people."

"David and Darlene ... Creed."

"Thank you," he said. "Also, I'll need you to provide me with a safe word or safe phrase," he said. "This is for when you want to exit the game. You say your safe word or phrase quickly three times."

"Uh ..."

"How about Miami Vice?" he said. "Miami Vice, Miami Vice, Miami Vice."

"Whatever you think is best."

"Lovely choice," he said "Now if you would please make your way to the cinema. There's a video you'll need to watch. Required viewing." He pointed across the room where there was a dark curtain and a small sign: *Cinema.*

"Thanks."

"You're welcome and, remember, it's up to you whether you want to live or die."

23.

"Welcome back, sir," the saleswoman said as Skelly burst back into the showroom. "We didn't think you'd be back so soon."

"Hey, when in Rome, right?" he said and flashed her a smile.

"We have two platforms open if you'd like to engage," she said and pointed towards the two vacant platforms.

"I'm okay, right now," Skelly said and pulled his phone out of his jacket pocket and looked down at it. "Give me a minute."

"Would you like to come back later? I can reserve a platform for you if you like."

"I'll wait," he said and unlocked his cell phone and pressed his fingers down:

SKELLY: *What's the word?… Erin?!!!!*

ERIN: *Reynolds is in there with him now. It's not going well*

SKELLY: *I need a name*

ERIN: *John Wayne Gacy*

SKELLY *That isn't funny*

ERIN: *Hold on*

Skelly shoved his phone back into his pocket. "I'm ready," he said to the saleswoman.

"Do you want to use the same platform as last time?"

"Sure," he said and followed her over to the center platform, which now had some strange treadmill in the middle of it. "What's that?"

"That's a new product. It's a 360-degree treadmill. It allows for you to walk freely within the game. It gives you more mobility and kinesis. Would you like to try it?"

"Okay," Skelly said apprehensively as he stepped onto the center platform and subsequently the 360-degree treadmill.

"We'll start you off at a slow speed and we can go up from there."

"Sounds good," he said as his phone buzzed in his pocket.

He pulled it out and answered it. "What?"

The treadmill started moving and Skelly struggled for a moment to get his footing.

"Barry Foster," Erin said on the other end of the phone.

"Yeah, I know that."

"And Garrett Alan," she said victoriously.

"Thank you," Skelly said. He hung up the phone and slid the headset on. "Let's go," he said and watched as the screen on the headset flashed.

When the flashing stopped Skelly found himself still sitting across from Don Johnson.

"A simple sign-up will give you access to the bar and rec area," Don Johnson said. "That's where we are now but we need to do a double-authentication in order for you to go anywhere else in *Stolen Planet*."

"I'm ready," Skelly said.

"Would you like to provide me with the names of two—?"

"Barry Foster and Garrett Alan," Skelly said.

Don Johnson looked down and ran his finger down what appeared to be a roster on his desk and stopped. He looked up. "Congratulations," he said and offered his hand to Skelly. "Welcome to *Stolen Planet*," he said and shook Skelly's hand vigorously and stood up. "How would you like to pay?"

"Pay?"

"The fee is five thousand dollars. American dollars."

"Will you take a check?" Skelly asked.

"Of course, not. But you knew that already. We take over two thousand forms of crypto currency. But feel free to pay later on. We understand that our members may be in some sort of financial constraints and we want to do what we can to help out."

"Yes, of course," Skelly said as Don Johnson led him past the water cooler and stopped at a set of double doors. They were tall and medieval. "Good luck in there," he said and patted Skelly on the back.

"Thanks," Skelly said as the doors opened.

Don Johnson gave him a light push and he soon found himself at the precipice of what he suspected was a lobby.

There was a bar on the far end that went across the entire room. Lasers shot up from the floor and provided light for the entire space, and plants and various seating arrangements were scattered throughout.

There were a few people sitting at the bar. They turned around and greeted him. "Hi, Skelly!" they said. Skelly responded with a feeble wave and walked towards the bar.

"Can I have a Jack and soda?"

"Nope," the bartender said. "Not until you watch the video." The bartender signaled towards a small theater at the end of the bar. "Watch the video and then you can have a drink."

Skelly leaned back from the bar a craned his neck towards the theater.

There was a narrow doorway covered by velvet curtains.

Skelly stepped away from the bar and made his way towards the theater.

The people at the bar started clapping when he reached the entrance.

He peaked his head in.

It was empty.

"Keep going," the bartender said.

Skelly went through the velvet curtains and took a seat in one of the comfortable recliners.

He looked around as the grainy black-and-white film leader counted down to one.

The walls were covered with broken televisions and he could only see one other person slumped down in the front row.

"Good evening, recruits. I'm Don Johnson," Don Johnson said as he appeared on screen.

"Give me a break," Skelly said and then was quickly *shhh*'d by the person in the front row.

"The negative impact of technology on our mental, physical and social lives is shattering," Don Johnson said as the video cut to an aerial shot of the Grand Canyon. "Remember what life used to be?" he asked. "Peace and tranquility were at our very fingertips, but now we're oppressed by our desire to stay connected. Our social, mental, physical, and environmental health is suffering. Yes—it's true—we have reaped the benefits from the recent Digital Revolution. But at what cost?" Don Johnson asked as a series of images flashed across the screen: stress, anger, fear, bullies, suicide, a wide array of smart devices, and then finally a man sitting alone at a table eating a bowl of cereal. "Is this what you want from your life? Is this what America wants? The world wants? A world in which our jobs and livelihoods are taken over by the Robot Revolution? Don't be misled, folks. At first, the wide array of devices and technological advancements at our fingertips were here to help us. Help us eat better, walk farther, and meet more people. But we know better. If we didn't, we wouldn't be here," he said. "These big corporations are taking our personal information, our data, our preferences, and pictures and selling them to the government. What for, you ask?" An image of Johnny 5 appears on screen. "Don't be misled by this image. Johnny 5 is not your friend. Johnny 5 doesn't want to have a beer with you. Johnny 5 hates you. These corporations are using our data so they can build robots that will eventually replace us.

"Don't believe me? Ask my good friend, Travis Holt," Don Johnson said as Travis Holt appeared on screen.

"Thanks, Don," Travis said as he sipped a glass of wine. "You may recognize me from the evening news. Truth is, I'm the result of years of focus groups on what audiences want and don't want in an evening news broadcaster. The result? I'm boring and predictable, I spend hours calculating weather and crime patterns throughout the United States all so you'll stick around through the commercial break, and impulse buy Caribbean cruises and erectile dysfunction medications. Things you never knew you needed until we told you about them. Do you think it's a coincidence that the erectile dysfunction commercial ran right after I did a segment on how testosterone levels are decreasing around the world? It's not. And, I still have a drinking problem and I'm a robot!" He started to laugh and took a swig of wine. "Don, why don't you tell them about the game."

"*Stolen Planet* is a massive multiplayer online role-playing game where you have the freedom to explore, meet other residents, socialize, build, create, shop, and trade virtual property. While here you will be given different tasks and objectives. Once you complete those tasks you will be able to advance and get closer to identifying the secret organization."

"We'll give you a hint," Travis said. "All of the tasks have to do with how technology is destroying your life."

"That's right. I forgot to mention that," Don Jonson said. "It's fun and educational. Now, make your way to the bar and have a drink and the bartender will give you your first objective!" he said as the soundtrack kicked in and credits started to roll on screen. Skelly got up and walked out of the theater and sat down at the bar.

The bartender handed him his drink. "Jack and soda, right?"

"That's right," Skelly said and took a sip of it.

The bartender handed him a small black envelope.

"Enjoy your drink and open this when you're ready," the bartender said. "There's no rush."

Skelly opened the envelope and took out a small laminated card:

I pledge, as a member of Stolen Planet, *to do everything in my power, in this game and IRL, to remove technological advancements from our society so we can live fuller and more prosperous lives.*

"Are you guys serious with this?" Skelly asked as he set the card down on the bar.

"Do you pledge?" the bartender asked. "If you pledge, then you can get out of this dive and see what *Stolen Planet* has to offer."

"Have you seen a guy by the name of Barry Foster come through here lately?" Skelly asked.

"You have a picture?"

"He's six feet tall, has dark brown hair and blue eyes. Narrow nose that slopes down towards the floor. Broad shoulders. There's your picture."

"That could be anyone," the bartender said. "The drink is two bitcoin." Skelly feigned looking for his wallet. "Don't worry about it. You can settle up later. You have the opportunity to earn money as you play."

"You ever heard the name Garrett Alan?" Skelly asked.

"Can't say that I have. You going to take the pledge or what? If you pledge, they comp the drink."

"I don't think so," Skelly said.

"Then what are you doing here?" the bartender asked and leaned in closer to him. "Cold feet or something?"

"I'm working on a case."

"Here?"

"In real life," Skelly said like an old pro.

"Oh," the bartender said and leaned back and looked around.

"These two guys, Foster and Alan, they were playing—they were here, I think—the night a girl was murdered outside their motel room."

"In the game? This hotel?"

"In real life."

"Ah, that's some advanced player stuff, right there."

"What does that mean?" Skelly asked.

"Look," the bartender said as he got real close to Skelly. "I just work here, oaky? I got a wife and two kids in college IRL. I don't care what goes on after people leave here, when they move on to the higher levels, but, I've been around and I hear things."

"What kind of things?" Skelly asked.

"They're training for something," he said and put his arms up in resignation. "But that's all I know."

"Training for what? To find the secret organization?"

"Did you hear me? I said that's all I know and I don't know about you but I want to keep my job. If I'm lucky, I clear a bitcoin a night. Sometimes I feel like I want to hunker down and hang a catheter up next to my bed and have my wife spoon feed me so I can stay here for days on end. Then I can make four bitcoin a day. I'm not above it, and my wife understands, and I'm making way more money than I would IRL. The bar I worked at got some bionic bartender. It's fast, efficient, and it never messes up a drink. How am I supposed to compete with that?"

"That's it? Four bitcoin a day?"

"That's pretty good," the bartender said and then saw the look on Skelly's face as he examined his drink. "One bitcoin is equivalent to six hundred American dollars. You are American, right?"

Skelly nodded. "You?"

"I traveled around a lot when I was a kid. I live in Germany right now. I have a son at Oxford and a daughter at Harvard in the States."

"Good genes."

"Smart kids. My daughter runs the Harvard Biorobotics lab. The irony, right?"

"It's the future."

"Not here it isn't."

"This is a twelve hundred dollar drink?" Skelly said.

"How do you think they pay for all of this? *Stolen Planet* can't pay for itself," the bartender said. "Don't worry, there will be plenty of opportunities to make that money back in the game."

"What happens in Level 8?"

"I can't tell you that."

"Tell me a piece of it," Skelly said. "We're just two friends exchanging thoughts and ideas from different cultures. Pretend we've been friends for a long time and you haven't seen me in a while and there's something you really want to tell me." Skelly took a sip of his twelve hundred-dollar drink.

"You ever heard of Nitro Zeus?" the bartender asked.

"No." Skelly said. "What is that?"

"It's a game changer."

"Game changer?"

"It's the reset button of all reset buttons and everyone here wants to get their hands on it."

"Nash Bridge, Nash Bridges, Nash Bridges."

24.

The screen in the small theater went dark.

The lights came on quickly.

I slowly stood up and stepped out of the theater and made my way into the saloon.

There was a long oak bar that ran along the back wall, at least twenty or thirty yards, and a few tables scattered around the center of the room. A few people saw me and waved. "Hi, Peter!" they said and continued on about their business. I went over and took a seat at the bar.

"Did you enjoy the film?" the bartender asked.

"Yes, very much so. Informative," I said as I looked around. The room was large and spacious. Plants were scattered throughout to give the setting a more natural feel. It smelled like discarded cigarettes.

"You're being polite. What can I get you?" the bartender asked and handed me a small envelope.

"I'm not sure," I said as I looked over the endless shelves filled with at least a thousand different types of alcohol. "It stinks in here," I said as I waved my hand in front of my nose.

"No problem, Peter," he said. The smell of discarded cigarettes quickly dissipated and was replaced with a floral scent. Lilacs maybe.

"You like that?"

"Better."

"No problem. It's an easy fix," he said and waved his hand in front of the bar. "We have everything," he said. "Open the envelope and think it over," he said and moved down the bar to help someone else.

I opened the envelope and pulled out a small laminated card. I read what was printed on the front.

This is a strange place, I thought. I looked over at a gentlemen sitting a few seats away from me. He held his glass up and nodded at me. He was wearing a pink shirt and white pants with pink socks and a pink belt. He looked familiar.

"Hey ... hey—" I said to him. He turned back towards me and looked at me intently. I motioned for him to lean closer to me. "Are you Elvis?" I asked in a voice that was slightly below a whisper.

"Excuse me?" he said as he squinted at me.

"Are you Elvis?" I said a bit louder.

"Why, yes. Yes, I am," he said and put his hand out in my general direction. I took his hand and shook it.

"I'm Peter Richards," I said.

"Very pleased to meet you, Peter."

"Derek, leave Mr. Richards alone, will you? He's new," the bartender said as he made his way back over to me. "That's Derek. He's a regular."

"But he said—"

"I know what he said. Derek lives in Portland, Oregon. He has a wife and a newborn baby girl, but somehow he manages to spend all of his time here," he said. "Elvis is the avatar he uses in the game. Similar to how you decided to play this game as a middle-aged nondescript white guy with a central weight problem. Wanted to know how the other half lives, right?"

"No. I'm me. No avatar. I didn't know I could do that."

"It's pretty common. You have the opportunity to live in an alternate reality, the virtual world, and actually be someone else. Most people choose to be someone else, but you do what you think is best," the bartender said. "What did you decide?"

"Sure," I said and gently put the laminated card back in the envelope.

"Sure to what? The card or a drink?"

"Both," I said and handed him back the envelope.

"Congratulations, you passed the first level," he said loudly. A few people in the bar started clapping. Elvis pointed his finger at me and nodded. "You're room is ready if you want to go and get freshened up," the bartender said.

"Sure," I said. "And then what?"

"You'll receive instructions at the appropriate time. In the meantime, enjoy yourself," he said. "You're in Room 24, on the right," he said.

I left the saloon and headed down a narrow and darkly lit hallway. The walls had pictures of various historical events. The first was a black and white photo of an enflamed Hindenburg followed by a picture of the Space Shuttle Columbia free falling in the sky. The last picture was a black-and-white print of an oversized box with various cables and wires connected to it. There was a small sign below the photo, which read: *ENIAC*. I tried to sound it out.

"It stands for Electronic Numerical Integrator and Computer," Don Johnson's voice said inside my headset.

Okay, thanks.

"It was the very first all-electronic and digital computer. It was invented in the mid-nineteen-forties and was called the Big Brain," Don Johnson said. "For all intents and purposes, it was the beginning of the end of mankind."

I stopped when I reached Room 24. The door was cracked and there was a sticky note on it that said: *Level 2 starts now.*

I gently pushed the door open to reveal my room.

It was dark and cool and smelled like fresh-cut grass.

A slight breeze drifted across my face and I felt like I was standing outside.

A queen-size bed was in the center of the room and a small television sat on a dresser across from the bed. The television was playing news footage of a large city burning to the ground. A reporter appeared on-screen. "It's worse than we thought," the reporter said. "Military officials are telling us that the Red Mercury is expected to wipe out at least half of the population." The TV screen cut to fuzz for a few seconds then went back to the reporter.

I went over to the bed and turned on the bedside lamp.

Next to the lamp was a picture of me with Paula and the girls sitting in front of Santa Claus. I looked up and found a picture of Paula on the other side of the bed and a few more pictures of my family around the room. Before I had time to process any of this, there was a soft knock on the door. "Peter. It's us. Let's us in," a voice said on the other side of the door. "It's David and Darlene."

"Be right there," I said as I looked at the pictures of my family.

I went over and opened the door.

David and Darlene were standing there, but they looked younger. "David?" I asked as I looked him over. "You look … different."

"I'm younger," David said and adjusted the full crop of hair on his head.

"This is us twenty years ago. You can be whoever you want here … or did David not tell you that? We are us twenty years ago. Better versions of us," Darlene said. "When David told me that you came over I had to get online." She laughed as she made her way into the room.

"What are you guys doing here?"

"We wanted to see how you were getting acclimated," David said as he stepped towards me. "Do you like it?"

"Sure. Yes," I said.

"I don't believe you," David said and smiled at me and gently patted my shoulder before heading in to the room and jumping face first on to the bed.

"What is this place?"

"It's all part of the game," Darlene said. She was sitting in the lounge chair on the far side of the bed with a corkscrew shoved into the top of a magnum of champagne. "You want some?"

"Yes, please," I said and then felt something in my hand. I looked down. I was holding a glass of champagne. "Thanks."

"We're in London. Outside your window you'll find yourself in Piccadilly Circus. The hotel has any amenity you can imagine," David said as he rolled over on the bed. "We're going to live here after the annihilation."

"The annihilation?"

"Metaphorically speaking, of course."

"David is messing with you," Darlene said and took a gulp of champagne from the bottle. "It's more like an uprising."

"The uprising?"

"Yes, it's this weekend," she said. "Saturday."

"What happens then?"

"We're going to wipe out all technology. We're going to hit the big reset button," David said as he leaned over so Darlene could pour champagne into his mouth. "We need your help."

"All technology?"

"Yes. It would be thoughtless if we only destroyed some of the technology. It would be futile, actually. Technology is advancing at an uncontrollable pace and it's being used against us. It's being used to suppress us and it's making us inert and accepting of what's going on around us," he said and pulled up his shirt to reveal his flat stomach. "Man, look at those abs. It feels great to be young again."

"It's going to be exciting," Darlene said. "We'll finally be able to get back to the good old days. We can read books and sit in silence and we won't have the Miles Cooperative breathing down our damn backs every time we have indiscretions online."

"Miles can't see us in *Stolen Planet*. Everything we do here is off the grid, so to speak," David said. "You're on the forefront."

"What he is so eloquently trying to say is that we need your help," Darlene said as a piece of dust flew into my eye. I pressed my eyelids together to loosen it but nothing happened. "You all right?" Darlene asked.

"I got some dust in my eye," I said and continued to press my eyelids together.

"Real dust or game dust?" David asked.

"How the hell am I supposed to know where it's from?"

"It's probably real dust. What developer puts dust into their game?" Darlene said. I kept my eyes shut for a few seconds and then opened them. "Better?" she asked. I nodded.

"Why do you need my help?"

"Peter, you are a very unique individual. You are one of the very first people to undergo a real-life human-to-machine integration."

"There were over six hundred people who did the same thing I did and there have been thousands more since then."

"Don't sell yourself short. Miles and Ә-zero and a hundred other companies are collecting information about us so they can perfect us and design robots that will eventually replace us. You may think you're human now, Peter, but just you wait. A few upgrades and you won't be able to tell your thoughts apart from the machines. It needs to stop."

"The machine part of my heart doesn't have thoughts."

"Not yet, it doesn't. Wait and see what Ә-zero does with you."

"They would never do that."

"Not knowingly they wouldn't. No. But it's happening."

"I thought Miles was working on a new world civilization."

"A new world civilization of robots," Darlene said.

"It's either that or a new world civilization for them to live in while the robots do all the work," David said. "That's my theory right now."

"Who is 'they'?" I asked.

"Oh, the evil board of directors of the Miles Cooperative," David said. "They invented secret and suspicious meetings."

"Doesn't matter," Darlene said. "Robots will rule the world and you'll be dead in some cubicle somewhere updating the firmware on your second wife. That's all you need to know."

"I don't think you're right though," I said. "I think Miles is actually doing something innovative. If you don't like it, that's one thing, but you can't threaten to destroy all technology, which I don't think is actually possible."

"We're going to stop it. We have the tools and you're going to help us."

"Okay, go ahead, but leave me out of it. I think you're wrong about Miles."

"You'll see. David told me about how Miles invited you to the meeting. He wants you to legitimize them. Why would he tell you what's really going on?"

"Because I'm a respected journalist. I'm admired in my field."

"Ha! That's funny," David said as they both laughed at me. What did they know anyway? "When the conference starts on Friday we'll need you to take something with you," David said and motioned for me to come sit on the bed with him. I didn't move.

"He won't bite," Darlene said.

"We're already impressed with what you're doing,"

"I'm not going to take anything with me."

"It's a small thing. You won't even notice."

"That sounds like a bad idea. It's like letting someone watch your bag in the airport," I said. "You guys seem really nice and—whatever— but this is a strange request. You want me to bring them something and you won't even tell me what it is?"

"We're helping each other out here," David said.

"I don't even know if I'm going to do that—go to that conference or whatever it is," I said. "I haven't told them one way or another yet."

"The secret and evil conference."

"Tell them yes!" Darlene exclaimed.

"Look, Peter, let's be honest," David said and reached out and put his hand on my knee. "You need this as much as we need it. You'll be helping your friends out and you'll be serving a purpose—finally doing something legitimate with your life. Do something significant, and maybe Paula will talk to you again and take you seriously again, and maybe, if you're lucky enough, she'll acknowledge your overall existence."

"Excuse me?" I said and took a step back. "I don't know what you two are up to, but I don't want any part of it."

"You're overreacting," David said as he stood up and looked at his physique in the mirror next to the bed. He pulled his shirt up again and flexed his stomach muscles.

"Paula and I still talk," I said.

"My bad," Darlene said. "Abbey must have her facts wrong. She said that Joyce told her that Paula doesn't talk to you anymore and that she hasn't in a long time. She says you guys don't think they notice, but they do," she said.

I looked down at the floor.

The floors were some type of very thick and plush animal skin.

From the hints of yellow and brown I thought maybe the rug was made from lion skin. I guess in a virtual world you could have anything you wanted.

I was embarrassed. Embarrassed about the overall situation with Paula and embarrassed these weirdos knew about it because my kid talks to their idiot of a child. "It's okay. It happens, Peter. Everybody understands," she said.

It was true. About ten years ago, I wasn't doing everything in my power to take care of my family. I was making selfish decisions and only thinking about how I could advance my career. Paula said I wasn't family-focused and we drifted away from each other. We lived apart for a while but I moved back in when it became too hard on her to manage a thriving career and growing business selling cosmetics to her inert neighbors while taking care of the girls. She went out with her friends more often and did more stuff with the girls by herself. So, yes, I guess at some point we stopped talking and interacting with each other. We had our good moments, but they were few and far between. Joyce was right. It's too bad she noticed.

"Paula and I are going through some stuff. It's not really your business," I said.

"Do something that will make her proud. Do something where she'll say, 'Damn, I didn't know Peter had it in him,' and she'll jump your bones," Darlene said.

"Oh, stop it," David chimed in.

"It's true though, David. I can't remember the last manly thing you did. I can barely look at you," she said and let out a small smile.

"The things you do in *Stolen Planet* don't have any effect in the real world. Drink, eat, screw whatever you want," David said and Darlene let out a loud laugh. "You like to screw things, Peter?" David said.

I felt uneasy and David's close proximity to me didn't feel sincere and comforting. It felt invasive and threatening.

"Stop it, David! You're making him uncomfortable."

"No. I'm not. We're just talking here. Man-to-man and friend-to-friend. You like to fuck things, Peter? I know I do."

"Can't remember the last time you did. At least properly," Darlene chimed in.

"The desire is only natural and there's nothing to be ashamed of," David continued as I ran my foot back and forth across the lion skin rug. "In *Stolen Planet* you can fuck whatever you want. If you wanted to you could fuck the lion this rug is made out of. You can do that," he said as a lion roared outside the door to my room. "Do it while you're still human and you can tell the difference between your desires and the desires Ə-zero programmed for you. In the game you can feel and experience things you can't in real life. You can go anywhere and experience things the limits of reality won't let you experience. But you can only do this if you help us with Miles. Can you do that for us?"

"Sure," I said cautiously. "Why not, right? It is, after all, just a game." I might as well get things taken care of while I was still human. I knew Ə-zero had at least three upgrades planned for the next month. They were mostly software-related, but their technology was developing at a rapid pace it was hard to keep up with each innovation. I also wasn't feeling myself lately. In fact, I'm not sure what the real Peter Richards felt like anymore. I felt detached and oddly routine about everything in my life. Eat this, buy this, run this mile and so on. Maybe that was a result of me being part robot. I was fading away one innocuous update at a time. "This will be good for me. I can do this."

"Attaboy, Peter!" David said and laughed. "That's what I'm talking about. You and I are going get along fine in here. Post-revolution Peter and David will be best friends."

"Let's go to Africa and find that lion!" I said.

"Easy there, buddy. We can do that but, we have to stay focused on the game right now."

"Bring that thing to the Miles meeting? Whatever you want. I'm down for it. I want a front row seat to the annihilation," I said. "This is part of the game, right?"

"There's a little bit of a gray area there, Peter," Darlene said. "It's for the meeting, but it's also part of the game. Get it?"

"I guess, but whatever. I'm down," I said.

Finally something I can do that will help Paula understand.

"Before you do that, we need you to do something for us."

"Right. Miles. I gotcha. The lion will have to wait."

"No. Something before you do that. Something that will prove to us and everyone else in *Stolen Planet* that you are really committed to our cause and that'll you'll go the distance to help us out."

"I'll go the distance."

"Nope," Darlene said.

"Peter, you can't just say you'll go the distance. You actually have to do it."

"I will go the distance. You have my word."

"Still nope on that one," Darlene said.

"Peter, we're going to ask you to do something to show that you're committed to us, and once you do it, we'll really know. Do you think you can handle that?"

"Sure," I said as my heart started beating. My palms were sticky. "What do you want me to do?"

"We want you to kill your wife."

25.

Skelly pressed the button to the Medical Examiner's office a third time. He was getting impatient.

He called Nicole and told her he was headed over. She said that would be fine, but had to hang up because someone just got there. He knew she was there, but she was ignoring him and he didn't like it. He raised his hand up a fourth time to press the button, but when his finger made contact he heard a series of locks being undone. "Sorry," Nicole said as she opened the door. "Something came up and I couldn't—it doesn't matter."

"Everything okay?" Skelly asked.

Her hair was frizzy from the humidity.

"Yes. Everything is fine. What can I help you with?" she said. She was being abrupt.

"Can I come in? I need to ask you about something," Skelly said. "It's somewhat sensitive. At least, I think it is."

"Something your girlfriend couldn't answer for you? You had to find a real woman?" Nicole said and then realized what she had said. "Sorry, there's been a lot on my plate with these … killings. Please come in." She took a step back and held the door open for Skelly as he walked in. The lab was dark and there was only one light on in the corner.

Molly Cooper's body was on the center table.

"Couldn't put her away, could ya?" Skelly asked. "Miles didn't come yet?"

"I bought some time. I wanted to make sure I didn't miss anything," Nicole said and took a seat next to Molly Cooper. "What's going on with you, Skelly?"

"Nothing. How's Molly? Find anything new?"

"Shock," Nicole said and handed Skelly a lab chart.

"Shock?"

"As the cause of death," Nicole added. "Shock to the system, or better known in my field as circulatory shock."

"So, a heart attack?"

"No. A heart attack is coronary thrombosis when oxygen to the heart is blocked. Shock is a total shut down to the system and has no relation to emotional shock, like when someone sees a ghost or whatever. It usually happens to people with severe illnesses and medical conditions."

"Which Molly didn't have."

"Right," Nicole said. "Which makes me think this is emotional shock."

"But you said—"

"I know what I said, Skelly. Bear with me here, but I think she saw something and it scared her to death. Literally. She saw something and it scared the shit out of her and her system shut down and went into shock."

"Have you heard of something called Cotard delusion?" Skelly shook his head. "It's a condition where someone thinks they're dead."

"Jesus. Is that what you think happened?"

"I'm my medical opinion, yes, and I put it in the report. Twelve years of schooling and now I'm working with a corpse who was frightened."

"Thanks, Nicole. You've really given me a lot to work with here," Skelly said. "I guess I'll go look for scary stuff and interrogate that—or them—whatever."

"Stop."

"Maybe I should ask her parents if she scared easily. 'Why yes, she did scare easily and thanks for asking, but it was usually scary stuff that scared her.'"

"Shut up, Skelly. You don't have to be an asshole about it."

"I'm just saying."

"Did you come here for something or did you want to waste my time?"

"Ever heard of Nitro Zeus?" Skelly asked and let the tension in the room settle.

"No. What is it?"

"I was hoping you would know."

"Context?"

"It's a game changer is what I'm told," Skelly said. "Have you been drinking?"

"What? Me? No." Nicole said. "I don't know why you would think that."

"Don't be defensive about it. I was just asking. Something stinks."

"Your attitude."

"Fine. So nothing on Nitro Zeus?"

"Who told you about it?"

"A bartender."

"Oh, great."

"A bartender in a virtual reality game."

"You play?"

"Just this one time. *Stolen Planet*. It's for a case—Molly Cooper's case. Some kids were playing it at the hotel the night she was killed. Maybe they were playing it. I don't know. They aren't talking."

"You aren't giving me much here, Skelly."

"I guess we're even then," Skelly said.

"I can help," a voice said from the other end of the lab. Skelly jolted up in his seat.

"Who was that?" Skelly said and put his hand on the holster of his weapon.

"Dammit," Nicole said as a hand popped up from behind the exam table at the far end of the lab.

The hand grabbed on to the table and pulled a person up behind it.

It was Travis Holt.

Former person.

"Hey, Skelly," Travis said and waved at him. He seemed to have trouble getting his footing.

"Hey, buddy, what's going?" Skelly said and smiled. "Did you know he was back there?" Skelly said and looked at Nicole, who was mortified.

"Travis, you should go," Nicole said.

"Uh, sure," he said and pulled up a bottle of Fireball and took a swig from it. "Whatever you want, Babe."

"Babe?" Skelly said.

"It's nothing," Nicole said.

"I wouldn't call this nothing," Travis said.

"Travis—stop, please, and go."

"She got a little jealous of you and your ... partner."

"She's not my partner. She's helping out."

"That's right. Skelly doesn't partner up," Travis said as he made his way towards the door.

"Aren't you gay?" Skelly asked.

"I'm going through a bit of an identity crisis, if I'm being honest."

"Hey. Wait a minute, Travis." Skelly said as he thought of something. "What can you tell me about Nitro Zeus? In that expansive brain of yours."

"Nitro Zeus? Sure." Travis said and looked back at Skelly. "When President Obama took office, his administration developed a program that would release a cyber attack on Iran in case the diplomatic efforts to limit its nuclear arsenal failed and subsequently led to war."

"Right. Stuxnet."

"No. Stuxnet was a computer worm design to infiltrate industrial control systems in Iranian nuclear facilities. Nitro Zeus is designed to disable Iran's air defense systems, communications systems, and the power grid. It has the capability to shut down the infrastructure, and not only in Iran, but everywhere. It's a game changer," he said.

"So I heard," Skelly said. "How is it implemented?"

"The American government spent tens of millions of dollars to develop the computer code and place electronic implants in the Iranian computer networks."

"So it's only effective on a system that has one of those implants?"

"Theoretically, yes. But it's very difficult and costly to have covert agents go from computer system to computer system. There have been some theories that the government had back-room deals with some of the large technology companies to include the implants in the actual manufacturing process. Companies like Cisco, IBM, Lenovo, Ɔ-zero, and even the Miles Cooperative have been rumored to include these implants in their manufacturing, so when they build a new storage system, for instance, the system would by default have a government-designed implant. New phones, watches, cars, everything."

"So it's possible that anything those companies manufacture has an implant that could be activated with Nitro Zeus?"

"Correct."

"But only in Iran?"

"Highly unlikely. If the government did in fact do this, they probably told the companies to put them in all of the devices that were being made so as to not draw attention to Iran specifically. Covering their tracks."

"So Nitro Zeus shuts these systems down?"

"Total shut-down."

"Can they come back online?"

"Highlty doubtful."

"Great. You've been most helpful, Travis."

"Cool, dude. Can I go now?" Travis asked.

"Please," Nicole said and went and opened the door for her as Travis went up to her and kissed her on the cheek. Skelly started to snicker and covered his mouth.

"It's not funny," Nicole said as she shut the door.

"Sorry," Skelly said as he put his hands up in resignation. "It's not what I was expecting."

"Is it ever what you're expecting, Skelly?"

"I suppose not. I didn't think you were on the market for anything."

"I'm not. You have Erin. I have him."

"What's left of him."

"He gives amazing head. I mean, he's like a robot and won't stop. It's insane."

"He is a robot, is what you mean to say," Skelly corrected.

"Touché."

"Explains the lovely breath you have, though."

"Did you get what you came here for?"

"I did yes," Skelly said and sat there and looked at Molly's body. "Nitro Zeus is part of *Stolen Planet*. Something about when people get to Level 8 and Nitro Zeus. Not sure what it is, though."

"What happens at Level 8?"

"I don't know. He wouldn't say."

"The bartender?"

"Right. The bartender."

"Maybe you should ask him again or go back and get to Level 8 and find out for yourself."

"What do you think Molly Cooper saw that scared her to death?"

"I don't know, Skelly. Too bad she can't tell you herself."

"Maybe because it's a game?"

"Maybe but probably not," Skelly said as he looked down at his phone. There was a message from Erin.

Erin: *COME DOWNTOWN ASAP.*
GARRETT ALAN WANTS TO TALK.

26.

"I'm not doing that," I said. "I'm not going to kill my wife."

"Oh, come on. I want to kill David all the time," Darlene said as she sipped champagne. "It's marriage. It's only natural."

"There's a difference between wanting to do it and actually doing it."

"Is there? In *SP* anything you can imagine is possible. It's all right at your fingertips."

"I'm not going to do it. It's totally messed up and you two are monsters. I don't even know why I have to do it."

"To prove to us that we can trust you."

"I told you that you could trust me!"

"But in order to play this game, you have to *show* us. We've identified the secret organization and we need your help infiltrating it. If you're going to help us we need to trust you. Those are the rules. Everyone else did it, so I see no reason why you should receive an exception."

"Yeah, and what happened to those people?"

"They're around doing their thing. Their thing just isn't as important as your thing."

"What sort of answer is that? Are they in jail? That's probably what you meant to say."

"No, they aren't in jail. They proved themselves to be loyal and they each have their assigned task."

"What about the disappointing recruits you mentioned earlier?"

"Not everything works out as planned."

"Like killing someone? They didn't want to kill their best friend or partner or whatever? That sounds insane if you ask me. What's wrong with people?"

"What we're doing here is very important—it will change the

world—so we need to make sure you're onboard. Not everyone has been onboard."

"Did the other people also have a connection to the Miles Cooperative? Did they have access to this super-secret meeting?"

"Nope. They sure didn't," Darlene said. "We heard rumors about it, but didn't know it was real until ... right before we changed our identity."

"That's why we did it," David said. "There was so much noise about Miles, but we decided to make the final step—the big step—when we knew for sure it was real."

"Then you need me more than I need you and I won't do it."

"It's not real, okay?" Darlene shouted at me. "You bring her into the game, and you do it in the game, so can you get off your high-horse and man-up and kill your wife?" she said and locked her eyes on me. "Do you spend your whole life like this? Thinking things over and analyzing every possible scenario? You're so busy planning and freaking out that you aren't ever doing anything. If I was married to you I wouldn't talk to you either. Such a waste, even with your access to Miles," she said and took a minute to calm herself down.

"How do I invite her into the game?"

"Invite her over—she can come to our house—and she tries the game out and then, BLAMMO, she's dead, and then we can move on to the bigger and more important stuff."

"Seems arbitrary."

David let out a small breath of air and lowered his head. "Well, we tried, didn't we Darlene? We thought Peter was our guy—our number-one guy—but we were wrong. Maybe we should go to the castle and recruit one of the employees there. We'll find another way into the conference. We'll get a real man who understands how to take care of business."

"You should go ahead and say your safe phrase, Peter," Darlene said. "We have no use for you, so you should probably leave. You're of no value to *Stolen Planet*. A game isn't a game if you aren't willing to play. You're more robot than man. It's what we feared the most. We needed a winner, but instead we got a loser."

It's just a game, I thought.

It's just a game, Peter.

Get over yourself and start living in a world of yes.

Maybe killing Paula will be cathartic for me.

Maybe it will help me get out whatever frustration and anger I have towards her and the situation.

Maybe it will help me and her move on and we can look back fondly on this moment.

"Yes," I blurted out. "Yes. I'll kill my wife."

"What?" David said and raised his head. "Really?"

"Yes, for the game. For you guys, I'll do it. I'll kill her for *Stolen Planet* and then you can give me whatever it is and I'll take it to the conference. Deal? I'm down and I want to win!"

"That's the best thing I've heard all day. Peter wants to kill his wife!"

"But only in the game, right?" I asked.

"Yes, of course. It's only in the game, Peter. She'll be fine IRL. But don't let us down. We need you and the conference is the key to our mission in *Stolen Planet*."

"I understand."

"You'll be lauded a hero once this is done, Peter."

"What happens when the game is done? When we end modern civilization as we know it?"

"You'll be famous. More famous than you could have ever imagined."

"I have a pretty extensive imagination," I said and then something occurred to me. "What will happen to me?"

"What do you mean?"

"I'm part machine, part technology. What will happen to me when this is all said and done?"

"Oh, you'll most likely be dead."

"Yeah, probably," Darlene added. "Or we could take your heart out."

"But only in the game, right?"

"Sure."

27.

"He said he wants to talk to a detective," Erin said as she and Skelly stood outside one of the interrogation rooms downtown. "He came in about thirty minutes ago and he's pretty freaked out."

"Did he say anything?"

"Nope. He wouldn't talk to me."

"Right, because you put him in an interrogation room. No one ever wants to talk when they're in there. You have to level with people and connect with them on a human level. You can't put them in a cage and expect them to dance."

"I'll be sure to write that down later. Good advice."

"You could have put him in the rec room or sat him at my desk," Skelly reached for the door handle. Erin put her hand out and put it on his wrist. "Reynolds is in there with him, just so you know."

"What? Why?"

"He's representing him."

"He's not even a lawyer anymore!"

"He knows that, but when you asked him to get Barry Foster to talk he got clever. He went out and found this Garrett guy and told him that the police were looking for him and wanted to talk to him about the events that night at the Blue Bonnet." Skelly banged his fist on the door lightly. "You know what he wants, so make sure he doesn't get it, okay?"

"Okay," Skelly said and tapped on the door for a brief moment before opening it.

Garrett Alan was sitting at a steel four-by-six table. He was wearing workout clothes and drinking a cup of coffee. Reynolds pulled a chair up next to him and was leaning forward in the chair so he could be close to him.

"I'm Detective Skelly," Skelly said and proffered his hand to Garrett.

"Garrett Alan," the kid said and shook Skelly's hand.

"Thanks for coming in. You know this guy isn't an actual lawyer, right?"

"What?" Garrett said and looked over at Reynolds. "Is that true?"

"He hasn't practiced law in at least ten years. The last time he saw a courtroom, you were in elementary school."

"Come on, Skelly. That's a low move even by your standards," Reynolds said and turned towards his client. "I have a law degree. I went to Harvard, for Christ's sake."

"He doesn't care, Reynolds."

"What do you do now?" Garrett asked.

"I'm a political adviser."

"I'm surprised you haven't hanged yourself yet," Garrett said and Skelly laughed. He liked him.

"Garrett, I want to ask you a few questions about the night Molly Cooper was found outside the Blue Bonnet," Skelly said. "You came in here on your own recognizance and you aren't a suspect and you aren't under arrest so you can walk out any time you want. You don't need a lawyer to tell you that. How does that sound?"

"He told me that you were going to try and get me to say stuff I wasn't comfortable saying and that I needed a lawyer to make sure I wouldn't incriminate myself."

"You came to us, so I'll let you lead the conversation. How does that sound?"

"He said that police tend to be corrupt and they seek out information they want to be there."

"Seriously?" Skelly said and looked at Reynolds.

"You need to watch more television, Skelly," Reynolds said.

"Putting me in an interrogation room automatically makes me a suspect."

"It was the only room available and it doesn't make you a suspect. It's not a representation on how the department or I feel about you. If you like we can go and sit at my desk with or without your lawyer."

"Fine. I can do that," Garrett said.

"Great," Reynolds said and slapped his hand on his knee.

"Not you," Garrett said.

"What?"

"You heard him. Get out of here," Skelly said.

Reynolds stood up and slowly worked his way towards the door.

"You and I still have some stuff we need to discuss, Skelly."

"No we don't," Skelly said and opened the door and motioned for Reynolds to leave.

"We do. You said you'd think about it."

"I did think about it, and the answer is no." Skelly said and shut the door. He turned and smiled at Garrett. "Where were we?" he asked.

"I killed the girl," Garrett said.

28.

"She made us cut through his stomach," Maya said from the depths of her VR headset.

We were sitting at the kitchen table. Maya had a frozen fetal pig in a Tupperware container sitting on the table in front of her. She pulled the top off the container. "I'll show you," she said and picked the fetal pig up to show us. *Could she see through the headset?*

"That's so gross," Joyce said and covered her mouth.

"I'm with Joyce on this one. That's pretty disgusting."

"It's science, Dad!" she shouted at me.

"Easy with the volume there, honey," I said as the front door opened.

Paula came in carrying a bag of groceries and set it on the counter.

"Mommy!" the girls shouted and ran over to her and the tension in her shoulders waned. The girls gave her hugs and ran upstairs.

Paula unpacked the groceries.

I got up and went over to help her. "How was work?"

"Fine," she said and took some stuff out of the bag and went to the other side of the kitchen.

"The girls know."

"Know what, Peter?"

"About how you and I don't talk. About how you shut me out."

"I don't know what you're talking about. Life is busy," she said.

"You're icing me out, Paula. I don't like it. You pretend like I'm a ghost in my own house."

"You were a ghost once before. You should be used to it."

"I was never a ghost."

"The girls are smart. They pay attention and know what's going on. Besides, we have our good moments every now and then. Did Joyce bring it up?"

"No. David and Darlene said something about it."

"The suspicious ones from the news you keep talking about?"

"Yes, correct. From the news and also from gymnastics. Funny world we live in. Their daughter, Abbey, told them because I guess Joyce told her because she's canny and she pays attention."

"What do you want me to do about it?"

"Let's find a solution."

"After you."

"David and Darlene—these shady people I keep talking about— invited us over this evening. You, me, and the girls."

"In the eyes of Peter Richards we're all shady," she said. "Anyway, Joyce has a lot of homework tonight. Maybe another time." It was her way of telling me it was never going to happen.

"You know what. I totally understand. I might still go over there for a while. They have one of those new VR headsets. It's super cool."

"Enjoy yourself," she said and closed the refrigerator door. She tapped a button on the display screen on the outside of the fridge that showed us what we needed to get at the store and then went upstairs.

I stood at the kitchen counter and listened to the girls laughing upstairs. I could hear Maya running back and forth.

My wrist buzzed.

I looked down at my wristband.

The screen was a dark red, which meant that the battery was about to die or there was something seriously wrong with my internal levels.

I tapped on the screen.

A message popped up on the screen: *Sodium at 3,500 mg* followed by a small sad face.

That didn't make sense. I knew I had tendencies to break away from the doctor-prescribed diet but 3,500 mg was extremely high and equivalent to about a pound of bacon. I tapped on the screen again and held my finger down to reset the monitor.

As I was waiting for my wristband to reset the display screen on the fridge flashed and text slowly scrolled across:

INCOMING MESSAGE. ACCEPT/DECLINE.

"Accept," I said and a woman's face appeared on the display screen. "Please hold for Miles," she said and then the screen switched over to the older gentleman I met at the Driskill.

"Hi, Peter," he said. He was eating something. "I got these kimchi fries from this truck downtown that was selling food. Have you heard of these?"

"Food trucks? Yes."

"It's amazing. I think I got into the wrong business. Anyway, you should try this kimchi stuff. It's incredible."

"I can't. Doctor's orders."

"Oh, right. I forgot about that. You're living on the sidelines of life," he said and laughed at his own quip. A spot of kimchi came out of his mouth and landed on the screen. "Nevertheless, Peter, I really wish you would take my advice and stop messing around. The suspicious stuff starts in less than twenty-four hours."

"Excuse me?" I said and leaned closer to the screen on the refrigerator. I tried to wipe the stain of kimchi off even though I knew it was on the other side of the screen.

"About the conference. I trust that we'll see you there," he said. "Falkenstein Castle. Are you familiar? Number eight on the Travel Channel's list of 'Best Places in the World to Host Secret and Suspicious Meetings'."

"I haven't decided yet," I said softly, so the girls couldn't hear me upstairs.

"Peter, I hope you understand the opportunity you have here. I hope you've really had the chance to think about it."

"I have," I said.

"We're really counting on you here. I want you to know that. We think what you're doing is important and we want you there. Besides, it could open a lot of doors for you," he said and took another bite of his food. "Also, you'll need to keep yourself occupied without the girls around."

"What was that?" I asked. I couldn't hear him over the noise of the kids running around upstairs. For a second there I thought he said without the girls around.

"Without the girls around, Peter. What will you do with yourself?" Oh. I did hear him correctly.

"I'm sorry. It must be a bad connection."

"There's no such thing."

"For a second I thought you asked how I was going to keep myself occupied without the girls around."

"I did say that! You got Cleft's client list, didn't you?"

"Yes," I said apprehensively.

"They're on there, Peter."

"Excuse me?"

"Paula, Joyce, and the other one. All three of them," he said and let out a small burp. I ran to the other side of the kitchen counter and grabbed my bag. "Where did you go?" he asked.

I dumped the contents out on the counter and quickly went through them and pulled out Cleft's client list.

I quickly flipped through the pages and looked at the hundreds of client names on the left. I stopped when I reached:

RICHARDS, Paula
(+ two minors: 2 girls), Austin, TX.

"You okay, Peter?" Miles said from the screen.

I ran my finger across the page and stopped at:

OLESAY, Natalya
(+ two minors: 2 girls), Gazetnyy per, 9c5, Moscow, Russia.

My pulse started to race and I felt as if I was about to hyperventilate.

"You okay, Peter?" he said. "You look faint."

"Give me a second," I said and grabbed the edge of the counter so I wouldn't pass out and fall over. I took a few short breaths and collected myself.

"So, you in or what, Peter?" he asked again. I could sense his growing impatience.

I glanced at Paula's name on the client list again. + *two minors.*

"I'm in," I said.

"Great," he said. "I'll see that your sodium levels go back down to their normal levels so your doctor stops bothering your wife," he said and the screen went blank.

"Peter!" Paula shouted as she was running down the stairs. She came into the kitchen. "Are you okay?"

"I'm fine," I said and closed the client list and shoved it back into my bag. I didn't look up at her. "It's a reporting error. Absolutely nothing to be alarmed about."

"Are you sure?" she asked. I couldn't tell if she was concerned or if she was disappointed because she wasn't going to get my life insurance. At least not yet.

"All good here," I said and gave her a weak thumbs up.

"Let's go then."

"Go where?" I asked.

"To David and Darlene's house," she said and looked at me like I was insane and we had a whole conversation about going and planned everything out and I just forgot about it.

Silly me.

Joyce agreed to watch Maya for a little bit while we went over to visit with David and Darlene. I collected myself and agreed to go over.

Paula had heard so much about virtual reality and wanted to know what Maya was experiencing through the headset she had on eighteen hours a day. Paula felt like she was really missing out by being stuck in a lab all day. How could she possibly turn down an opportunity like this? Also, I suspected, she saw an opportunity to sell her skincare products to Darlene. I made this astute deduction because Paula brought along her rolling suitcase filled with skincare products.

"We didn't realize how close you two lived," Darlene said as she opened the front door. "Planning on staying long?" she asked when she saw Paula's rolling suitcase.

"I hope you don't mind, but I brought some skincare products that I think you'll love. Lash boosters, filler patches, I have it all."

"I thought Peter said you were a biologist."

"Yes, and this on the side. It's what I'm passionate about. It's the American dream."

"Yes, of course it is," Darlene said. "David is upstairs." She led us into the living room.

Two headsets were sitting on the coffee table. "We were just playing. Have you ever played?" she asked, getting right to the point.

"No. I'm afraid I haven't," Paula said politely.

"It's amazing," Darlene said. "What sort of biologist are you?"

"I work for a company that studies biological data. Bioinformatics. It's super boring. How about yourself? What do you do?" Paula asked.

"Oh, please," Darlene said and waved her off. "David! Our guests are here!" she shouted up the stairs. "Have a seat." She pointed to the couch.

"David and Darlene have this thing that they do," I said. "Where they don't engage in any sort of technology whatsoever. Mennonites."

"Luddites," Darlene corrected.

"Oh, right."

"You two have discussed this?" Paula asked apprehensively and darted her eyes from Darlene over to me.

"Peter knows all about it," Darlene said.

"Oh really?" Paula asked and looked down at the headsets sitting on the coffee table. "Those are technology."

"We abstain from specific technologies. Everything but that."

"I get first try!" David said as he rushed down the stairs. He stopped when he saw Paula. "You must be the lovely Mrs. Richards," he said.

"It's Miss Olesay actually. Natalya Olesay," Paula said. Getting back to her Russian heritage. Distancing herself.

"Oh, wow," David said. "It's exotic. I like that."

"Seriously?" I asked. It's one thing when Miles tells me she's changing her name, but hearing it from her own lips was absurd. Clearly she didn't care.

"Like two months ago, Peter." Paula said. "You need to pay attention. This is what I've been trying to explain to you," she said, but I didn't recall those conversations. Surely I would remember those. Olesay was her family name in Russia. She changed it when we met and got married. Joyce is also an Olesay, but I've come to love her as my own.

"Good thing you dropped the Richards. So boring," David said.

"Tell me about it!" Paula said and they all started to laugh at me.

"Go ahead—try one on," David said and handed Paula a headset.

"So that's what we're doing?" Paula asked. "We came over here to put headsets on and play a game? No human interaction at all?"

"Is there something else you'd like to do?" Darlene asked. "Something you want to discuss with us?"

"No. This is good," Paula said and looked at them suspiciously.

"She's always wanted to try one of these," I interjected.

"What are we playing?" Paula asked.

"There's a bunch of different games, but the one we like is called *Stolen Planet*," Darlene said. "It's an anti-government, anti-technology funhouse!"

"I don't mean to be rude, but I don't think that game is for me," Paula said. "Anything else?"

"We also like a game called *Swing Town*," David said.

"We're not playing that!" Darlene said loudly.

"Maybe they would like it."

"No, David. Only you like that game."

"You don't know unless you ask, honey."

"That's a pass for me," I said.

"I'm down," Paula said.

"Honey."

"What, Peter?" she said firmly.

"I don't think that's appropriate."

"Who are you to decide what is and is not appropriate?" she said as Darlene whispered something into David's ear. "They wouldn't have brought it up if it wasn't appropriate."

"We can show you," David said. "If you want."

"You can go first," Darlene said and smiled at me. "Peter and I will watch. Do you like watching, Peter?"

"That's his whole life. He sits on the sidelines and takes it all in," Paula said and turned towards David. She moved her hair out of her face and smiled at him. "How does this work, David?" she said as she picked up one of the headsets and examined it.

"Do you want a cocktail, something to set the mood?"

"Let's get on with it. We're on a tight timeline."

"I don't have anywhere I need to be," I said.

"Of course you don't," Paula responded.

"Do you want to select a character for me? It's common for people to have avatars. You can choose mine for this game, since you'll be—"

"Be yourself, David," Paula said as she put the headset on. "I can handle it."

"Very well. Let's get right to it," David said as he winked at me and picked up the other headset and put it on.

"It's a new game," Darlene whispered to me. "Apparently, it's very popular."

"Where are we David?" Paula said through the headset as she moved her head back and forth. "This place is amazing."

"It's my mansion. The kitchen is commercial-grade with a butler's pantry and a sub-kitchen for when you have company over. The appliances are totally kickass."

"You're missing the point of the game, David," Darlene interjected.

"Don't worry about it," he said. "Paula, do you want to go upstairs?"

"Do we have to? Let's stay down here," Paula said and lowered her voice. "Come over here."

"Go on, David. Go to her," Darlene said as she leaned back on the couch and watched him. She reached over and ran her hand up my leg. "You like that?"

"I'm good," I said and brushed her hand away gently.

"You're so soft, Peter," she said and grimaced at me.

"Oh, wow, David," Paula said as she let out a devious smile. "It's so big."

"It's part of the game. It's not really that big. It's quite disappointing actually," Darlene said.

"Can I touch it?" Paula asked and reached her arm out.

"All right," I said and stood abruptly. "Can we stop now?!"

"Yes, right there, David. Oh my—that feels so good," Paula said.

"How is she feeling anything? It's not even real, Paula!"

"Right there. Come on, come on, David."

"Supposedly, they have sensors you can buy to put into—" Darlene said and made an obscene gesture with her finger. "Never mind, you probably wouldn't understand anyway, but they're supposed to be super-effective."

"Damn, David! Right there!" Paula screamed and slammed her hand down on the chair.

"Stop!" I said and reached over and took her headset off. "Enough of this!"

"Stop, Peter!"

"That's enough! We're married!"

"Oh, lord. Get off your high horse for once will you? Why do you have to be such a martyr? Can you chill out for two seconds and enjoy life?" Paula said and grabbed the headset from me.

"You're such a bore," Darlene said as she flipped her hand at me. I was dismissed and of no value.

"We're married," I said again.

"We're all amongst friends here," David said and came over to me. "We can do the other game if Peter doesn't want to do this."

"He never wants to do anything," Paula said and crossed her arms in an attempt to shut me out physically and emotionally.

"Peter, you can screw my wife," David whispered into my ear as he handed me the headset. I pushed the headset away. "Seriously?" he said. "Do you know how many people would kill to be in your position?" He proceeded to smile and wink at me. I don't think Paula noticed.

"That's how Peter is," Paula said. "He doesn't know how to have any fun. He is unable to get out of himself."

"Peter, come on," he said again and pressed the headset into my chest. "If you say yes, I'll even let you try out the jockstrap."

"The jockstrap?"

"It's a device that you put over your—you know—to enhance the experience. Designed and manufactured right here in central Texas. It has tiny little fingers that do all the work."

"Does it work?"

"Yes, except for that time when a woman put a razor blade in her husband's jockstrap when she found out he was going online and meeting transvestites," he said. "Let's just say he didn't do that again."

"I'm down for the anti-technology fun house," Paula said. Finally.

"Great," Darlene said. "Why don't you and Peter go first?"

"I'd actually prefer to ... not do it with Peter," Paula said.

"Are you kidding me?" I said. She shrugged.

"This is a different game, honey," Darlene said.

"Still. No change," she said and looked over at me.

"You know what?" I said and stood up. "I'm out."

"No, no," David said and put his hands on my shoulders and tried to push me down. "Don't be out. Be present. Be here. You're letting your emotions get the best of you."

"She doesn't want to."

"Be reasonable. Both of you," Darlene said. "It's just a stupid game."

"I'll do it," Paula said. "But only under one condition."

"What is it?" I asked.

"Not you, Peter." Paula said as she locked her eyes on Darlene. "Would you be interested in buying some skin care products?"

"Oh, shit," I said.

"Shut up, Peter," Paula snapped at me.

"Skin care products?" Darlene said tentatively. "But, of course?"

"Great," Paula said. "I'll send you a price sheet later on. You have to, at least, buy the rejuvenating mask and sleep extender."

"Deal. What's the sleep extender?"

"It's amazing. You won't regret it. If you don't buy it, I'll hunt you down for eternity," Paula said and put the headset on. "Where do I start?"

"You'll see when you get in there," I said. "Whatever happens, know that I love you."

"That's a bizarre thing to say, Peter. Normal people don't say that sort of stuff," she said and pressed down on the power button.

She was engaged.

I looked over at David and Darlene. "How am I supposed to kill her?" I whispered.

"What did you say?"

"We left instructions for you in your hotel room," David said as I put on my headset and pressed down on the power button.

The screen flashed and I found myself in my hotel room with the lion skin rug and pictures of my family.

The sound of city life pulsated through the window.

I went over and pulled the dark cotton curtain back to reveal Piccadilly Circus draped in darkness. Cars and people filled the streets. It was raining. A bolt of lightning struck the Tower of London.

I closed the curtain and looked at the mirror across from the bed. There was a note written on it in what I suspected was lipstick:

When you kill her do it with this

An arrow pointed to a small handgun.

There was a knock at the door.

"Peter?" I heard Paula say on the other side of the door. "Let me in! This place is weird. Don Johnson is everywhere!"

I tucked the gun into the back of my pants and opened the door.

It was Paula.

"It's you," I said.

"Obviously it's me," she said. "Were you expecting someone else?"

"No, it's ... you can be whoever you want in the game and you're ... you."

"I like who I am," she said. "What's your excuse?"

"I haven't decided yet."

"Do you like who you are, too or do you lack the originality gene? Peter Richards surprises the world and plays it safe," she said and took a cautious step inside the room. "Is this your room? I'm across the hall," she said and looked around. "I have the same pictures in my room." She looked down at the rug. "Nice décor."

"The rooms are customized based on your personality."

"They really nailed you," she said as she looked down at the lion skin rug underneath her feet. "Did you go to Africa and kill this yourself?"

"I like to think it speaks to my potential," I said.

"Let me know how that turns out for you. Where are we?"

"The Robo-Motel," I said "We're in London, a post-apocalyptic London. That's my working theory, at least."

"I like the other game better," she said as she looked at herself in the mirror. "That's cryptic," she said as she looked at the note attached to the mirror. "Kill who? Whose lipstick is that?"

I took a small step towards her and pulled the gun out and held it up. "I'm sorry, Paula."

"Peter, what are you doing?"

"They said I needed to kill you—to prove myself."

"Prove yourself to who?"

"They have a very special assignment for me. I am going to change the world."

"Peter, put the gun down," she said.

"Why are you leaving?"

"What?" she said and feigned confusion.

"Why are you leaving? I know that you're changing your name and taking the girls back to Russia."

"Peter, I don't know what you're talking about. I'm not taking the girls back to Russia."

"I saw Cleft's client list. I know that you asked him to get you and Joyce and Maya new identities. I should have known you would do something like this to me."

"I don't know what you think you saw, Peter, but we're not going to leave you. We just used Cleft to change our name, so they could be more in touch with their ancestry."

"Stop, Paula! That is such a load of shit. He had an address for you. In Moscow."

"Woe is me. I'm Peter Richards and the world is out to get me," she said and flung her hands up in the air. "Just because you saw it on a list doesn't make it true, Peter. Do you think I'm some sort of insane person who would take your children away from you? What sort of monster do you think I am?" she said and took a step towards me on the lion skin rug and reached her hand out for me to take it. "Take my hand, Peter."

"No," I said and let my hand drop a little bit. My hand was getting tired from the weight of the gun. "You always wanted me to do something with myself. Well, this is it."

"Said the crazy man waving a gun at his wife."

"I'm not crazy, Paula!" I said and raised the gun back up. "Back off!"

"You're being radical, Peter!"

"Don't say that! That's a horrible word."

"We all see it," she said. I could hear the panic in her voice as she took another step closer to me. "Put the gun down, Peter."

"Don't shut me out, Paula!"

"You shut yourself out. It's not me. You isolate yourself and marginalize me and you don't even notice because your head is so far up your own ass."

"Stop," I said and rubbed the tip of my finger around on the trigger of the gun. I could feel the cold hard metal and it felt nice. The hand sensors I had on were incredible. *It's just a game*, but boy will she be pissed when this is done.

"You're such a waste."

"I'm sorry," I said and pulled my finger back on the trigger twice.

Two bullets flew out of the gun went across the room and landed straight into her chest.

Blood spurted out of her chest and landed on my cheek.

She dropped to her knees as a look of disappointment crossed her face.

"What did you do?" she asked as she grabbed her chest.

I panicked and dropped the gun. "Paula!" I screamed and went over to her and rolled her body over and shook her. "Paula! Answer me!" I kept screaming at her, trying to get her to listen to me.

I felt the softness of the lion's skin under my knees and stopped.

I looked at the pictures of me and Paula and the girls and then stood up and looked out the window and saw the reflection of the moon in the Thames. The city was pitch dark and then I remembered: This wasn't real.

Paula and I were still in David and Darlene's living room.

This wasn't a hotel room.

This wasn't post-apocalyptic London.

This was a game, manufactured from the mind of human beings.

I took a breath and relief washed over me.

"Miami Vice, Miami Vice, Miami Vice," I said softly.

The screen flickered rapidly and I heard the soft hiss of the pressure seal being released.

"Wow, Peter." David said as I pulled my headset off. I looked over at Paula but she wasn't there. "You did it. I didn't think you had it in you," he said as I looked down at the floor.

Paula was lying there with her headset on. She wasn't moving.

"What happened?" I asked.

"What do you think happened? You killed her."

"But ... I thought it was only in the game," I said. I was confused and didn't understand what was going on. "We were in the game. I shot her, in the game."

"There are some gray areas." Darlene said. "Some people suffer shock in the game and it kills them IRL."

"Stop saying that!" I screamed. "I killed her?!"

"Appears that way, doesn't it?"

"I didn't mean to kill her. I thought this was—"

"You probably didn't mean to, but you did aim the gun at her and you pulled the trigger and you probably really wanted to, right?"

"We're gonna need to get rid of the body," David said.

29.

Skelly collected himself before he responded to Garrett's confession.

Skelly was certain it was false and Garrett was scared.

Maybe he was confused.

Twenty-year-old kids at prestigious universities don't confess to murder, even if they did do it. There was simply too much on the line for them. They hire lawyers to go to court for them with the hopes they can beat the system and sometimes they do. Maybe Garrett was stupid and didn't have enough foresight to appreciate how good his life was.

"Excuse me?" Skelly asked.

"I killed her," Garrett said. *He was stupid.*

"I thought I misheard you there for a second," Skelly said and wrote some stuff down in his detective notebook. "Do you want to tell me what happened?"

"I can try. I'm not sure you'll understand though," Garrett said and let his shoulders relax.

"Why don't you start with what you were doing at the Blue Bonnet that night."

"We go there every Saturday night. Barry's family owns the hotel and he worked out some sort of deal with the manager," he said like it was no big deal and that was how most people go about their daily lives. Entitlement.

"And what are you doing there each Saturday night?"

"We have a group. There's about four or five of us, depending on the week, and we play VR games. My dad owns a store up in the Domain that sells VR equipment."

"Head Room?"

"Right. Are you familiar with it?"

"I get out every now and then."

"It's a leader in its class. Anyway, Barry gets the hotel room and I provide the equipment and we play. Usually we play through Sunday."

"What are you playing?"

"All sort of games, but lately we've been playing this game called *Stolen Planet*. For the past two or three months probably. We're really into it."

"Tell me about that."

"It's a multiplayer game where you're trying to defend the country from—something—and throughout the game you are given challenges. When you complete a challenge you move to the next level and each challenge has something to do with the adverse effects technology has on our lives and how we need to reset ourselves and start over."

"The irony, right?"

"Excuse me?"

"Never mind," Skelly said. "So what's the objective?"

"Of what?"

"The game, Garrett. Why are you doing the tasks and moving up? What's the end point?"

"Total annihilation," he said.

"Oh. Annihilation of what?"

"Why would I tell you that?"

"Garrett, you came here to confess. There must be something you want to share with me."

"You wouldn't understand."

"Try me," Skelly said and waited as Garret thought for a second.

"On campus we use imageboard websites to share ideas and jokes and pictures—whatever—anything we think is funny. I post a lot of stuff about Barry because Barry is an idiot. We've been doing this for a while. Years, it feels like. Then one day I started seeing advertisements on the site for this game called *Stolen Planet*—*What Miles Doesn't Want You To See*—*What Miles is Doing With Your Data*—is what the advertisements said. We all knew Miles was tracking us and what we were doing online, but we didn't care or, we cared but knew there wasn't much we could do about it. So Barry and I started playing *Stolen Planet*. Most VR games have some backroom deal with Miles to collect and analyze user data, but *Stolen Planet* felt different. *Stolen Planet* felt like it was designed specifically so no one could know what people were doing in the game.

We felt safe in the game, and what we were doing in the game was almost secondary to the fact that no one knew we were doing it."

"You don't think the developers of *Stolen Planet* are selling your info and monitoring your every move?"

"No. They would never do that," Garrett said and looked down at the floor. He tapped his foot against the leg of the table. "Advance to Level 8 and become part of the annihilation. September fourth," he said quietly to himself.

"What was that?"

"September fourth."

"Right. Saturday."

"Are you listening?" Garrett said. "That's what we're doing at the Blue Bonnet. We're saving the world."

"From what?"

"The Miles Cooperative."

"Molly Cooper would probably disagree with you," Skelly said. "Tell me about that."

"One of the things they asked me to do in the game—to prove myself—was to kill someone. They wanted me to find someone and bring them into the game and then kill them," Garrett said delicately. "They said that if I killed them in the game it wouldn't matter. They would die in the game but they would still be alive in real life and that it didn't make a difference. What happens in the game is just a game. They called it a training module," he said and stopped.

"Training module?" Skelly asked.

"That's correct. They needed a lot of people so they designed a game in a virtual world to find the right people and assess the skills they had and then give them the skills they needed. It's virtually undetectable and Miles has no idea."

"Training you for what?"

"Like I said, September fourth. Saturday."

"What happens on September fourth?"

"The annihilation," Garrett said. He was getting irritated with Skelly.

"Oh, right. Gotcha," Skelly said and wrote *September fourth—Worlds End* down on his notepad. "I'm going to have to make sure I remember that," he said and then underlined it. He might have to reschedule his drum lesson.

"This isn't a joke," Garrett snapped at him. "You're the problem."

"Excuse me?"

"You and everyone else who doesn't seem to know what's going on. It's a big problem. You're going to wake up one day and everything will be different and you won't understand why."

"Why will everything be different?" Skelly said.

"The Red Mercury that went missing," Garrett said. "You know what I'm talking about?"

"Yes, I heard something about it. It disappeared from a research lab in North Carolina."

"Miles has it," Garrett said. "And they're going to use it on September fourth."

"Use it for what?"

"To wipe us out. New York, Dallas, Houston, Chicago, London—everywhere—obliterated."

"You understand what you're saying, right?" Skelly asked. "It's against the law to make threats against our country."

"I'm not making any threats," Garrett said and put his hands up. "I'm just telling you what I've seen."

Skelly set his pen down gently on the table and pushed his chair back. He looked up at the surveillance camera. Maybe someone on the other side was watching and heard what Garrett said.

"Red Mercury is incredibly dangerous. Maybe one of the most—"

"I know what it is!" Garrett shouted at him. "That's why I brought it up! Miles has it and they're going to use it to wipe out most of the civilized world."

"How do you know this?" Skelly asked.

"*Stolen Planet*. It's all in the game, dude," Garrett said. "Miles is going to wipe us out and start to rebuild. The ones that are left will rely on Miles for guidance and leadership. They won't have a choice."

"But it's just a game, right?"

"Think what you want, Detective," Garrett said. "You can rationalize it any which way you want, but it's still the truth. Miles wants to destroy us and *Stolen Planet* is going to stop them."

"How is *Stolen Planet* going to do that?"

"We're going to hit the reset button," Garrett said. Skelly thought about what Travis told him. *The reset button of all reset buttons.* "We have the ability to wipe out all technology and stop Miles."

"Can we move on here?" Skelly said and picked his pen back up. "I'd like to get back to the confession part of this where you told me you killed Molly Cooper."

"Red Mercury is odorless, tasteless and extremely dangerous powder. One kilogram costs two point three million dollars on the black market and when heated to a specific temperature, it can kill up to a thousand people when airborne and smells like burnt corn. Miles spent over a hundred million dollars on the black market for the powder and another fifty million for devices that will make the powder form airborne. Miles figured out how to weaponize it."

"I'm going to get a cup of coffee," Skelly said. He'd had enough.

"Miles has a conference in Austin this weekend," Garrett said. "A conference where a bunch of world leaders get together, smoke cigars, and talk about how they want to build the next civilization."

"Do you want any coffee? You seem like you might."

"But the conference is total bullshit," Garrett wasn't stopping. "The conference is for them to talk about the New World Order and about replacing humans with robots and moving to Turks and Caicos with all their money, all while they're launching Red Mercury. They built these cities—not for us—but for themselves. It's MetLife on crack."

"You seem like more of a sedative guy, actually," Skelly said.

"We're going to launch a virus that will cripple the devices that Miles has to weaponize Red Mercury and there isn't anything they can do to stop us," Garrett said. Skelly thought again about what Travis said. "You follow?"

"Nitro Zeus," Skelly said carefully.

"You've heard of it," Garrett said and smiled. "Red Mercury is very dangerous and we need Nitro Zeus to disable it."

"And then what?"

"Then we start over. Miles wants to destroy us—wipe us out—and Nitro Zeus is the only way to stop them."

30.

"You probably didn't mean to, but you did aim the gun at her and you pulled the trigger and you probably really wanted to, right?" Darlene said in the background.

I was standing over Paula's body.

I couldn't feel my legs or my arms and I felt disconnected from my body. It was as if I was watching this on TV.

It wasn't real.

It couldn't possibly be real.

This sort of stuff doesn't happen.

Paula isn't supposed to be dead.

"We're gonna need to get rid of the body," David said in manner that sounded like he was thinking about what he needed to get at the grocery store. Pick up milk, eggs, and dispose of the incredibly inconvenient corpse.

"Has this happened before?" I asked.

"Congratulations, Peter. You made it to the next level," Darlene said. She seemed relieved.

"I thought you said that it wasn't real," I said and dropped to my knees next to Paula. I grabbed her shoulders and started to gently shake her. "Paula! Can you hear me?! I'm sorry!" *Dammit.* "You need to come back now!"

"There's really no use at this point," David said as he sat down and stretched his legs out. "We know you were fortunate enough to come back from the dead. I guess she isn't as lucky as you." He put his hands behind his head.

"It was just a game! That's what you told me!"

"Relax, Peter. It is a game and you did a great job playing the game.

You are moving up in the world. There was just a little technical challenge. With technology, it's bound to happen. As if we needed a stronger argument to oppose its advancements. Case in point right here," he said and nodded towards Paula.

"You must be a little relieved, right?" Darlene asked. "You wouldn't have done it if you didn't think this was going to happen. A small part of you probably—probably—wished for a scenario like this."

"Is this what happened when you died, Peter?" David asked. "Is she on the other side now or does it take a while to get there?"

"It's not like you're getting on a plane and flying halfway across the world," I said. "You people are insane!"

"It's a fluke in the game," David said nonchalantly. "It's been known to happen every now and then. Honestly, I didn't think it would be an issue."

"We actually didn't think you would go through with it."

"A fluke in the game?!" I screamed at David.

"There's something that happens when a person realizes they are going to die in the game. It triggers something in their nervous system. I can't remember what it's called, but there's a medical term for it. It's a totally legitimate and above-board thing," he said and snapped his fingers together lightly as he tried to remember. "In a day or so it'll be moot."

"Cotard," Darlene said softly.

"That's right," David said.

"Excuse me?" I asked.

Oh God, the girls. I need to go home.

"Cotard delusion. It's a mental illness where someone thinks they're dead. They're a living and breathing human being, but they believe they're a ghost walking amongst the people. Surely, you must know what that feeling is like, right Peter?" David asked. "In this situation Paula believes she's dead because she saw you kill her and it caused the systems in her body to shut down. She believed she was dying, so by design, she died."

"It's weird. Her mind tricked her body," Darlene said. "It's remarkable how calm you are considering the circumstances."

"Peter," a voice said softly.

I looked down.

It was Paula. "You're such an asshole," she said and she opened her eyes.

She was covered in sweat.

She must have been out for three or four minutes total.

Enough to go to the other side and come back.

"Paula, are you okay?" I asked and leaned down towards her and put my hands on her shoulders.

She responded with pushing her arm out full force and slamming it into my nose.

I heard a soft cracking sound and tumbled back. "Ow! You broke my nose!"

"You tried to kill me, Peter!" she screamed at me.

"I can explain!"

"Yeah, explain it to the police!" she shouted at me as she left and slammed the front door.

31.

"Tell me about when Molly Cooper was killed," Skelly said.

"You don't want to listen, that's fine by me," Garrett said and looked up at the camera. "He doesn't want to listen to me, for the record!"

"They don't care about you," Skelly said.

"They should," Garrett said and cleared his throat and looked back at Skelly. "I brought her into the game. I was wearing the headset and I walked out of the room. I was told to find someone and I wasn't going to pick one of my buddies and I was high, okay? I walked out and she was standing there. I think there were some guys with her but I don't know. I scared them away," he said triumphantly. "Is that what you wanted?"

"You asked her to come in and play?"

"Yes. I asked her and there wasn't a struggle. We saw the kids harassing her and Barry sent me out there to bring her in. It was the perfect opportunity."

"How's that?"

"We had no connection to her and she was in the right place at the right time. At least, it was the right place and time for us. She probably feels differently."

"She's dead, in case you forgot."

"Right. Anyway, I went out with the helmet on and told her who I was and what we were doing in the room. I said VR and told her I needed her help."

"Why didn't you take the helmet off?"

"Because Miles is always watching," Garrett said and waved his hand towards the surveillance camera. "When I left the room I knew I was exposed and I didn't want anyone to know it was me. Same reason why you can't tell who went into the room. The owner let us in through the back where there aren't any cameras. There was no way to tell it was us."

"I have a warrant sitting with Miles, so they will hand over all the footage in the area that night. I can put the pieces together."

"Did they give you anything yet?" Garrett said but Skelly didn't respond. "That's what I thought. They probably won't either," he said and took a breath. His shoulders relaxed.

"I don't need them to give me anything. I already have some footage," Skelly said and reached into his jacket and pulled out his phone and set it on the table. He pressed the screen and the surveillance footage from the camera across the street from the Blue Bonnet started to play.

Garrett leaned over and watched intently. He winced when he saw the figure grab Molly by the throat and throw her to the ground.

"How did you get this?" Garrett asked cautiously.

"It's from an old surveillance camera that Miles overlooked," Skelly said. "Do you want to revise your story? You already confessed so you might as well go ahead. This doesn't look like you asking her to come inside."

"I didn't ask her," he said softly as his arrogance diminished. "I grabbed her by the neck and pulled her into the room. Barry and I held her down and someone else put the headset on her. Happy now? She was terrified and we forced her," he said as Skelly relaxed and retrieved his pen. "Once the headset was on her I went back into the game and got the rope that was given to me and tied it around her neck and strangled her," he stopped and looked down. Skelly thought the boy was about to cry, but he wasn't going to ask.

"And then what?"

"We brought her in to kill her. It's what they wanted. We needed to kill her to show that we were loyal to the game. It was only supposed to be a game. Like that woman at H-E-B."

"Excuse me?" Skelly asked and tapped his phone to stop the video.

"The woman they found dead at the grocery store. Same thing, except they killed her IRL and not in the game. Idiots. Some people will do anything to get off. People are monsters."

"Who did that?"

"Raul did that," Garrett said. "Manager of the meat department. He heard about *Stolen Planet* and wanted to play, but they wouldn't let him, so he killed someone IRL to prove his loyalty. He thought they would let him in once he killed her but he was wrong. See what I told you? People are monsters. It was off protocol and if people wanted to play and wanted to be included they needed to follow the rules but Raul didn't think the rules applied to him. If you couldn't follow some basic and clear rules you couldn't be trusted to help fulfill their objective."

"The annihilation?"

"You're catching on."

"I'm waiting on Miles to send the footage over from the store," Skelly said confidently.

"You won't get it. Raul figured out a way to disable the camera in that section of the store. He said so himself. He thought he was being clever. The murder was never recorded and Miles won't give you anything because they don't want to admit they messed up."

"What happened after you strangled her? In the game, I mean."

"Immediately after I was escorted to a night club and given copious amounts of alcohol and the company of some very beautiful women. They said it was my reward for completing one of the last levels."

"That's nice."

"That is until they charge you for it."

"What do you mean?"

"They charge you for stuff in the game, and it's expensive. They say they'll pay you back once you've completed the mission."

"Bitcoin or something, right?"

"That's what I thought until I checked my bank account. They were actually withdrawing money from my account. Thousands of dollars, and I'm not some rich kid like Barry. I can't afford a loss like that. Anyway, after I killed her—after the nightclub—Barry took my helmet off. He literally ripped it right off my head and pointed to the dead girl in our room. The girl we brought in there—the girl I strangled in a game—she was laying on the floor dead," Garrett said as the realization of what he did washed over him. "I killed her. Then we took the body outside and left it behind the hotel."

"You didn't call 911."

"Nah, man. They can trace that. With Miles watching everything, we figured they'd find the body soon enough and tip you off."

"Wow," Skelly said.

"What else was I supposed to do? She was dead."

"You should have taken responsibility for it!" Skelly shouted at him. "You should have not killed her and never been in that situation in the first place!"

"When I killed her I didn't think she would die! That's not how the game is supposed to work," Garrett said and Skelly thought about the Medical Examiner's report and how it determined that shock was the cause of death.

"Why are you confessing, Garrett?" Skelly asked. "Tell me. Why exactly are you here?"

"I can't stop playing," Garrett said. "I'm responsible for her death, I know that, but I can't walk away from the game. They have all my money. I need to finish the game. Once September fourth happens and we're successful, I'll get my money back, plus interest."

"What makes you think you'll get it back?"

"That's what they told me. Be a good soldier and you'll be rewarded. I've done what's required of me. I proved myself to them. I showed them that I was of value, but they said I have to wait just like everyone else. Once we launch Nitro Zeus and everything comes to a stop, we'll all go back to *Stolen Planet* and celebrate. The celebration that will put all other celebrations to shame."

"But if you're successful, you won't be able to play *Stolen Planet*," Skelly said. "Get it?"

"No. Nitro Zeus is designed to wipe out the technology infrastructure. Phones, televisions, the electric grid, computer networks, air traffic control. The reason why it can do this is because—"

"The implants," Skelly interjected, thinking back to his conversation with Travis.

"Right. *Stolen Planet* took those implants out. Took them out of the helmets, the consoles, the generators, everything. It's impervious," Garrett said. "If you aren't a member of *Stolen Planet* by September fourth, you'll be left to fend for yourself in what's left of the real world under the watchful eye of Miles. Are you a member of *Stolen Planet*, Skelly?" he asked.

Skelly shook his head. Based on what Travis told him, at least ninety-eight percent of the technology in the world had those implants.

"Has the routine of everyday police work worn you out and you're

tired of fighting the Miles Cooperative?" Garrett said. "Do you want
to be part of the revolution first hand? I can get you in."

"I don't need any favors from you. I've been to *Stolen Planet* and it's
a total hell hole."

"Nothing's perfect. Why did you go?"

"It's part of my investigation," Skelly said. "Just a formality."

"But you're intrigued, no?" Garrett asked but Skelly kept staring at
him. "What's your safe word, Skelly?"

There was a knock on the door.

"You got a second, Skelly?" Erin said as she leaned her head in.

"Sure. What is it?"

"There's a call for you."

"Great. Who is it?"

"It's Peter Richards's wife."

"Peter Richards?" Skelly said. "Give me a break."

"She sounds pretty upset."

"Who's Peter Richards?" Garrett asked.

"Mind your own business," Skelly snapped at him.

"You want to take it?" Erin asked.

"Sure. Give me a second, okay? Also, can you see if someone can
take him to county?"

"Come on, man!" Garrett said. "After all that I've done for you? I
need to be in San Antonio in twelve hours!"

"San Antonio?"

"Yes, I need to be there to make sure Nitro Zeus infiltrates success-
fully. I'm the eyes on the ground there."

"Oh, and can you also get someone from Homeland Security on
the phone?" Skelly asked.

"Sure," Erin said.

"Tell them it's about—" Skelly said and stopped. He looked over
at Garrett.

"Red Mercury," Garrett said.

"Right, that's it," Skelly said and snapped his fingers.

"That sounds scary," Erin said.

"There's going to be a ... some sort of event. Right, Garrett?"

"September fourth. Saturday."

"That's this weekend!" Erin said and smiled.

"Brace yourself," Garrett said.

"In San Antonio, apparently."

"Everywhere!"

"It's some right-wing gamer conspiracy nonsense, Erin. Don't think twice about, it but let's cross our t's on this one and be thorough. I want to be able to sleep at night knowing that everything is okay," Skelly said and looked at Garrett. "Do you also think global warming was invented by the left-wing extremists to help promote and sell green energy?"

"I do think that. Don't you? Didn't you know that Pope Francis was picked by the New World Order?" Garrett said. "They need a consistent and inspirational figure to reinforce their agenda. What sort of propaganda have you been reading?"

"Oh, I see how this works," Skelly said. "You think the danger is some secret elite government group who wants to take all of our money, right? That must it be it, otherwise it would be the armed faction of the narco-Nazi-jihadist international terrorists who want a Krispy Kreme on every street corner."

"Don't patronize me."

"My bad. It's probably the Jewish-Marxism mafia working with the CIA and Mossad to decide who the lead in the next James Bond movie will be. Am I getting close?" Skelly asked.

"I can come back," Erin said.

"No. We're finished here," Skelly said and got up from his chair and walked over to the door and turned towards Erin. She was standing against the door frame with one leg up so her knee was sticking out. Skelly thought she smelled nice. "Don't let him leave the room until an officer can take him to the jail."

"You got it," she said and flipped her hair from one shoulder to the other and smiled at him.

"Thanks, and let me know when you get Homeland on the phone. I want to make sure we don't have a global catastrophe on our hands."

"Sure. Can't have that, can we?" she said. "It's after eight on a Friday. I'll see what I can do."

"Get the NSA and the FBI's cyber-security task force, too, while you're at it."

"Why?" she asked. Skelly saw the concern on her face.

"I'm following the necessary steps. Doing what's expected. Everything's okay, though. We could be saving lives here, Erin," Skelly said as he walked out of the room and over to his desk.

"Peter's wife is on line two," Erin shouted out as he picked up the phone and pressed down on the talk button.

"Hello?"

"Is this Detective Skelly?" a woman's voice said on the other end of the phone. She was breathing heavily and Skelly could feel the panic on the other end of the phone.

"It is. Is everything okay, Mrs. Richards?"

"No. It's not," Paula said. "Peter tried to kill me."

"Excuse me? What happened?"

"We were ... we were playing a game and he shot me."

"What? What game?"

"Yes. Virtual Reality. It's when you enter a world where—well, it's a different world—it's not real. Something altered."

"I've heard of it. Where are you right now?"

"At the house."

"Is Peter with you?"

"No."

"I'll be right there," he said and hung up. He turned back to the interrogation room. Erin was standing in front of the door, guarding it. "Erin, let's go!"

"What about this guy?" she said and tapped on the door with her middle finger.

"Get one of the traffic guys to sit on him. We need to go now!"

32.

"How do you feel?" Darlene asked me. She was standing across from me in their living room. David went to relieve himself.

"I feel strange," I said as a tingle went down my left arm. "She looked pissed."

"She was pissed," Darlene said. "But she'll get over it."

Paula ran off minutes ago, and when I went after her she turned to me with a defiant look on her face that said, "Don't you dare come after me." Usually that wouldn't stop me and I would chase after her but she took the car and screamed, "You're a dead man, Peter!" out the car window as she drove away. "This is just a small blip in a much bigger and more important timeline. She'll come to understand one day. You'll be regarded as a hero."

"Did I prove myself?" I asked.

"Global assurance in the dollar is a great example of collective faith in something abstract," Darlene said. "And besides, who are we to say where the line is between our life and a game or reality and virtual reality? Isn't it all the same anyway? Same feelings, same motivations and aspirations. Whether you tried to kill her in the game—a world generated and produced on computers from the mind and imagination of mankind—or whether you tried to kill her out here in real life. The intent was still the same."

"Lest you not forget, Peter," David said as he came back in to the living room zipping up his pants, "they betrayed you."

"All three of them," Darlene added. "Paula, and Joyce and Maya by association. They want to go back to Russia and leave you here by yourself. You're a lone wolf now."

I felt as if I was suffocating and water was slowly rising around me.

The proof was there in Cleft's client list. My wife and daughters had requested a new identity. Better yet, they requested Paula's and Joyce's Russian family name so they could move back to the homeland and start all over again without Peter, despite Paula's explanation otherwise. "What do I do now?" I asked.

"Get them back, of course," David said. "So many people think good enough is good enough, but it isn't, Peter. Every word matters. Every action matters and thought matters. Every pixel matters and details govern everything. Average loses. Own it." He put both hands on my shoulders and looked me in the eye. "Are you gonna be a man or a loser?"

"A man," I said. I felt a small fleeting sense of relief.

There was a solution to this problem and it was up to me to solve.

"Great. Then show them. Call Miles and tell him you'll be there this weekend."

"I told him before we came over. I already made that decision."

"That's what I like to hear. There is a man in you after all," he said and vigorously shook my shoulders.

"What next?" I asked.

Darlene was about to respond, but there was a knock on the door. David took his hands off my shoulders and went over and opened the door.

"Cleft," I said to myself. "Jesus."

"Peter, Cleft. Cleft, Peter," David said as Cleft stepped in. He was carrying a black steel briefcase. "I believe you two know each other."

"Hi, Peter," Cleft said. He was wearing khaki shorts and a burnt orange fishing shirt. Tomorrow was the season opener. Texas versus Maryland.

"Hey, dick," I said back to him. "Your beard implant looks like garbage. You aren't fooling anyone."

"Easy there, Peter. He's here to help."

"Oh, yeah? He's been so helpful before. What are you going to help with?"

"I'm going to remove your heart."

33.

"Excuse me?" I said and looked at Cleft, hoping he would elaborate.

"If you keep your ɘ-zero heart, you're susceptible to Nitro Zeus," Cleft said.

"Quiet," Darlene said and held a finger up to Cleft's lips and motioned to Cleft's wrist.

"Oh, right," Cleft said and slipped off his watch and handed it to Darlene. She went into the kitchen and placed it in the Faraday box.

"Don't you need to put that in the shed, too?" I shouted.

"Look who's paranoid now," Darlene said.

"The radio frequency identifiers in your heart will pick up the signal Zeus sends out. Once they receive the signals your heart with shut down so we need to take it out. It's not paranoia, it's caution," Cleft said.

"You know about this?" I asked Cleft and gestured towards David and Darlene. "You know what my new best friends are up to? Crazy VR games and alternate worlds."

"Just recently and only pieces of it. They were pretty tight-lipped about it," Cleft said. "David called me up and said they needed a surgeon who is available now and who can be paid under the table, and well, I have a lot of connections."

"Yet there is no one with you," I said defiantly.

"Oh, but there is," he said and raised the black steel case he was holding.

"What is that?"

"This is Kimberly. She has an MD from the Harvard School of Medicine and did her residency at the Mayo Clinic."

"You're holding a briefcase, Cleft," I said.

"But it's so much more than a briefcase, and let's keep the talking to

239

a minimum, shall we? Avery and I have a party to get to. Tomorrow is the first game. My time is valuable."

"Avery? Avery hates football," I said.

"Yet he humors me every year," Cleft said.

"It's vulnerable," David said. "If you keep your Ə-zero there's a chance you won't make it out of this alive. We're going to remove your Ə-zero system and replace it with Nitro Zeus."

"Replace it?!"

"We don't trust you, Peter," Darlene said. "And I know what you're thinking—'We've been through a lot'—but we still think you're a flight risk."

"No," I said and put my hand up to signal to Cleft that I wasn't having it. "I'm not going to do this."

"Let me remind you of something, Peter." It was David's turn now to persuade me. "You've spent the last ten years of your life with that thing, and what has it gotten you? A better, healthier lifestyle? A better sense of who you are and more years on your life? For what? Five or ten extra years to spend with your kids? We know how they feel about you, don't we?"

"Screw you guys."

"You raised your kids. Joyce is great and Maya is going to be fine without you. You need to think about doing something for yourself and something for the good of mankind."

"He's not even that healthy now," Cleft interrupted. "I caught him the other night eating red meat and drinking bourbon."

"Shame on you!" Darlene said and looked at me with dissatisfaction.

"Do you mind?" Cleft asked and pointed towards the kitchen.

"By all means," David said and led Cleft and Kimberly into the kitchen. Cleft set the briefcase down on the kitchen counter. It was approximately one foot by two feet and could easily fit into the overhead compartment of an airplane. Cleft rolled his fingers around on the combination lock until the locks on either side of the case popped open.

"Is it *Fuck Peter?* Is that what the combination was?" I asked.

"Yes," Cleft said and opened the case.

Darlene and I leaned over and looked inside.

"What is that?" Darlene asked.

There was a small battery pack tucked into the top of the case and the main compartment had a silver lining and contained two metal arms that were folded across each other.

A prosthetic hand was attached to the end of each metal arm. One of the prosthetic hands was holding a scalpel and the other was holding a five-inch medical clamp.

"She's a heart surgeon. She can do a triple bypass in under an hour," Cleft said. "Did I mention she did her residency at the Mayo Clinic?"

"I was uncertain before but it's clear as day now," I said. "Cleft Duvall hates my guts."

"You did good, Cleft," David said.

"Who knows, Peter, maybe you and Kimberly will make a love connection. One robot to another," Cleft said.

"Do you know what these two are up to?" I asked Cleft. "Do you know the extent of my involvement with them?" Cleft shook his head. "If you're helping them out, it's important you understand why."

"They paid me and you'll suffer so I'm happy," Cleft said.

"They're going to launch a virus that is going to wipe out all technology."

"You too, Peter," David said. "Don't try and distance yourself now. We've come so far together."

"It's going to destroy our infrastructure and cripple our economy and economies around the world," I said. "Did they tell you that?"

"Don't be ridiculous," Cleft said and waved me off. "David and Darlene used to own a pool cleaning company in Florida and they came to Austin to escape some bad debts."

"That's not true," I said. I was exasperated. "They are members of an online community—a virtual reality community—that's recruiting people to become part of a revolution."

"Annihilation," David corrected.

"Can't it be both?" Darlene asked. "Can't we be escaping bad debt and be part of an online community that wants to destroy technology?"

"Virtual Reality?" Cleft asked. He looked at David and Darlene and started to seem concerned.

"It's a game that was designed to be undetectable by Miles because it wants to destroy Miles," I said.

"That's interesting," Cleft said and then smiled at David and Darlene. "He's ridiculous, isn't he?" Cleft started laughing. David and Darlene started laughing with him and they all looked at me like I was some sort of a nut case.

"I am so tired of your bullshit, Peter! It's always you versus the world. You're such a wronged man."

"Cleft, you're not being a very good friend," I said.

"Oh, Peter. You're always such a martyr," Cleft said and pulled a syringe from an inside pocket in the briefcase.

He took the cap off and squirted some of the fluid into the air and then quickly jabbed the syringe into my shoulder.

"What was that?"

"It's a horse sedative," he said. "You'll feel the effects in ten or twenty seconds and you won't feel anything once you're out. Given your history of addiction and questionable choices, you'll probably enjoy it. You should come around in an hour or so, as soon as Kimberly is finished sewing your chest back up."

"You're a terrible friend," I said.

"I'm the best friend you have. You'll thank me later," he said and that was the last thing he said before I arched my arm back, swung it around and pounded my fist into his left cheek.

I heard a small crack and blood and saliva shot out of his face and landed on David's shirt.

I watched as Cleft dropped to the floor and smacked his head on the laminate.

He deserved it.

I heard David and Darlene shouting. They were outraged, but their voices slowly faded and their faces soon became fuzzy.

The sedative took effect and I blacked out.

34.

"Hit the damn gas!" Skelly shouted at Erin as they weaved their way south on Red River Street towards Cesar Chavez.

It was late Friday night and Red River was packed with students and suburbanites out to catch the latest in the Austin music scene. Erin slammed on the brakes as two kids passed in front of their cruiser and flipped them off. "The gas, not the breaks!" Skelly shouted at her. He was lit.

"I almost ran over those assholes."

"It's a write-off," Skelly said. "Take this down to Cesar Chavez and take a right."

"It's too crowded."

"It's the only way."

"Yes, sir," she said and looked out her window. They were stopped in front of Esther's Follies, a modern-day vaudeville-style theater. "You ever seen a show there?" She pointed across Skelly's chest.

"Comedy is dead, Erin," he said. "Everyone knows that."

"You're a downer," she said and smiled at him.

He smiled back.

The moment was interrupted by a buzzing in Skelly's pocket. He pulled out his phone and answered it.

"This is Skelly."

"Detective Skelly, this is Agent Kyle Brisco with Homeland Security," a young voice said on the other end of the phone. "How are you this evening?"

"I'm good," Skelly said.

"Do you have a few minutes to chat, sir?"

"Sure. What's up?"

"In person, Detective."

"I'm sort of in the middle of something right now."

"It's regarding what you called about. Your partner left a message."

"Oh, the Red—" Skelly started to say and snapped his fingers at Erin.

"Skelly, can you tell your partner to make a stop at the Four Seasons. I'll buy you and your lovely partner a drink."

"The Four Seasons?"

"That's correct. It will only take a few minutes."

"I'm sorry Agent Brisco, but we are—"

"See you shortly, Detective," Agent Brisco said and hung up the phone.

"Who was it?" Erin asked.

"Some juvie who said he was from Homeland Security and wants to buy us a drink."

"The Four Seasons?" Erin asked and quickly glanced over at Skelly.

"If you like that sort of thing. Sitting in a hotel bar watching transients from every walk of life," Skelly said. "It's no JW. I'll tell you that."

"I won't discriminate if you won't," Erin said.

"We don't have time," Skelly insisted.

"We'll make time," Erin said as she took a hard right on to Cesar Chavez and then an immediate left into the entrance of the Four Seasons hotel.

The Four Seasons used to be the go-to luxury hotel of downtown Austin. That was until the market saturated and hotels started opening on every street corner. The Four Seasons was still a luxurious and top-of-its-class brand, but it was now almost indistinguishable from the dozen or so other luxury hotels in the downtown area. Given the smorgasbord of options, Skelly didn't understand why people still chose the Four Seasons. He suspected the federal government gave its employees a discounted rate. In fact, he thought anyone staying there was getting some sort of backroom deal.

"Are you checking in?" the valet attendant said as Skelly and Erin emerged from the car.

"We'll be a quick second."

"Of course," the attendant said and handed Erin a valet ticket.

"Thanks," she said and took the ticket. "If we aren't back in ten, you can forget about us, if you get my drift," she said and smiled.

"Of course, ma'am."

"We'll be back in five," Skelly said as they entered the vacant lobby. He looked around. Past the lobby a band was playing in the bar area. Past the band a young man was standing by the bar. Skelly locked eyes with him and he raised his glass in Skelly's direction. "Let's go." Skelly signaled towards the bar.

"Detective Skelly, I presume? I'm Agent Brisco," the young man said. Skelly thought he was thirteen, maybe fourteen, years old. His head was shaved, with the exception of a small patch of hair down the middle. Surely they don't let kids into bars these days.

"This is Erin. She's my partner," Skelly said.

"Nice to meet you," Agent Brisco said and proffered his hand in Erin's direction.

"Likewise. Skelly and I always go to the JW up the street. This is nice!"

"We got your message," Agent Brisco said.

"Message?" Skelly asked as the bartender came over and set down two highball glasses.

"Fuzzy navels?" the kid asked and gently pushed the drinks near Skelly and Erin.

"Don't mind if I do," Erin said and picked up her drink. She looked over at Skelly. "We called them about the ... Red Mercury." She mouthed the words.

"Right," Skelly said and considered his drink and then looked up at the kid. "Couldn't deal with this matter over the phone?"

"No. The connection isn't secure, as I am sure you know," Agent Brisco said. "Nothing is secure these days. There's no way to tell who's listening in on our calls."

"But yet here we are sitting in the wide open of a hotel bar," Skelly said and looked up at the closed circuit cameras over the bar.

"Nah. We're okay. The security cameras here have been broken for at least six months," Agent Brisco said as a thought occurred to him.

"Everything okay?" Erin asked and took a sip of her drink.

Agent Brisco reached down below the bar and lifted up a Gucci gancini-embossed computer case.

"Fancy," Erin said.

"Hand me your phones."

"Excuse me?"

"I'm going to need you to hand me your phones," he said.

Skelly pulled his phone out and handed it to him.

Agent Brisco put the phone in the computer case and looked at Erin.

"Fine," she said and handed it over. He put her phone in the case and pulled out a small black cube and set it on the bar. He pressed down on a small button on the top of the cube.

"It's a white noise machine," Agent Brisco said. "It distorts any frequency a device might pick up within ten feet."

"Red Mercury," Skelly said. "What can you tell me about it?"

"Nothing," Agent Brisco said and then saw the impatience appear on Skelly's face. "Because it doesn't exist."

"What do you mean, it doesn't exist?" Skelly said pointedly. "I got a guy sitting in a room downtown telling me it's real and that it disappeared from a research lab in Sweden—"

"North Carolina," Erin corrected.

"It's a Chinese thing."

"A Chinese thing?"

"I mean, the Chinese invented it," Agent Brisco said.

"So it is real."

"To the contrary. The Chinese invented it to undermine American interests."

"I'm not following," Skelly said.

"The Chinese government flooded their media channels with stories about how the United States was developing an odorless and tasteless powder that could wipe out an entire city within minutes. It was to protect Chinese investments abroad and limit the amount of defectors. Ultimately it was a bluff and was about power."

"Fear America. Be faithful to China," Erin said.

"Pretty much," Agent Brisco said. "Whatever this guy in the interrogation room is telling you is totally bogus. He must have read about it somewhere. There's no doomsday scenario here."

"Thanks for the insight, Brisco. We have places to be," Skelly said and took a long hard sip of his fuzzy navel. He felt slightly relieved.

"Safe travels, Skelly," Agent Brisco said as he pulled out the Gucci gancini-embossed computer case and handed them their phones.

Skelly and Erin left the bar and got back into their cruiser.

Erin drove them west across Cesar Chavez towards the west side of town. She bypassed Mopac and drove past Zilker Park and then cut down through Rollingwood, an affluent suburb outside of downtown.

She gently slid the car into the driveway when they reached Peter and Paula's house.

The garage door was open and a car was parked in the middle of the garage at a slight angle.

The trunk was open.

Erin and Skelly got out.

Skelly went and looked inside the trunk of the car as Erin approached the front door and rang the doorbell.

"Trunk is empty," Skelly said.

"What did you think was going to be in there?" Erin asked.

"You know they never found Hoffa," Skelly said. "In fact, they never really found Elvis either or Amelia Earhart or D.B. Cooper. There's a reason why people don't like flying."

"Who's D.B. Cooper?" Erin asked as Paula opened the front door.

"Took you long enough," she said.

"Traffic," Skelly said and motioned his hand towards Erin. "This is Erin. My partner. She doesn't know who D.B. Cooper is."

"Who's D.B. Cooper?" Paula asked.

"You two will get along great," Skelly said.

"Your trunk's open," Erin said politely and gestured towards the garage.

"That's right. I'm leaving."

"Where are you headed?" Skelly asked.

"Come with me," Paula said and made her way back into the house and into the kitchen. "The girls are asleep upstairs."

Erin and Skelly followed her. Erin looked around. "I like your house."

"Some post-future shit Peter was into," Paula said. "That's what you get when you marry half a man."

"Are you leaving the girls here or are they going with you?"

"Of course, they're coming with me," Paula said with a short and calculated tone. "Can I get either of you something to drink?"

"I'm good. Thanks," Erin said as she looked around the kitchen. There was a large suitcase sitting on the kitchen table.

"Tell us what happened, Paula," Skelly said.

"Peter tried to kill me and I would like to press charges."

"Where is he now?"

"Who knows? He took me over to an acquaintance's house to play some incredibly ridiculous game, and he shot me!" she said incredulously.

"He shot you?" Erin said and looked Paula up and down. "Are you okay?"

"Of course I'm not okay. My husband tried to kill me!" she said. "It was in the game but I could feel it."

"*Stolen Planet*," Skelly said softly.

"Oh, you know of this! You must be an insane person too, right?" Paula said, but Skelly didn't respond. He looked at Erin and then back at Paula and the suitcase on the table. It was packed to the brim with clothes and various pictures of Paula and the girls.

"What is it?"

"Did he say anything to you? Before he tried to kill you."

"He said they had a very special assignment for him and he was going to change the world."

"Peter is up to something."

"No shit he's up to something!"

"Who are the acquaintances? I am going to need their address and names," Skelly said, but before Paula could respond, they heard a voice say, "Mommy."

"What was that?" Erin asked.

"Nothing."

"Mommy," the voice said again and the door that lead to the garage opened slightly and Joyce peaked her head in. "Are you coming?" she asked softly. She was wearing pajamas.

"I'll be right there, honey," Paula said. "How's your sister?"

"She's still asleep," Joyce said.

"Go back to the car."

"Where's Dad?" Joyce asked as she looked at Erin and Skelly.

"Go back to the car, okay?"

"Sure, Mommy," Joyce said and shut the door.

"I thought you said they were asleep upstairs," Erin asked but Skelly put his hand out to stop her.

"Who are the acquaintances?" Skelly asked again. "I am going to need their names and address."

"David and Darlene—whatever. Their daughter goes to gymnastics with Joyce. Peter saw them and thought they were suspicious so he decided to stalk them."

"Suspicious?" Erin asked.

"Yes. Suspicious-looking, making doubtful choices. I don't know! It's how my husband sees the world."

"Where do they live?"

"Over on Johnny Miller Trail. Second house on the left," Paula said. "Can you make sure my husband suffers for what he tried to do to me?" Skelly gave her an indecisive nod. "Give me a second. I need to check on my girls." Paula grabbed the suitcase and went into the garage.

"What is it?" Erin asked Skelly.

"There's a connection between them and Garrett and what happened at the Blue Bonnet," Skelly said. "I think Miles is planning on doing something dangerous."

"Red Mercury?"

"It's possible."

"But you heard him. He said it didn't exist."

"I know what he said, but that's what he's supposed to say," Skelly said as they heard the garage door close. Skelly went to the front of the house and looked out the front window.

Paula backed the car out of the garage and drove away.

"Shit."

"It's okay. Let her go."

"Where do you suppose she's going?"

"Somewhere far away, probably," Skelly said and pulled his car keys out and went outside to the cruiser. Erin followed him and they drove slowly through the hills of Lost Creek and over to Johnny Miller Trail. Erin took a right onto Johnny Miller Trail and stopped in front of the second house on the left.

It was engulfed in flames.

35.

I felt emptiness in my chest cavity when I came to.

At first I thought I was dead. At long last, Peter Richards was finally dead. For sure dead, and absolutely positively dead this time. There was no purgatory and no uncertain middle ground in this scenario. I could smell rotten week-old peanuts and the sweat of athletic socks drifting through the air. That was the smell of death that I knew and loved so well. No more responsibility and no more worrying about my children's well being and the mortgage on my house. No more sleepless nights thinking about where my next paycheck will come from. Relief and satisfaction washed over me like waves attacking the shoreline.

I felt relaxed and absolved from life's responsibilities.

Death would be nirvana and freedom from the discomfort of life.

Paula would be better without me.

She would be happier. The girls would struggle, at first, but they would grow up and the images and memories of me would slowly fade. It would be expedited when Paula met a man and fell in love. Maybe he would be a real man, a full human with no robotic accompaniments. Or perhaps Paula would find herself falling for someone more advanced and in touch with his own technological capabilities. For certain though, whomever Paula fell for would ask her to tell him about the late and great Peter Richards and what he did to save the world. He'd ask so incessantly that Paula would get agitated with him and long for the days with a do-nothing Peter Richards.

The memories were interrupted by the sound of a car running over gravel.

I opened my eyes and I found myself curled up in the back seat of David and Darlene's car.

The sunlight hit my eyes.

David was driving and turned back to look at me. "Hey, buddy," he said.

"What time is it?" I asked.

"You were out for a while. Almost twelve hours."

"Where's Cleft?"

"He left last night. Today is game day, sport," he said and held up his hand and bent his middle and ring fingers down under his thumb while leaving up his pinky and pointer to make the ubiquitous "hook 'em" sign that Texas football fans know and love. "Am I doing that right?" He took his eyes off the road.

"Perfect," I said as I lifted my head up and gazed out the window. We were still in the neighborhood. I thought for a second that I saw Skelly drive past us but I couldn't tell for certain. I felt light-headed and woozy and my chest was burning.

"Not much of a football fan?" David said as Darlene snickered. "They lynch you in Texas for saying stuff like that."

"Where are we going?" I asked.

"First, we are going to stop and get some tacos and coffee and then we're going to go out to Burnet to Falkenstein Castle. Miles is expecting you," David said as we continued through the neighborhood. I looked down at my hand.

My Ә-zero monitor was gone. "Where's my monitor?"

"You don't need it anymore, Peter," Darlene said.

I reached my hand into my pocket to pull out my phone but it wasn't there. Darlene held it up so I could see it and then tossed it back to me.

I looked at the screen.

There was a text message from Miles: See you soon, Peter.

"When did he send this?"

"A few minutes ago," Darlene said. "We also threw out your medications, too."

"Why did you do that? I need those."

"You thought you needed your Ә-zero, too, but you seem to be doing fine without, am I right?" Darlene said as we pulled into a crowded parking lot on the outside of the neighborhood. I was familiar with this place and used to spend my mornings here sipping black coffee. How I longed for the good old days. David pulled the car into a handicap spot and Darlene jumped out and ran into the coffee shop.

David looked back at me. "When this is all done, and you do your thing and we do ours, let's meet here," he said.

"Where? Here?" I said.

He pulled a folded light blue sticky note from his pocket and handed it to me. "Here," he said. I unfolded it.

Robert Mueller Municipal Airport

"The old airport?" I asked.

"The studios behind the airport. Stage four," he said. The Robert Mueller Airport was the first municipal airport built in Austin and was replaced by the Austin-Bergstrom Airport a few miles northeast of downtown. It was named after Robert Mueller, the city commissioner who died while he was in office. The old airport has been turned into a residential community that shares the old airport with Austin Studios. "You clear on what you need to do?" he asked. I nodded. "Great. Darlene and I will drop you at the entrance to the castle. Miles added you to the guest list so you shouldn't have any problem getting inside. You won't be allowed to take anything inside with you. No phone, no watches, computers. You get the idea. You're going to go through a scanner and the alarm will go off. When they take you aside, tell them it's your mechanical heart, and if they give you a hard time tell them to speak to Miles."

"But you took it out."

"So you lie. We replaced it with the virus but don't tell them that, for obvious reasons."

"So the virus is setting off the alarm?"

"More like the metal box containing the virus is setting off the alarm."

"A metal box?!" I said, suddenly becoming acutely aware of a small metal box that was recently added to my chest cavity.

"Darlene videotaped the whole thing if you don't believe us," he said and reached over the seat to hand me his phone.

"Maybe later," I said.

"Don't worry so much about the details. They aren't going to cut you open right there. Tell them to get Miles and you'll be good," David said. "Do you always worry this much?"

"Is it inside me?" I said as I moved my hand up to my chest.

I pressed my hand down on my heart. My skin and nerves felt tender but I couldn't feel any sort of metal box. I pressed down again. Still nothing except a slight twinge of pain. I was going to have to take his word for it, unfortunately.

"Easy there, buddy. I don't want you setting that thing off before you absolutely need to."

"How do I set it off? When it's time, I mean."

"Just say these four little words," he said and handed me a piece of paper with four words written on it: *The future is ours.* "The wireless signals will do the rest."

"The future is—"

"Jeeze, don't say it now, Peter. That would defeat the point of doing this."

"The box recognizes my voice?"

"Correct. Once you activate it, it will send a signal to all the sub-boxes. Atlanta, San Antonio ... they're all connected. You get the point."

"And that's it?"

"Cleft left this for you," David said and handed me a box of 1972 Topps One baseball cards. "He said you shouldn't leave valuable stuff lying around your house." I took the box from David and ran my hand over the shrink-wrap. "Wait until later before you open it, okay?"

"Sure," I said as Darlene got back in the car with two medium-sized paper bags and two cups of coffee. She handed one of them to me along with one of the bags. I looked inside. It had two cinnamon rolls and three breakfast tacos.

"Eat up," she said and smiled at me. "Let's see what the real Peter Richards it made of, shall we?" She handed the other cup of coffee to David as we left the parking lot and headed west on Bee Cave Parkway and began our journey out towards Burnet. The trip took a little over an hour and was forty-five minutes too long. David drove ten miles under the speed limit the entire time. He said he didn't want to draw attention to us, but I think he was buying time so he could finish the audio book he was listening to. *Be Obsessed or Be Average.*

I could sense that Darlene was irritated but she wasn't saying anything.

We conveniently reached our destination when the last chapter was finished. David stopped the car at the bottom of the road that led up to Falkenstein Castle, a massive stone structure that stood in the middle of Texas hill country.

"This is as far as we take you," David said and pointed to the door for me to get out. I reached over and gently pushed the door open.

"Where are you guys going?"

"Oh, one more thing, Peter," David said and looked at me. Darlene turned and faced me, too. "Godspeed, my friend."

"OK," I said and got out of the car and shut the door.

"See you on the other side," Darlene said as they drove away.

36.

"This is Detective Skelly. Badge two-thirty-six. I need fire and rescue. Address is twelve nineteen Johnny Miller Trail. Can you go quickly on this? We don't need the whole neighborhood catching on fire," Skelly said into his phone as he and Erin got back into the patrol car. "They say they'll get around to it by Monday." He put his seatbelt on. "Let's go." But Erin didn't turn the car on. She wasn't even putting on her seatbelt. "Let's go Erin. What's the problem? I don't need to sit here and watch the house burn down."

"Skelly," Erin said gently and pulled something out of her pocket and set two folded pieces of paper down on the dashboard.

"What is that?"

"The tickets to Vegas Reynolds gave us," she said. "Flight leaves tonight."

"He gave them to me, actually. You sort of managed to work your way into the situation simply by being in the same place as me at the right time."

"Come on, Skelly," she said as a ball of fire shot out of the downstairs window in David and Darlene's house. Skelly could feel the heat on his cheek.

"Fine," Skelly said. "You can take someone if you want. You've done a fairly sufficient job helping me out here. It's the least I could do for you. I'm perfectly capable of handling this doomsday scenario on my own."

"It's not a doomsday scenario. The FBI guy said so himself," Erin said. "People want to think the world is ending so they can rationalize buying more of the shit they don't need."

"You're starting to sound like me. Take the tickets. Have fun.

Everything will be fine here," Skelly said and reached his arm out and put it carefully on her shoulder and gave it a soft quick squeeze.

"But that's the thing. I want to go with you," she said. Skelly looked at her and then at the house as it slowly crumbled to the ground.

"The fire department sure takes a long time. It's really an infrastructure issue, if you ask me. Not enough space on the road for the fire trucks."

"Are you listening to me? I told you I want to go with you to Vegas. I want you to take me."

"To Vegas?"

"Yes, Skelly," Erin said with a tinge of impatience in her voice. "I think we have something." She reached her hand out and put it on the edge of his thigh. He let his legs and knees relax a little bit. "You feel it too?" She moved her hand closer to his crotch.

"Erin," he said softly.

"What, Skelly? I know things are complicated. If that's what you were going to say. I like things when they are complicated. I like solving problems."

"We should go."

"Come on," she said and reached her fingers out until they stopped on his crotch. "Are you worried about what I might think about you and Nicole?" She rubbed her fingers lightly on the outside of his department-issued black pants. "I don't care about you and Nicole so don't even think about going there right now."

"This is highly unprofessional, Erin."

"I'll tell them you went easy on me at the interrogation panel," she said and kept rubbing. "You know Nicole and Travis are screwing each other right?"

"I do," Skelly said and looked up at the ceiling of the patrol car and closed his eyes.

"That's right. Of course you do. That's what detectives do. They dick around and figure stuff out."

"God, that feels good."

"You want to dick around?"

"Don't stop."

"I bet he's a shit lay. Rumor has it these robots can't control themselves. State of the art technology and they can't last two minutes," she said. "But I bet you can."

"Keep going."

"You want me, Skelly?"

"Right there, Erin ..."

"Damn, you're hard as a steel. Take me, Detective," she said.

Skelly opened his eyes, stared at the ceiling of the car and put his hand down on her wrist to make her stop. "Don't make me stop, Skelly. You like this."

"I can't, Erin," he said and moved her hand carefully away.

"Don't be so gentle with me. I can handle you," she said and reached for the zipper on his pants but he held her hands back. "Let go of me!" She pushed his hands away and then let out a small smile.

"Erin, you're not paying attention," Skelly said. "We need to go right now. We can finish this later."

"God, you're so cerebral. This is devastating. You need a damn safe word or something?"

"What?" he said.

"You need a safe word to make this easier for you? In case you hit troubled waters," she said.

"Nash Bridges," he said and let go of her hands.

"Excuse me?"

"What?"

"You said Nash Bridges."

"I did?"

"You totally did," she said as she pulled her hands back.

"Don't stop."

"No. You're right. We need to go," she said and started to turn her body back towards the steering wheel of the car.

Skelly reached out and grabbed her and pulled her back towards him. He kissed her and pulled her in closer to him. The next few minutes were a blur. Erin unzipped his pants and he pulled her over so she was on top of him in the passenger seat. He pushed her skirt up until it was past her hips and ran his hands over the outside of her legs. The humidity outside made them sweaty and sleek. Skelly liked that.

"Come on, Skelly. Clock is ticking," she said as he pulled her panties down and slid inside of her. "Jesus. Skelly. Damn steel," she said. He pushed his hands down on her lower back and thrust inside of her. She let out a soft moan and clenched her lips with her teeth. Skelly took one hand and ran it up her chest. "Keep going," she said and he thrust inside of her again and pressed his pelvis against her. "Damn," she said as they came.

When they finished, Erin started laughing and punched Skelly's chest. "That was good," she said and rolled back to the driver's seat. "It's hot in here."

Skelly looked over at the burning house. "Erin, let's go."

"I'm on it," she said and started the engine and drove down the street.

They took their first right and passed a fire truck as they headed out of the neighborhood and drove an hour west towards Burnet. When they hit Burnet they went north for another twenty minutes until they reached a winding road that took them up to Falkenstein Castle. The castle was built by a local developer in the mid-nineties who was inspired by the castles in Germany. Skelly thought it might be nice to have that kind of disposable income.

They went by a dozen or so police cruisers and large SUVs as they made their way towards the entrance. Skelly nodded at the police officers, but didn't recognize any of them.

Erin slammed on the breaks when they reached the entrance to the castle.

A security guard came over to the driver's side window. He had two hand guns in his utility belt and semi-automatic strapped around his back. "Turn the car around, lady," he said as he leaned down and looked inside the car.

"I'm dropping him off," Erin said and pointed at Skelly.

"What's your name?" the guard said and looked at Skelly.

"Detective Skelly. Austin Police," he said and waved his badge.

"Turn the car around, lady, and go home," the guard said. "No police."

"Come on," Skelly said and the guard set his eyes on him and didn't flinch. Skelly kept his badge up.

"You're blocking the gate," the guard said.

Skelly looked past the guard and at the security office next to the gate. There were a few guards inside talking to a man that Skelly recognized. Average height, average build, slight slouch, and no distinctive attributes at all. He was so bland he was unmistakable.

"Richards," Skelly said.

"What?" Erin said.

"That's Peter Richards," Skelly said and pointed at the guard house. "I know that guy." He unbuckled his seatbelt.

"Stay in the car, sir!" the guard said as Skelly opened the door and emerged from the car. "Get back in the car!" The guard drew his firearm. A guard on the other side of the car drew his firearm.

"I need to speak to that man, right now," Skelly said.

"Get back in the car or we'll have you arrested," the guard said.

"I'm a cop!" Skelly shouted and waved his badge. "Peter! Peter!! It's me!!" Peter looked out and locked eyes with Skelly. "Peter! I need to talk to you."

Peter was about to say something, but a door to the guard's office opened and an older gentleman walked in and shook Peter's hand.

Skelly didn't recognized him.

Peter and the older gentleman exchanged a few words and Peter pointed towards Skelly. The older gentleman looked out and signaled to the guards.

They lowered their firearms.

"You're free to go," the guard said and turned towards Skelly.

"I need to speak to that man! He's under arrest."

"Please go."

"Who was that?!" Skelly said. He was confused. "He waves his fingers at you and I have to leave?"

"Secret meeting. Members only," the guard said firmly and took a step towards Skelly.

"Whatever you say," Skelly said and got back into the car. "Jesus." He looked over at Erin. She was looking down at her phone. "What's the problem?"

"There's been an explosion in New Dehli," she said and showed Skelly the screen of her phone: *Explosion Rocks Chandi Chowk Bazaar*. "It's just after eight p.m. there."

"What the hell is going on?"

"They said hundreds are feared dead," Erin said.

Skelly looked back towards the entrance to the castle as Peter and the older gentleman got on a golf cart and drove away towards the entrance to the castle.

"Was it the Pakistanis?" Skelly asked.

"No," Erin said and showed him her phone again: *Second Explosion rocks Dream World Resort in Karachi*. "They're connected." She started reading from her phone. "'The first responders describe the scene as horrific. People within a hundred yards of the blast were killed immediately or suffered from hearing loss and third degree burns and missing limbs.' It goes on to say that people in the surrounding area of the blast experienced swelling of the face and bleeding from the mouth and nose. They also describe the air as smelling like burnt corn." She looked at Skelly.

"Burnt corn?" he said and pulled out his phone. "Red Mercury."

"You heard what Agent Brisco said, though," Erin said. "There are no doomsday scenarios."

"Brisco. This is Detective Skelly. We met earlier," Skelly said into his phone.

"Yes, Detective. How are you?"

"Not great. Have you seen the reports about the explosions in India and Pakistan?"

"I have yes. Is there something I can help you with?"

"It's Red Mercury."

"Is there a special request or are you just passing along information?"

"Excuse me?"

"Is there something I can help you with, Detective Skelly?" Brisco asked him. He sounded impatient and rushed.

"I think there will be more attacks and I think I knew who's connected to them."

"You'll need to go into the local field office and file a formal complaint. I am sure you can understand that. Our hands are rather full these days."

"Are you listening to me?" Skelly shouted at him. "There are going to be more explosions and the Miles Cooperative is responsible! That's my complaint."

"Detective Skelly, as I am sure you know, Homeland Security and Miles Cooperative have a long and successful working relationship that spans many years. It would be a conflict of interest—"

"God damn you, Brisco."

"Thanks for calling, Detective. It's been really nice catching up with you. If you do decide to file a complaint with the field office, please let me know. Turnaround time is four to six weeks," Agent Brisco said and quickly hung up.

"Screw you," Skelly said and shoved his phone back into his pocket. He looked over at Erin. "Call downtown and tell them there's an imminent threat. Make sure they evacuate the stadium, too."

"There are over a hundred thousand people in the stadium, Skelly. You can't possibly expect them to just take your word for it."

"Convince them," he said.

"And what are you going to do?"

"I'm going to go inside and stop them," he said and looked at the entrance to the castle. He turned back and pulled Erin in close to his chest and kissed her.

She put her hand up and gently touched his shoulder.

"I'm coming with you," she said and kissed him back.

37.

It was just after eleven in the morning and downtown Austin was vacant. Kick-off was in less than an hour and the streets, which were usually packed with people dressed from head to toe in burnt orange, were empty.

Cleft and Avery walked north on a street parallel to the Texas State Capitol. Cleft had on a burnt orange fishing shirt and khaki shorts. Avery was wearing blue jeans and a plain white T-shirt.

"It wouldn't kill you to wear some burnt orange now and then," Cleft said. "You went to school here. It's the least you could do."

"I go to the games with you, Dad. Isn't that enough?"

"I suppose it's not, actually."

"You bleed orange, so it's hard to compete," Avery said and looked up at his dad and smiled.

"You do too. It's in our genes," Cleft said and reciprocated the smile as a few people rushed past them and headed into Scholz Garten, a local German bar that was popular with football fans.

Cleft looked across the street to a parking lot that was filled with pickup trucks, big screen TVs, and two large smokers. The hundred or so people in the parking lot were all staring at the various televisions that were set up. The usual excitement and energy around game day was gone. There was an odd deafening silence outside and Cleft felt a sudden wave of nausea come over him.

"What are they watching?" Avery asked.

"I don't know. Let's go in here," Cleft said and they reached Scholz's and went inside.

The bar was filled with people and the shaded back patio was empty. Everyone was inside watching the televisions above the bar. Everyone

265

was silent except for Travis Holt, who was on television. Even his robotic shell had an ominous tone.

"Atlanta Police have also called in Homeland Security and the FBI to investigate," Travis said.

"What's going on?" Cleft asked someone standing next to him, but they didn't respond and kept their eyes locked on the television. The camera cut away from Travis and went to an aerial shot of what appeared to be the remains of a baseball stadium. It was engulfed in flames and black smoke. "Where is that?" Cleft asked.

"Atlanta," a voice said. "Braves game. There was an explosion."

"If you're just joining us," Travis said as the screen went back to him. It kept showing the baseball stadium in the upper-right corner. "There's been an explosion at SunTrust Park in Atlanta where the Braves were playing against Miami. The source of the explosion hasn't been determined, but footage from the game suggests it originated at home plate. Thousands are feared dead. We're waiting on an update from the Atlanta Police Department. But in the meantime, we have a statement from the Miles Cooperative about this attack and similar attacks that have happened throughout the world in the last hour."

The screen cut to an older gentlemen. He had long white hair and a beard that was neatly trimmed around the edges.

"For those of you don't know me, I'm Miles, the founder and CEO of the Miles Cooperative. You may have heard of us or recognize the name from a wide variety of surveillance and public service equipment throughout your fine city. The main goal of the Miles Cooperative is to make sure that every man, woman, and child on this planet is safe. We have a proven track record of helping cities reduce petty crime and homicide rates over the past ten years. The recent news has shown the world that there is a new type of danger out there. A danger that we were not prepared for mentally or physically. As the CEO of Miles, I apologize to each and every person on the face of this fine earth that we will do everything we can to protect you. Additionally, we have housing available in over a hundred cities that we will make available to survivors of these terrible attacks. New York, Chicago, Sydney, and London are among a few of the epicenters that will be used for salvation and recovery through these incredible troubling times."

"What cities were attacked?" Cleft asked.

"New Dehli, Karachi, and just now, Atlanta," a patron said and shook his head.

"Why is he talking about Sydney and Chicago then?" Cleft asked. A handful of people turned and glared at him. "Were those cities attacked? What? Sorry but—"

"Dad," Avery said and put his hand on Cleft's arm. "Just watch, okay?"

"These micro communities are part of a new world initiative that the Miles Cooperative has been working on for the past decade. We weren't planning on making an announcement, but given the current tragedy, we felt it was necessary to help. Representatives of the Miles Cooperative will be reaching out to the refugees of these attacks immediately. If you have questions, concerns, or need to talk to someone, please call the number on the bottom of the screen," Miles said as a number flashed across the bottom of the screen.

The screen went black and then a mattress commercial came on.

"That's crazy," Cleft said. "When did these attacks happen?"

"Within the last hour," Avery said.

"How is it even possible then that he made this video? I'm not following."

"Are you kidding me?" a woman at the bar said and looked back at him.

"Don't you think it's strange? These attacks just happened and he's offering support to people in cities that weren't attacked."

"That's a really terrible thing to even suggest," the woman said.

"What are you suggesting?" someone asked. "Are you insinuating that Miles had something to do with these attacks?"

"It certainly appears that way," Cleft said. "At least to me." He looked around and felt a sea of people dressed in burnt orange staring at him and Avery.

"You should keep the right-wing conspiracies to yourself, buddy. People are dying out there."

"It's not—I'm not conspiring. I'm looking at the evidence."

"You have a funny way of seeing things, asshole," a guy said.

"Dad, let's get out of here," Avery said and started making his way to the door as Travis appeared on screen.

"We have breaking news," Travis said as the crowd in the bar turned back to the television. "A train entering King's Cross Station has exploded."

"Let's go," Cleft said and followed Avery out of the bar.

"Where are we going?"

"We're going to get your mother. There are going to be more attacks and we need to get out of here."

"Where are we going to go?"

"I have a safe house in Waco that we can use. It has enough food and supplies to last us a good five years."

"Five years? Why am I just now hearing about this?" Avery said. "I can't get up and leave for five years." He was stunned. "You're being alarmist, Dad."

"I'm not being alarmist. There will be more attacks. Terrible and horrible attacks. You need to come with us."

"Do you know something I don't know?"

"No, God no," Cleft said. "I'm being responsible for my family. I can't let anything happen to you or your mom." Cleft took the car keys out of his pocket. Avery stared at him with a look of surprise on his face. "Are you coming?"

"I can't, Dad. I have a job, employees and things I'm responsible for," Avery said. "People need me and I can't just get up and leave everything."

"Tomorrow none of that stuff will matter," Cleft said and reached his hand out.

"You don't know that."

"Trust me. I know it, Avery."

"I'm sorry but I can't do it, Dad," Avery said. "Come back into the bar with me and we'll have a drink and let this pass. There are tens of thousands of people here who think you're crazy."

"It's not over yet," Cleft said as people started dispersing from the tailgate across the street. They were headed in different directions and away from the stadium. A handful of people rushed out of the bar and Cleft stopped a student. "What's happening?"

"Police told everyone to evacuate the downtown area," the student said and rushed across the street. Cleft turned around and looked up at the stadium. It was a massive venue that was an integral part of the Austin landscape.

"There must be fifty thousand people there already," Cleft said. He felt sick.

"Dad. You okay?" Avery said. "You're white as a ghost."

"Let's go, son," Cleft said and walked back towards Avery and down the street.

"I'll drive," Avery said and put his hand out for the keys.

Cleft reached out to give Avery the keys as a loud booming sound erupted behind them. The sound was followed by a huge wave of dark smoke that came from the southern edge of the stadium and barreled its way towards Cleft and Avery.

Cleft reached his arm out just in time to cover Avery's head as the plume of smoke hit them and knocked them to the ground. Cleft went down hard and hit the side of his head on the curb. He watched as Avery landed next to him in slow motion.

The wave of smoke rushed past them.

It sounded like Avery was screaming something, but Cleft couldn't tell for sure. Between the smoke blocking his line of sight and the blood seeping down his face, he couldn't tell what was happening. He struggled to say something, but felt weak and disoriented. Avery was panicking and Cleft wanted to reassure him. Everything was going to be okay. Cleft gently muttered the words. He could hear himself talk but wasn't sure if Avery could hear him.

Cleft watched Avery as his vision suddenly became blurry. He couldn't make his son out anymore. He thought for sure there was another explosion and then all he could see was blackness.

A blackness that didn't have any space for light or sound.

38.

"That's a cut," a thirty-something hipster said. He had a long beard and was wearing a pair of Warby Parker glasses and stood next to a video camera and monitor.

Miles was sitting on a bar stool in front of the camera. His gray hair was slicked back and he had large potato chip bag clips on the back of his jacket to keep the front wrinkle-free.

"Thanks," Miles said and shook his hand. "Let's wait for confirmation before we send this to the networks."

"Of course, sir."

"I'll give you the go ahead when we have the all clear. We can't have this out there until we're ready," Miles said as he reached around and took the clips off his shirt and walked over to me.

"Peter, let's go this way," he said as we walked out of the small conference room and down a long and crooked hallway. I leaned down so my head wouldn't scraped against the serrated ceiling.

"You play much golf, Peter?" he asked. I shook my head. "The objective of golf, in my humble opinion, is to play as little of the game as possible. See, the less you play the better you are at the game. It should be about relaxing and spending time with your friends and colleagues. The good stuff. People waste so much time trying to figure out how to play."

"Good advice," I said.

"Maybe you and I will go out and play this afternoon," he said and then stopped and turned towards me and put his hands on my shoulders. "Thanks for doing this, Peter," he said. "I don't think I mentioned that to you yet, but I appreciate what you're doing here. Helping us.

Exposing us and giving the world a better understanding of what we do."

"Listening and observing. That's what you wanted," I said and felt my heart pound against the wall of my chest. I ran my hands together and rubbed the sweat off my palms. I was terrified.

We were still in a narrow hallway. Surrounded by jagged stone walls and unfulfilled dreams.

"Don't under estimate your role here. The Miles Cooperative is on the brink of something amazing and we need the people of the world to understand and accept that."

"Yes, of course, sir," I said.

"We set up an interview for you with Travis Holt for later today. You can tell people about all the good things we're doing," he said. "Besides, it's what's in here that counts." He pressed his index finger against my chest, right on the outside of my heart and the virus that was meticulously concealed inside of me. "You seem like you have a good heart, Peter." Maybe he was on to us. Maybe he was being sincere and I was prone to constant worry due to an unchecked imagination.

"That's a very nice thing for you to say."

"Just remember those four little words."

"What?"

"I love you," he whispered.

"That's three words," I said.

"Yes, and your point?"

"You said four."

"It's the sentiment that counts, Peter, not how many words it is."

"Right, but—"

"Let's go meet everyone," he said as he headed down the hallway. I followed him a good fifty feet until we reached two large wooden doors at the end. There was a security guard on either side of the doors. Each was dressed in a black suit and tie and had a holster around his waist. They pulled the doors open.

"After you," Miles said and gestured as I walked into a large meeting room with oak flooring and dark cedar walls.

A chandelier hung over a large circular table and let out a soft yellow light. There were twelve tall brown-back leather chairs positioned evenly around the table. All but two of them were occupied.

"What took you so long Miles?" an elderly and fairly rotund man sitting at the table exclaimed. His forehead dripped with sweat. "We've been sitting here for at least an hour waiting for your lazy ass to show up."

"We had to call Louise's secretary so she could run out and get us more cocaine. That's the situation you've put us in," said a woman wearing a dark blazer with dirty blonde hair tucked behind her ears. She was young and looked like she was from New York City. I knew the type. The type was distant and preoccupied with how to get to the fishmonger, butcher, and cheese guru all before they got home to watch seven episodes of *Law and Order*. "New Yorkers don't really like that show" is what they would say whilst erratically changing the channel to *Sex and the City* or *30 Rock*.

"His commute takes longer when the fate of the free world rests on his shoulders," said a gentleman sitting next to the woman. He was around the same age and his dark trimmed glasses made him look like an intellectual who sat on the board of a handful of prominent educational institutes.

"Touché," the woman said.

"Miles, can you tell me what my wife was looking at on the internet last night?" the educated man with glasses asked.

"It couldn't be any worse than what you looked at last night," Miles said. A few people around the table started to laugh. Miles raised his fingers to his mouth and the assembly of people quickly quieted down. "Ladies and gentlemen, I'd like to introduce you to Peter Richards." He put his arm out towards me.

My heart was beating rapidly and I could feel the edges of my heart pound aggressively against my chest cavity. I took a slow and measured breath and looked around at the various people sitting at the table. I recognized two of them immediately. The head of the IMF was sitting to my left. She was in her mid-sixties and had short brown hair with bangs and looked like she could moonlight as a New York theatre critic. She sipped on a cocktail. Across from her was a morbidly obese man who looked familiar. He was chatting privately with an elderly gentleman sitting next to him. "Peter is here to document the wonderful things we are up to and what the future holds for us and our initiatives," Miles said. A few of the people at the table clapped and nodded at me.

The future is ours, I thought, as Miles motioned for me to take a seat next to the head of the IMF.

"Hi, there. There's a buffet in the other room," she said and leaned in towards me. She had a round face and was wearing a black peacoat and smelled like Greenwich Village on a fall Sunday morning. Musty with a vague suggestion that it might be garbage day. "You know everyone here?" she asked.

"You look familiar and he looks familiar," I said and pointed over to the morbidly obese man as he pulled fried chicken out of a brown paper bag and ate it.

"I'm the head of International Monetary Fund and that's the President of the United States," she said. "Surely you recognize him."

"Right. Of course," I said. "Everyone else I recognize on the periphery."

"What I wouldn't do for another cocktail," she said and let the last word roll slowly off her tongue.

"Louise, can you call your lady and see where she is with the eight balls? I find it very hard to sit around here without anything to do. I'm getting restless," the smart guy with glasses said as a door on the far side of the room quickly opened.

A robotic butler rolled out with a serving tray and went over and took the empty highball glass from the head of the IMF and replaced it with a full glass.

"It's about time," she said. "Whose idea was it to have the judgy robots?"

"Talk to him," the President said and pointed up at Miles. "He says it's the future. We'll outsource to the machines and live our lives in utopia. He's either a genius or an absolute madman."

"What's your name?" I asked and looked at the head of the IMF.

"I'm Eleanor," she said and proffered her hand towards me as the robot rolled back to the door and opened it. "It's nice to meet you. You're here, so you must already be a winner. Miles wouldn't have it any other way." I shook her hand and watched as the robot went back into the anteroom, where there was a wall filled with a dozen monitors. The monitors were showing news footage of cities in pure chaos and burning to the ground.

Across from the monitors was a table with a team of robots working away furiously on computers.

"What's in there?"

"It's the future, Peter, and it doesn't concern you," the President said to me. "Can someone keep that damn door closed please?"

The door quickly slammed shut.

"That's Alan Anderson. He's a professor of economics at Harvard," Eleanor said and pointed to the gentleman sitting next to the President. "That's Gretchen Albertson, Damian Halvestad and Randall Brokon and Louise LeCareaux." She pointed to the array of characters sitting around the table. "Louise likes her cocktails like she likes her men. Up and dirty."

"Any other way would be criminal," Louise said and pushed her hair behind her ears.

"What does she do?" I asked.

"Ask her yourself," she said and then shouted across the table. "Louise! You in Sydney these days?" She lowered her voice. "The plebe wants to know what you do."

"God, no. Sydney is a terrible place to watch the downfall of the free world. I currently buy and sell companies on the black market," she said and laughed.

"She used to run an accelerator program for high-tech companies."

"Screw that. I live on a Zaha Hadid yacht in Indian Ocean. It has two artificially intelligent butlers."

"I bet Cliff enjoys that."

"Who's Zaha Hadid?"

"Oh, Cliff? I left him ages ago. It's okay and totally fine. These butlers can take me at the same time and I think they kind of enjoy it."

"That's right." Eleanor laughed and took a gulp of her newly arrived cocktail.

"Are you still working, Eleanor?" Louise asked.

"Hell no. I haven't done anything since I told this sucker to raise interest rates."

"You insisted!" the President said.

"Why is he here?" Louise asked and looked over at me.

"Peter is a journalist," Miles said. "He's here to document what we're working on." He put his hands on my shoulders.

"You mean—?"

"Yes, the new world civilization we're working on. Peter is here to debunk the thinking that we're out to get everyone's money. He's going to legitimize our initiative," he said and took one of his hands off my shoulder and firmly patted my chest.

"God help you, Peter. Can you also clap with one hand?"

"Why? Do we have a public relations problem?" Louise asked.

"There may be a few people out there who have suggested that we have less than ideal intentions."

"Why? What do they know? This is a secret meeting in a secret castle."

"They do weddings here."

"How are we expected to get anything done if this was a public forum? People would criticize every decision we made."

"Good point, Randall," Louise said. "We need productive imaginations working within the vast and complex minds of powerful people in order to produce a highly selective and aristocratic culture. Human progression and evolution cannot be determined by the majority of common folk."

"Could you imagine what would happen if the people's vote actually meant something? The world would literally cave in on itself."

"I need to protect my money. If we let regular people make decisions we would all be broke within a week and what good is that?" the President said.

"I like my money!" Damian exclaimed.

"Good for you, Damian, but can we all give a nice big hello to Peter and thank him for coming here?" Miles said.

The group at the table gave me a few half nods and side glances.

"I gave public radio a considerable donation last week. They said they would mention my name during the morning news," Louise said proudly. "Peter, you seem like a good man with a good heart."

"Actually, Peter is one of the very first people to receive a mechanical heart," Miles said. "He's half-robot."

"Why do you have a mechanical heart?"

"Heart attack. Ten years ago."

"You don't look a day over forty."

"I didn't take good care of myself. Too many cocktails and white flour."

"What? You walked around and ate white flour?"

"No. I walked around and ate pasta and bread."

"Apparently pasta is very good for you these days. Everyone is talking about it."

"Peter, try this," the President said and threw a drumstick across the table. It landed in front of me and grease flew up and brushed my cheek. "It's from a startup in Venezuela and it tastes like ... pussy."

"Jesus Christ," Louise exasperated. "You think everything tastes like pussy."

"God. That's a terrible word. Can you use any other word?"

"You can't say stuff like that!" someone else said as the table erupted in objection.

You're a damn monster.

What the hell is wrong with you?

"Monster of the free world," the President said and raised his hands in concession. "Would you rather I said it tasted like the tip of a castrated elephant penis?"

"Holy shit."

"What does that taste like?" Randall asked.

"You should ask Damian. He'll tell you all about it. Isn't that right, my friend?"

"Cheers, sir," a man in a corduroy jacket and kerchief said and raised his glass to the President.

"They get the chickens from a farm where they feed them with the ashes of Pete Rose."

"Peter Rose isn't even dead," Damian said.

"Top-secret information, or what we like to refer to as beyond classified," the President said.

The group at the table rolled their eyes as the door on the other side opened and a robotic butler came in and whispered something into Miles ear.

"What do you mean it's already started?" Miles asked. The robotic butler whisper something else into Miles ear. "Dammit."

"Can we keep the damn door closed please?"

"Everything okay?" Louise asked.

"Yes, everything is perfect. It's just a small technical problem," Miles said and looked down at me. "I'll be right back. Feel free to ask them anything you want. They're willing to be totally transparent." He leaned down and whispered something into my ear. "You remember those three little words, my friend?"

"What?" I said and looked back at him. "'I love you'?"

"Oh, right. Shit. Four words. You remember those four little words?" he said and pressed his mouth right up next to my ear. "The future is ours."

"But ..."

"Relax, Peter. Don't overthink it," he said quietly.

"Overthink what?" I asked.

"Nitro Zeus."

"You know?"

"Of course, I know. Why else would you be here?"

"Miles. There are no secrets in the secret meeting. You know that!" a person who I suspected was Gretchen said.

Miles ignored her and faced me.

"Can you do this?" he asked. I gave him a gentle nod. "Good. I knew you could. This is important. It's probably the most important thing you will ever do."

"What are you talking to him about?" the President exclaimed. "We can't hear you mumbling over there and can someone please close the damn door?!"

"It's sooner than we thought, but you know what to do."

"What? Now?"

"I'll give you a signal," Miles said and quickly excused himself from the room.

The large door on the other side shut behind him and the room went silent and everyone turned and looked at me.

I was alone.

"Any questions, Peter?" the President asked me. "Do you like the chicken?"

"It's delicious. Thank you," I said and held the drumstick up in between my fingers. I hadn't taken a bite yet.

"But does it taste like ...?"

"Can you stop it please?!"

"There is one question I would like to ask," I said. "What is your opinion of a One World Government? Specifically, that you are all here to discuss and finalize the formation of a One World Government." I pointed at the President. "You first."

"Who, me?"

"Naturally."

"Personally, I love the idea."

"From the perspective of the IMF, it's a great idea," Eleanor said. "We force communities and governments to convert to a global currency and we make billions. This is off the record, of course."

"Say something different please," Damian said.

"How does that work?" I asked.

"I'm not sure I follow. I thought you were here to ask questions about our future cities, right? Legitimize us and what we're trying to do. You are being rather hostile towards us," the gentleman next to the President said and looked around the room. A few people nodded in support. "We want people to live off a resource-based economy where they are able to utilize natural resources and have sustainable development. We are going to create a world where people can do that. There will be no war and homelessness will be obsolete. Big thinking here." His tone was rather belligerent. It was clear he read the handout and brushed up on the mission statement.

"It's the only way for us to survive as a human race," Eleanor said. "Isolate and protect our wealth. Can I get another drink please?! We make a concerted effort to marginalize the middle and lower classes and use our education and knowledge to make as much money as possible. I mean, if they were smart they would do it, too."

"I couldn't have said it better myself," Damian said.

"If we don't believe in the institute of the state we are finished as citizens," the President said.

"People need us to guide them and tell them what to do," Louise said. "If they didn't have us, they would be lost and without purpose."

"What's the purpose?"

"I'm not following."

"What is your purpose?"

"Oh, right. You're one of them. You're a plebe and part of the common folk. You think if you figure out what it all means, you're better than everyone else," Eleanor said. "Let me put it to you this way. Your job as a citizen of the world is to live in constant fear of death and to buy shit and help us make money." She waved her hand around the room. "Our job is to reinforce your fears and take your money."

"Okay," I said as I waited patiently for my signal. I wanted to obliterate these monsters. "What else?"

"That's it," she said. "There isn't anything else. You may think there's something else, but that's so you keep your mind occupied long enough you don't think about the thing that scares you the most."

"What's that?"

"The thing that every living and breathing animal is afraid of. Dying," she said and stopped. "For the love of everything, where are my eight balls?"

"That's where you're wrong," I said as a robotic butler came out the back room with another drink. The door stayed open behind him. "I've already been dead. Three times, actually."

"What the fuck is going on back there?" the President said and looked into the back room at the monitors showing various cities burning to the ground. "Miles! What's happening back there?"

"Nothing, Mister President," Miles said and leaned his head out. His face was ashen and water was forming around his eyes. He was upset.

"Doesn't look like nothing. Did the Red Mercury go off already?"

"India and Pakistan and most of the East Coast are already offline," Miles said.

"Oh my," Louise said.

"It just started."

"Is that why you are so sad? This is a time for celebration."

"I thought we were going to do a toast or something. It's the end of the human race and we need a formal send-off."

"Let's get some champagne," Gretchen said.

"Where are the eight balls?"

"Are the helicopters here already? It's too soon. Miles, I thought you had this organized! Now you brought in some weirdo and we're already setting off bombs. It's very amateur."

"Yes, it's early. I thought we had at least another twenty minutes," Miles said and then looked over at me. "Peter, I love you." Our eyes locked and I knew what he wanted me to do. I knew why he wanted me here and my purpose was clear.

"I love you too, Miles," I said.

"What's going on here? This is total insanity," Louise said as I closed my eyes.

I stretched out my arms and reached for the ceiling and let out one large deep breath.

Pphoooooooooooph.

"The future is ours!" I screamed.

There was a faint clicking noise inside my chest cavity. I opened my eyes and looked at the group of people around the table. They were staring at me. Their eyes were filled with confusion and irritation. I wanted to say something but I didn't need to. The action was enough. The consequences were coming.

"What happened?" someone asked after a second or two.

"Miles? Who is this guy? Why is he here?" Louise asked as the monitors in the back room started to go dark.

One by one, the screens cut out and the slight hum from the power supply went quiet.

"Is this man a lover of yours?" the President asked.

"That would be rich," Damian laughed.

"We have a problem," one of the robots in the back room said as it leaned back in its chair. The robot was wearing a dark blue lab coat and had what appeared to be a printout of a human face pasted to his steel frame.

"What is it? What's the problem?" Damian said.

"The TV signals are cutting out."

"So what?!" Damian shouted. "You're a robot. Figure out how to fix it!"

"We also lost the signal to the devices in New York, London, and possibly Paris."

"What does that mean?"

"We can't reach them."

"Set the devices off, now!"

"We can't set them off if we can't connect to them. Our whole system is down," the robot said as the light behind his eyes quickly dimmed.

His head flopped down and slammed into the keyboard and a small flame erupted from the control pack on his back.

"Can you call someone?" the head of the IMF screamed across the table. "Can anyone call someone?" She looked around at the men in black suits on the edges of the room with sunglasses and earpieces.

They were non-responsive.

"My phone isn't working," Damian said as he tapped his fingers against it furiously.

"Mine is out, too. Miles, what's going on?"

"It's working," Miles said and looked over at me.

I felt a surge of power inside my chest and blood went in one side of my heart and disposed of oxygen in my lungs and shot healthy blood out the other side. I could feel the blood pushing through my veins and the disposal of carbon dioxide inside my lungs. I was acutely self-aware and cognizant of the machinery inside my body, and slowly becoming more aware of what I had just done. "Peter," Miles said and grabbed my shoulder. I was zoned-out, looking across the room. "Peter, you did it! It's working!" Miles vigorously shook me back to reality.

"I did?" I asked.

"What did he do, and what do you suppose is working? It appears that absolutely nothing is working right now!" Damian said as he threw his phone across the room.

It hit the wall and smashed into a dozen pieces.

"Nitro Zeus," Miles said and looked over the various people sitting around the table of power.

"What is that? Is it like the god Zeus?" someone asked as the lights in the ceiling went out.

We were covered in darkness.

"Oh, Miles! How could you?!" the President shouted. "We're all here because of you. This was your idea."

"How could he what?" the person asked again. "I've never heard of this—"

"I changed my mind," Miles said.

"You changed your mind?! About what?"

"About what we're doing here and what our intentions are."

"Oh, now you're starting to feel right about everything?" Louise quipped. "A little late for that if you ask me."

"You don't have the luxury to change your mind!" Gretchen said "You're a monster!"

"Why the sudden change of heart, Miles?" the President asked.

"You have become unfocused and obsessed with power. All of you. You forgot the true purpose of what we were doing here."

"What was that?"

"Money."

"Power is currency though."

"But if we just sit around talking about our power, what good is it?"

"Kill him!" Gretchen said and looked back at one of the Secret Service agents standing behind her. "I said kill him!" she screamed again, but the agent didn't move.

"If I told you, I would end up like Devon."

"Who's Devon?" the President asked.

"Former President of the European Central Bank."

"Oh, that guy? I thought we killed him."

"We did, but Miles is having a sober moment here and wants to talk about him."

"We'll kill you too, Miles," Damian said.

"Go ahead. I see you waving your finger at me but I've made far more money than any of you can ever imagine," he said. "And after all is said and done, I'm going to make even more money. You think you have it figured out, but you're wrong."

"Shut up, Miles."

"What about all the money we've invested? All the time and energy we've committed to creating these designer cities we'll live in when the world goes to shit which will be in about—" Gretchen said and looked down at her watch. "Ten minutes," she said and tapped on her watch. "Surely, you can't discount that, Miles."

"You are all focused on monetizing the human race. That's the problem. You're fixated on people and communities and suppressing cultures so you get the best return on your dollar."

"That's exactly how the world works. Create fear and gain profit."

"But that's where you're wrong. I'm focused on a post-human and post-reality world and I figured out how to monetize it. I tried to tell you but you wouldn't listen. So, respectfully, you can all go to hell."

"What's Nitro Zeus?" Louise said from the darkness.

"It's a super virus. It takes everything offline. Anything that has a power source can be terminated through radio frequencies," another voice said.

"Anything?"

"Yes, anything, and that includes Red Mercury," the President said as he looked over at me and Miles. "Above and beyond top-secret. In fact, most law enforcement agencies don't know a thing about it. Mostly because there isn't anything you can do to stop it once it starts."

"Shit," Gretchen said.

"You must be very proud of yourself, Miles," the President said, "and what you've done."

283

"As a matter of fact, I am," Miles said.

"What do we do now?"

"Not much we can do," the President said and looked back at the Secret Service agent standing behind him. "Can you get the helicopters, ready?" the agent nodded and left the room.

"The choppers won't work," Miles said. "Everything is offline now."

"You're a damn idiot, Miles," Gretchen said. "You've ruined everything."

"What about your pacemaker?" Louise asked.

"What about it?" the President asked.

"Is your pacemaker going to be okay?"

"Look at this guy," the President said and pointed at me. "He has a mechanical heart, and if he's okay, then I'm going to be okay, too. Let's face it, I'm always going to be okay. I'm invincible."

"I took my heart out. What's your excuse?" I said.

"You took your heart out?"

"That's right. They cut me open and took my heart out and replaced it with Nitro Zeus so we could come here and destroy you."

"That's incredibly aggressive. What's your name again?" Eleanor said.

"Peter Richards."

"I hope you're happy with yourself, Peter Richards. Seems like Miles really tricked you."

"He didn't trick me. I knew what I was doing."

"Oh good for you. I hope you're okay with the consequences."

"But now you all know that I was right and you were all wrong," Miles said. "I couldn't have done it without Peter Richards."

"You're welcome."

"I wasn't thanking you," he said and looked over at the President. The color was disappearing from his face.

"You okay?" the guy next to the President said and grabbed his shoulder and shook him.

But it was too late. His eyes rolled into the back of his head and he slammed his face down on the table.

"I need some electrolytes," Damian said.

"You did it, Peter! The future is ours!" Miles shouted out.

"Miles! What in the world is going on?!"

"Put us back online!"

"It's too late now," Miles said as the double doors swung open.

Detective Skelly was on the other side with his gun drawn. A woman was standing next to him, and behind her were at least two dozen federal agents.

"Richards," Skelly said and looked at me. "You're under arrest." He looked around the room and the power and influence staring back at him. Familiar faces that he couldn't quite put names to. "Is that—?" He pointed at the President, who was face down on the table. "Erin, call it in." Federal agents rushed towards me and tossed my body to the ground.

"Easy with him!" Miles shouted as one of the agents flipped me over and put handcuffs on me.

"There's a problem," the woman said as she stepped up beside Skelly. Her phone was out. "My phone isn't working."

"That's the idea," Miles said as we stood in darkness.

The only light in the room was provided by a narrow skylight thirty feet above us. "The entire infrastructure has been shut down."

39.

Skelly closed the door to the back of the cruiser and got in the front seat next to his partner.

A Homeland Security agent got in on either side of me and shut the doors.

I looked over at one of them. He was maybe fifteen years old and his head was shaved, with the exception of a small patch of hair down the middle.

"Let's go," the kid said and tapped on the glass separating the freedom in the front from the degenerates in the back.

Skelly held up his finger to indicate that he should settle down as he looked down at a folder his partner had in her lap. She opened it to reveal a picture of David and Darlene. She looked back at me and then pressed the picture against the divider window.

"Where are they?" she said. Her voice was muffled from the two-inch thick glass between us.

"I don't know," I said. My hands were cuffed behind my back. I was leaning against the door. The cloth and padding were removed and all I could feel was the cold hard steel against my forearm. It provided mild relief from the suffocating heat outside. "They dropped me off here."

"Where did they go?" Skelly's partner asked.

"I don't know," I said. "Where are Paula and my girls?"

"They're safe. You can see them in fifteen years when you make parole," Skelly's partner said. One of the agents started to laugh.

"I'm sorry but who are you?"

"I'm your worst nightmare," she said as she looked back at me. Skelly glanced over at her with a raised eyebrow and concerned look on his face. "I've always wanted to say that." She was still looking at me. "I remember you. We saw you outside that restaurant in Westlake. I asked Skelly who you were and he said you were a ghost."

"A ghost who's responsible for this disaster," the agent chimed in. "Delusions of inadequacy if you ask me. Fluke in the system."

"What's that?"

"He's saying you don't look the type," Skelly chimed in. "The type of person who would do something like this. You don't look capable."

"Stupid is what I was getting at," the agent said.

"We stopped Red Mercury."

"Barely. Most of India and Europe are off the map and there was an attack downtown about forty minutes ago."

"Also, in case you wanted to keep track, you took the infrastructure down."

"A small price to pay. I'm responsible for stopping Red Mercury. You saw what they were doing in there? The President was in there."

"The President is a lauded hero, so careful what you say," the agent said. He tapped his foot on the floor of the car. "Can we go please? I feel like I'm stuck in a casket here with you people."

"It's not going to work," I said.

"What's that?" Skelly asked.

"You won't be able to turn the car on," I said. "The infrastructure is fried."

"The car isn't part of the infrastructure, smarty pants."

"Doesn't matter. It's all connected. All the technology working together. Destroyed."

"You're responsible for this."

"You better believe it," I said as I looked outside the car.

We were parked on the grass on the side of the entrance to the castle and were surrounded by police cars and large SUVs and hundreds or so officers from various departments. Through all of the chaos all I could hear was a deafening silence. The normal hum from power lines and electricity traveling through something was gone. I watched as police officers tried to restart phones and reset their smart watches and wristbands. They were dismayed and confused, but they would understand the reality of it soon enough.

"The studios behind the old airport," I said.

"The airport?"

"Where David and Darlene might be. The old airport. Stage 4."

"How the hell do you expect me to get there?" Skelly asked as he turned the key in the ignition.

The car didn't respond.

"The castle has courtesy shuttles we can use. Anything fifteen or twenty years old should work."

"CTECC is over there," Erin said. "It's probably up and running."

"What's CTECC?"

"Joint operations center," Erin said. "It's designed for incidents like this."

"Okay," Skelly said cautiously. "Go get us a courtesy shuttle. We'll find David and Darlene and go to CTECC and figure it out from there." Erin nodded and got out. She made her way through the crowd of officers and disappeared.

"They're going to crucify you," the agent said. "Wait until we throw your ass to the networks."

"TVs don't work either. This CTECC place is probably a dustbowl by now," I said and thought about why Miles asked me to be there.

I thought about Paula and the girls sitting at home or wherever they were. Sitting in darkness and confusion and uncertain of what was going on.

Despite the rage, I was sure Paula was trying to reach me. But the phones wouldn't work and the cars wouldn't start and the neighbors wouldn't know anything. It's at least a twenty-minute walk to the nearest store, and what good will they be. By the time she gets over there, the store will have been ravaged a dozen times over.

As dire as this was, I knew Paula wouldn't panic.

She never panicked.

There was enough food and supplies in the house to last us at least a month—maybe two without me around. The community would come together and figure out a plan and find a way to get back up on their feet again. Maybe then I would go and find them. In fifteen years or so, and when the old painful memories were washed away.

There was a light tap on the driver's side window.

Erin dangled a set of keys in her hands.

"Well done, partner," Skelly said and got out. He opened the back door and pulled me out. "No sudden moves, Richards, you got that?"

"Yes, sir," I said as he slammed the door. "What about him?" I asked.

The agent pulled on the handle to his door. It didn't open.

"Safety locks," Skelly said. "He can stay here."

"Get me out of here!" the agent said and banged his fist against the window. "You'll regret this, Skelly!"

Skelly walked me over to the courtesy shuttle.

We got in.

Skelly put the keys in and twisted them forward. It took a second but the engine caught and we were up and running. We headed down the access road and drove away from the castle.

We went through Burnet and watched as the sun slowly set over the horizon.

The main street in Burnet was empty and all of the shops were vacant, save a few stragglers talking on the sidewalk, trying to make sense of it all. It was an hour drive through total darkness to Austin and another ten minutes until we made it to the studios near the old airport.

Skelly stopped the car when we reached the security booth. There was a sign:

AUSTIN STUDIOS

A man with black curly hair, and a newly pressed shirt stepped out with a clipboard.

Skelly pushed his badge towards the guard's face.

"What's that?"

"Police. That mean anything to you?"

"Not anymore, it don't."

"What did you say?" Skelly said and leaned his head out the window and looked at the guard looming over him.

"It's a new world," I said. "That badge isn't going to do you any good."

"Whatever, Peter," he said as he pulled his arm back into the car and tossed his badge onto the center console.

"Name, sir?" the guard asked.

"Detective Skelly," he said abruptly. He was annoyed.

"You can come in," the guard said and looked over at Erin. She offered her name and the guard looked down at the clipboard. "You can't come in."

"It's official business," she said.

"You're not on the list," the guard said and looked at me and then Skelly. "You two can go."

"Wait a minute. What list?" Erin said. "You didn't even ask him for his name."

"I don't need his name. That's Peter Richards," he pointed to a battery operated television. It was showing closed circuit footage of me standing inside Falkenstein Castle shouting, "The future is ours!"

"All your dreams coming true, Peter?" Skelly asked and cracked a small smile.

"What am I supposed to do?" Erin said. "Do you even know what's going on out there? Have you seen the news?"

"There is no more news, ma'am," the guard said and nodded at her. "The van needs to stay here, gentlemen, but feel free to walk. It's a hundred yards that way and on the right," he said and pointed back towards the old airport.

There was a parking lot on the left and an old airplane hangar on the right.

"We'll be right back," Skelly said and put his hand on Erin's forearm. "I can meet you over at CTECC."

"What about Vegas, Skelly?" she said as she set her hand on top of his.

"I'll be right back," he said and leaned over and kissed her on the cheek. "We'll go to CTECC and we'll talk about Vegas." He unbuckled his seatbelt and opened the door. "Follow me, Richards." He emerged from the car and opened the back door and let me out. He unlocked my handcuffs and walked towards one of the hangars. "You'll recognize these two when you see them?"

I nodded and looked around.

The studio was dark.

The heat was starting to break and a cool breeze ran across my face. We could see the outlines of the hangars under the dim and fading moonlight. "The moon is soft tonight," I said. I was a few steps behind Skelly.

"The light from the moon comes from reflections of the light below," Skelly said.

"Uh, I think it comes from the sun," I said.

"Don't ruin my moment, Peter," Skelly said. "Soon there won't be any moonlight and we'll be on our own." He stopped.

We were standing in front of a large airplane hangar.

We looked above the large doors on the front of the hangar.

STAGE 4

There were two guards standing in front of the doors wearing black tactical pants and bullet-proof vests. They each had an assault rifle.

They slid the door open for us as we approached. "Check-in is on the right," one of them said as we went in.

The place was the size of a football field and appeared to be empty. The temperature inside was stifling and the walls and ceiling were covered with thick sound-deadening foam.

"Look down," Skelly said and pointed.

We were standing on a metal walkway overlooking a wide open space that went five stories below the ground floor. The bottom level was packed with people. Two hundred to a row and five hundred rows deep. Each and every one of them was wearing a VR helmet.

"Over here, gentlemen," a woman said. "Take your pick." She waved her hand over a collection of headsets hanging from a wall behind her. She was wearing a T-shirt: *The Future Is Ours*.

"What is this place?"

"This is *Stolen Planet*," she said and smiled.

"I want that one," Skelly said and pointed to a black headset with a silver frame.

"Great choice. 7780 pixel display with a 360 degree of view and 900 frames per second."

"That's what I'm talking about," Skelly said and took it from the table.

"Skelly, what are you doing? She's waiting for you out there. You're never going to find them down there."

"I'm not looking for them. Even if I did find them, then what? Take them to CTECC and what—interrogate them? It would be futile. You're right."

"What are you going to do?"

"Richards, now is a good opportunity for you to leave," he said and put the headset on.

"There's a staircase behind you," the woman said. "You can go to spot 59-G. It's twenty rows from the back. When you get there, you'll see two tubes. One is a feeding tube and the second is a catheter. The feeding tube is blue, so make sure you don't mix the two of them up."

"Got it," Skelly said and made his way towards the staircase. He stopped and looked back at me.

"And for you?" she said and looked at me.

"I'm ..." I said and looked at the collection of headsets in front of me. I looked down at Skelly. "I'm good."

"Excuse me, sir?" she said.

"Come on, Peter," Skelly said. "We don't need this world anymore. We live virtually now."

"It's quantum suicide," I said to myself.

"What are you talking about?"

"This isn't what I want," I said and turned and walked out of the hangar. I waved at the guards, suggesting *I'll be right back, I just forgot this one thing* and hustled my way to the parking lot. Erin was sitting patiently in the van. I wondered how long she'd wait there for before leaving Skelly.

I reached the parking lot and made my way through a row of cars and stopped when I found David and Darlene's Explorer. It still had the temporary plates.

I opened the door and sat in the back seat and picked up the box of Topps One baseball cards in the originally sealed hobby box.

I ripped off the plastic covering, pulled open one side of the box and reached inside and pulled out a quart-sized plastic storage bag.

I dumped the contents on my lap: drivers license, cash, various credit cards, and a passport.

I picked up the passport and opened it.

It had a photo of me from a few years ago. I looked below the faded picture at the name:

ELVIS AARON PRESLEY

"Great, Cleft." I said and closed the passport and got out of the car.

I shut the door and made my way out of the parking lot and past the guard booth.

I looked west towards downtown. It was dark and deserted.

The silence was peaceful.

I turned around and slowly made my way down the street, trying to think of where I wanted to go next.

THE END

ACKNOWLEDGEMENTS

Sara Barney, Jack Barney, Claudia Chahin, April Litz & Katie Kaighin
Blake, Decker & Cookie Brenda (a triple threat)

ABOUT THE AUTHOR

Dana Barney is a Bostonian turned New Yorker turned Los Angeleno turned Austinite with a strong proclivity for the absurd and conspiratorial. He has a BA in writing from Bennington College in Vermont. He enjoys exploring the underlying, and sometimes inevitable, dark side of everyday life. He lives in Austin with his wife, and two daughters.

CPSIA information can be obtained
at www.ICGtesting.com
Printed in the USA
LVOW08s1802201217
560317LV00004B/621/P